OUT OF MIND

Catherine Sampson started her career in the BBC and has worked as Beijing correspondent for *The Times*. She now lives in Beijing with her husband and three children. *Out of Mind* is Catherine's second novel, following her remarkable debut, *Falling Off Air*.

Also by Catherine Sampson

Falling Off Air

CATHERINE SAMPSON

OUT OF MIND

MACMILLAN

First published 2005 by Macmillan
an imprint of Pan Macmillan Ltd
Pan Macmillan, 20 New Wharf Road, London N1 9RR
Basingstoke and Oxford
Associated companies throughout the world
www.panmacmillan.com

ISBN 1 4050 4081 5

1 3 5 7 9 8 6 4 2

A CIP catalogue record for this book is available from
the British Library.

Typeset by Setsystems Ltd, Saffron Walden, Essex
Printed and bound in Great Britain by
Mackays of Chatham plc, Chatham, Kent

For my parents

Acknowledgements

I would like to thank many people for their help and support. They include Martha Huang, Caroline Finnigan, Rupert Wingfield-Hayes, Lizzie Aylett, Joanna Bates, Jennifer Schwerin, Nancy Fraser, Lucy Kynge, John Turner, Isabelle Lee, Jean-Noël and Val Pommier, and my parents Joan and John Sampson. I am extremely grateful to my agent, Amanda Preston, and to my editors, Sarah Turner, Amy Einhorn and Kristen Weber. My husband, James Miles, has been a pillar of strength.

Prologue

She had resisted coming here, to this place where violence raped serenity. But the lawns covered in virgin snow, the valley seamed with silver, had lulled her into a sense of rare and exquisite security. As beauty always did. When would she learn that scenes of bucolic tranquillity were always the scenes of the greatest betrayal, that the rolling hills were the swell of fear, that the good earth hid butchered flesh, and that the steadfast face of a farmer was a mask of grief?

Now, with the brittle snap of a twig behind her, she knew she should never have come. Her body primed for flight, adrenalin flooding blood, oxygen fuelling muscles, senses screaming for information. Claustrophobia engulfed her, trees encircling, skeletal branches bearing down. She broke into a run, long legs covering the ground at speed, then, shoes suddenly skating on ice, feet sliding, she fell.

As she pulled herself upright, she heard the voice of reason in her head, speaking quietly beneath the high-pitched hum of panic: was there really someone there or did the snap of the twig invent him?

Then feet crunched across the ice, and he reached her and grabbed her. He pushed her to her knees, and the ground froze to the fabric of her jeans. He pulled a sack over her head and she was blinded, her arms flailing for balance. Her lungs cried out for air, but the sacking was tight around her nose and mouth, and the knowledge of death seeped into her gut. She delved inside herself for comfort, pushing her way back past the horrors she had witnessed, back past the suffering of others, and back to the beginning, to what was good and true.

One

When I awoke the twins were playing quietly in the patch of sunlight at the foot of my bed. I pretended to be asleep and through half-closed eyes watched them squatting, bottoms stuck out, in their pyjamas. Hannah and William are three years old. Hannah has the willpower of a Sherman tank and William the devastating cunning of a stealth bomber. They were sorting through my jewellery box, draping strings of beads around their necks. William had a bangle dangling from one ear and Hannah had devised for herself a crown. Once in a while Hannah would thwack William, and he would obediently hand over whatever treasure she coveted, then steal it back when she wasn't looking. They were so busy that they had forgotten even to demand food and drink.

Their father, Adam, was murdered nearly two years ago, and anyway had never really been a father to them. Perhaps, I thought wistfully as I watched them play, this was what parenting would be like as they grew older. They would require only the occasional meal or dose of moral guidance and I could recline on the sofa and admire them as they quietly bathed and dressed themselves and bent their heads dutifully over their homework.

Half an hour later, when Finney arrived, Hannah was sitting stark naked on the stairs and screaming, and William was clinging to my leg, trying to pull me towards his train set. Finney took in the scene with one sweep of the eyes, settling on

Hannah to give her a look he would usually reserve for the drunk and disorderly.

'We're going to be late,' he growled.

Long weekend drives in the country with my children on the back seat are not Finney's idea of fun, but I had asked him to come along because I needed the eyes of a detective chief inspector. And he agreed because he has fallen in love with me, even if he has not fallen in love with my children. We were heading south on the A23 towards Reigate, to a manor house on the edge of London, a place known among my fellow journalists as the War School. Here, in rural England, journalists learn from former elite forces soldiers how to duck and dive in deadly games of hide and seek. Or how to staunch the bleeding of a fallen colleague whose stomach has been blown open or his eye dislodged. His screams are amateur dramatics and the torn flesh is bread soaked in animal blood, none of which makes it any the less a matter of life and death.

Because of the number of journalists who have died in the past decade in war zones, news organizations now realize they must try to protect their employees, at least with knowledge, and sometimes with arms too.

'You know this is a wild goose chase,' Finney shouted over the children's yelling. I was driving and he was in the passenger seat, stoically ignoring Hannah, who was lying almost flat and stretching out her legs to kick the back of his seat. 'If there was anything to find, Coburn would have found it six months ago when she disappeared.'

Finney can be pretty scathing about the incompetence of his colleagues, even about DCI Coburn, who headed the investigation into Melanie's disappearance. But the police force is his family, not mine, and I didn't want to get into a fight.

'I promised Melanie's parents. I can't not go.'

*

Corporation camerawoman Melanie Jacobs had disappeared on 10 January, a Friday six months earlier, from the War School, which is officially called HazPrep. The Corporation employs thousands of people. It is like a very little country or a big school. You have a few colleagues who are blood brothers, lots of people you know to say hi to, and legions whom you know by reputation only. I worked just once with Melanie, but I was impressed by her seriousness and attention to detail. Since then I had heard colleagues speak with approval, and sometimes with disbelief, about her bravery in war zones. Shortly after she covered a particularly bloody civil war, I saw her in the canteen and went over to say hello. Melanie was tall and agile and strong. She let her dark hair grow long and straight, and when she was working she generally tied it back behind her head. That was when you could see that her left ear bore not one but a row of six gold studs. She nodded in greeting but did not smile. I looked into her eyes and saw that something had changed.

'It must have been hard,' I said. I don't know why I said it. It's not the sort of thing journalists normally say to each other.

'It's a job,' she muttered, shrugging.

I don't know if she intended it in the way that it hit me, but I walked away bathed in guilt. I had the same job as her. I'd started out as a television producer, but I'd learned how to operate a camera and sometimes I filmed my own material. We were both journalists. But I'd said no to war zones with scarcely a second thought because I am the single mother of two small children. Melanie had no children to hold her back and had taken the decision to risk her own life day after day to record human atrocity. It seemed to me that this was the purest form of journalism, to put the factual record above one's own survival. I did not know Melanie well enough to ask about her motivation. I could not believe that she sought glory – camera operators do not, in general, achieve glory, however good their work. But could such a dangerous decision be entirely selfless?

On another occasion I bumped into Melanie with her parents at King's Cross. So when she went missing a few weeks later I telephoned them to see if there was anything I could do to help. Melanie's mother, Beatrice, worried sick but polite nevertheless, thanked me for my concern and asked simply that I keep in touch, which I did. Beatrice and Elliot, Melanie's father, lived in Durham, and Elliot's health had deteriorated rapidly after his daughter's disappearance. Beatrice did not like to leave him for more than a few hours, but the lengthy train journey to London was more than he could stand. She was the sort of person who by instinct would have dug around to find out what had happened to her daughter, but her circumstances made her feel impotent and cut off. She was frustrated at the lack of news and upset that the police investigation seemed to be running out of steam.

'DCI Coburn tells me there's no evidence that she's dead. He says it's possible she's had a nervous breakdown and that she just upped and went, but I find that hard to believe of Melanie.'

Desperately apologetic, she'd asked me whether I would mind keeping my ears open within the Corporation for any word at all on what might have happened to Melanie.

'Who have you spoken to inside the Corporation?' I asked her. 'There must be someone who's the contact point for the police.'

'There is a man called Ivor Collins,' Beatrice said, 'who has been very kind. He came up on the train to see us and he brought us Melanie's things. He talked with us for a long time, but he seemed to be completely mystified too. He said he would let us know anything he found out, but . . .' Her voice trailed off unhappily.

'He hasn't contacted you?' I was incredulous.

'Oh yes, he has. He's rung us every week. He's been very kind, but he hasn't had any news for us. Maybe he feels, until there's something definite, he can't tell us. But that's not what I want . . . Melanie had friends, she had colleagues, they must be talking about her disappearance, people must have theories, there must be rumours. I want . . .' Her voice cracked and she fell silent. I could hear her trying to control herself, breathing hard and slowly into the telephone.

She wanted what I would want. She wanted every tiny speck of information, she wanted to know she had left no stone unturned. She wanted to know that she had done everything she could for her daughter.

I know the name Ivor Collins. Usually you glimpse him in the distance, like a star in the night sky. Occasionally, if there is a morale issue, Collins visits the rank and file to dispense encouraging words, pat backs and nose around to see where – or with whom – the trouble lies. When I had spoken to Beatrice, I looked Ivor Collins up in the directory, and found that Ivor was HCP (R, H), which stood for Head of Corporate Policy, brackets Resources comma Human close brackets.

The next day I made an appointment to see him and found his comfortably appointed office in the far reaches of the management empire. He greeted me with a warm handshake and invited me to sit in the armchair opposite his. He had startling blue eyes and snowy white hair cut very short. His body was narrow, and his long face seemed even longer because of its unusual thinness. He looked like an exclamation mark.

'You wanted to talk to me about Melanie Jacobs,' he said, cocking his long head on one side.

'Her parents are frustrated by the lack of news,' I told him, 'and they asked me to keep my ears open.'

He nodded thoughtfully. 'And what have you learned?'

'You're the first person I've asked.'

'Well . . .' He heaved a sigh and spoke in a voice that was so low it was almost not there. Whether this indicated a desire for ultimate deniability or simply a throat infection, I could not tell.

'I find it hard to speak to Beatrice and Elliot every Monday, as I do, when I can't tell them any more than they've read in the papers. All of us here have been helping the police in whatever way we can, but there has been little to tell them. Melanie was supremely brave, extremely talented, and we valued her highly. We have no idea why she disappeared.'

I left Collins's office ten minutes later, empty-handed. As I trod the lengths of corridor back to my office, I felt increasingly dissatisfied. Collins had not dismissed me, he had not tried to stop me asking questions, but he had met each of my enquiries with a sad shake of the head and an apology that there was nothing new that he could tell me, his blue eyes filled with a concern that looked genuine.

Surely, I thought, it was impossible that Collins had no more information now than the day Melanie vanished. I simply could not believe it. And as I thought it over, alarm bells began to ring in my head. When, nearly two years earlier, Adam Wills had been killed, I had become chief suspect, and the Corporation had failed to stand behind me. Was the Corporation now abandoning Melanie to her fate as it had abandoned me? I had been a suspect in a murder investigation, so perhaps it was understandable that my employers should want to pretend I had nothing to do with them. But there was no such stain on Melanie's reputation.

The next day Beatrice rang me and asked whether I would mind terribly going to HazPrep, and checking one last time whether there was something, anything, that the police might have missed. I agreed immediately. If Collins was not going to stand up for Melanie then I would have to. I found myself fired by an angry zeal that, had I been honest with myself, I would have realized had more to do with what had happened to me nearly two years earlier than with what had or had not happened to Melanie.

Now, as hedgerow gave way to a high brick wall topped with razor-sharp wire, I recognized the War School from the TV coverage of Melanie's disappearance. HazPrep had not allowed journalists inside to film in the grounds at the time, nor had it allowed its staff to give interviews, with the exception of the director, Andrew Bentley. So there had been a lot of pictures of this exterior wall and the blue metal gate. I called Bentley from my mobile, as he'd instructed, and the gate slid open.

We parked by the manor house, a sprawling stone building surrounded with topiary at the top of a small hill. Bentley was waiting. I had expected combat fatigues, but he wore a dark blue business suit and what looked to my amateur eyes like a regimental tie. All I knew of his history was that he had been an officer in the Special Boat Service. His short dark hair had receded to show a large circle of glossy bald head, his shoulders pushed the suit to its limits, and his unbuttoned jacket revealed a chest that sat above his waist like a V. I could see my face in his shoes.

'Hello?' Bentley greeted Finney with an interrogative, and shook his hand.

'This is Tom Finney,' I said and left it at that.

'Good God, you've got a carful.' Bentley peered into the back.

'It's the weekend—' I started, but he waved away my excuses.

'Plenty of space for them to run around. I've got kids myself.'

I was pleased to find someone who didn't blanch when they saw children, but by the time I'd managed to dislodge William and Hannah from the car, Bentley and Finney had turned and were already heading towards the house. It was an English summer's day, the early sun now overcast with clouds that threatened rain, and Finney was wearing a leather jacket and jeans. Unlike Bentley, who made a suit look like a uniform, Finney was incapable of making even a suit look like a suit. I hadn't introduced Finney as a police officer, but it seemed to me, as they strode off together that the two men had recognized in each other the formal manner of men who work in hierarchical institutions and the bearing of those who expect a certain measure of respect. They were deep in conversation.

I gathered the children up and hurried after them. Inside the house we followed Bentley along a ground-floor corridor, and he stopped outside a door, the top half of which was glass.

'This is one of our seminar rooms,' he said quietly. 'It's being used, but you're welcome to take a look. A lot of what we teach is risk assessment, and self-awareness. We need to tell camera operators like Melanie that their camera looks like a rocket-propelled grenade launcher. They may think their equipment looks innocent enough, but it doesn't. And a camera operator needs a minimum of four seconds of film, which is a long time to stick your neck out with bullets flying.'

I stepped up and looked through the glass. There were a dozen men in there, sitting in a circle on metal chairs chosen for function rather than comfort, each with a notebook at their elbow. Two of them were passing notes to each other. A third looked close to sleep. I recognized only one of them, a man called Max Amsel. Max is one of the Corporation's war correspondents. Short and stout, he is Austrian by birth and was once told by a Corporation executive that he would never make a broadcaster because his accent was too strong. Now he speaks a smooth standard English. Only if you listen very closely can you hear the slightest of clipped edges.

An instructor stood at the front of the class, holding up a flak jacket and describing its many fine properties. Props were stacked on shelves around the edges of the room – first aid kits, helmets, a pair of boots, as well as what I assumed were models of grenades, landmines and mortar shells. Two old-fashioned blackboards stood at the front of the room, and there was a large flat-screen TV mounted on the wall. On one blackboard were diagrams of explosions, of the trajectory of shrapnel, with stick figures crouching, ducking, running. On the second, there was writing in white chalk. 'Be the Grey Man.'

'Shut the Fuck Up or Die,' was scrawled in pink chalk beneath it. Someone had wiped over the words in a half-hearted attempt to erase them, but they were still clearly legible.

Bentley followed my eyes.

'In a group-hostage situation it's generally good policy to keep your head down,' Bentley murmured in my ear. 'I think the commentary was added by one of our clients. Some of them think they're real jokers.'

I moved aside to let Finney take a look through the glass and then we moved on. We climbed the staircase to the room Melanie had occupied. The single bed was covered in a grass green counterpane. There was a small chest of drawers beside it, olive green curtains hung at the window, and the carpet was moss green, the walls beige. It was a room in camouflage. This must be what happened when you left interior decoration up to former soldiers. A narrow wardrobe was empty of anything but hangers. Through another door a shower room was hung with pristine towels. The room had long ago been wiped clean of any vestige of Melanie.

'The police sealed it off.' Bentley was standing in the door-way, as though crossing the threshold might make him disap-pear as Melanie had. 'They turned it upside down, but as far as I know they didn't find anything unusual and there was no sign of forced entry. In the end someone from the Corporation came and packed up her things.'

'Who was that?'

Bentley shrugged.

'I don't remember the name. We shook hands. She was in her late thirties, perhaps early forties, light brown hair. I can check with my secretary if it's important.'

'If you could. Did you spend any time with Melanie?'

Bentley shook his head.

'I had meetings in London the first two days she was here. The course runs like clockwork. My instructors don't need me breathing down their necks.'

We followed Bentley downstairs and outside again, and along a dirt path from the dining room towards the woods. A light rain was falling and the children galloped around us, shrieking with delight as they got wet and the soggy earth began to cling to their sandals.

'Am I right in remembering it had snowed?' Finney asked. 'Did Melanie leave tracks?'

'The snow hadn't settled on the path around the house itself – there was too much foot traffic. After that, well, we don't know which direction she took, of course. The guard at the gate didn't see her. There was snow and ice on this path down to the wood, but no one even noticed Melanie was gone until midday on January the eleventh – when she didn't turn up at class the instructor assumed she was sick and had stayed in her room. So the alarm wasn't raised until the afternoon. By which time we'd had a dozen men and women tramping up and down here. I think the sun even shone. So all we had left was sludge. Look.' Bentley came to a halt and pointed up ahead. 'We call this the booby-trap trail; we want our clients to learn how to use their eyes, and their brains. Here, look, the path forks and one route has been blocked off with a log. You should ask yourself: who did that? Why did they do it? Is someone you can't see forcing you to choose this path through the woods? There's a hut over there, it would provide excellent shelter. Someone's piled fire-wood in the doorway – you'd have to clear it away before you could get in . . .'

'. . . and it would blow up in your face.' Finney finished the sentence for him.

Bentley nodded.

Bentley's analysis of what we saw around us was delivered with clinical calm. I felt a chill creep into my bones. The beech trees in these woods had been here for a century or more, their thick foliage keeping out what little daylight there was. Even the rain fell more thinly here.

'And here's our execution ground,' Bentley said, his voice

still bare of inflection. He stood in a clearing in the trees. A perfectly circular patch of ground had been concreted over and a high brick wall constructed along one section of the perimeter with rough windows built into it. It looked like a theatre set.

'Not that an execution ground has to look like anything in particular, but when we're doing this exercise we want our clients to be able to identify this as a defined area, a killing zone, in which their efforts to save themselves take place.' He paused, then added, 'Melanie took part in this exercise on January the tenth.'

William hurtled past me and out into the centre of the concreted area, then he stopped and shouted something unintelligible towards me. We all stared at him. I had to stop myself from bodily seizing him up and carrying him out of this godforsaken place.

'William wants a ball, Mummy,' Hannah said.

I told her that I didn't have a ball with me, and she ran to William to pass the message on. He started to scream and stamp his feet.

'What happened that day?' Finney asked Bentley. 'Did Melanie say the right thing? Did she talk herself out of it or would she have been executed?'

Bentley puffed out his cheeks, and I thought he seemed uncomfortable with Finney's question. When he spoke he had to raise his voice so that we could hear him over William's tantrum.

'We don't deal in right or wrong answers here. We preach first psychological preparation and avoidance and if that fails we teach problem-solving techniques. No one pretended to execute Melanie, if that's what you're asking. We're not here to terrorize people. There's no need. Our clients aren't stupid. They know what they are getting themselves into. As I understand it, Melanie had extricated herself from some tight situations.'

William had fallen silent and was gazing at the ground as the drizzle became heavier, the raindrops fatter. They fell and burst against the concrete stage like ten thousand tiny explosions. Bentley glanced at his watch.

'My men will be using this area for a training exercise in a few minutes. Let's go and get some lunch.'

The dining room was almost empty, just a few tables occupied by people who looked like staff getting an early lunch. We took a table by the window and sat down. Bentley pointed out the adjoining bar, where Melanie had last been seen. She had been on the course for three days, and was due to leave on the fourth. The bar had a separate exit into the grounds. It was through this exit that Melanie had left the bar at ten p.m.

'Why go outside at all?' I asked. 'Wouldn't it have been quicker to go through the dining room?'

'It would have been quicker. Also it was dark outside and cold. But there is another entrance by the bedroom wing, and people do take the overland route. Usually to have a cigarette or make a phone call. The entire building is a no-smoking zone, including the bar. And mobile phone reception is bad inside the building and marginally better outside. I seem to remember someone said they thought she was speaking into her mobile just before she left.'

'Her mobile . . .' Finney was thinking aloud. 'I don't think it's been found – am I right?'

'Right,' I agreed. My knowledge of the newspaper reporting on Melanie's disappearance was second to none. 'The police checked her phone records and there was an electronic signal logging off from the local transmitter shortly after ten that night.'

'Which means either that the battery ran out or that someone switched the phone off,' Finney said, 'but either way the phone was somewhere in this area at that point.'

'The transmitter's footprint covers a much greater area than just HazPrep, of course,' Bentley said quickly. 'And we shouldn't forget that she might have switched it off herself as she left the area, so she couldn't be tracked.'

'She hasn't used it since,' I pointed out.

'Anyone who's technologically literate would know not to use their mobile if they wanted to disappear,' Bentley responded. 'From what I've seen of these guys, camera operators are using sat phones and videophones, and GPS units, and digital editing. If she's out there, Melanie Jacobs knows what she's doing.' As he spoke, I felt a warm wet sensation spread over my lap. Hannah, more asleep than awake, had done the inevitable. I could feel the urine trickle down my legs and saw it splashing into a little puddle on the floor.

'Here.' I dumped William on Finney's lap and grabbed a handful of paper napkins from the table. 'I'm sorry, we're going to need someone with a mop over here.'

Andrew Bentley looked blankly at the pool, then waved a waitress over with some urgency. Hannah and I retreated to the ladies' to mop up in privacy, but she was embarrassed and would not stop howling. I picked her up and cuddled her, and looked at the two of us in the mirror. You wouldn't have thought we were related. Hannah had her dead father's dark good looks. Huge tears were running from swollen eyes down her plump freckled cheeks, and her mouth was wobbling. In the mirror I was pale in comparison, my red-blonde hair cut in a short, messy bob. My eyes were huge with tiredness and I was thin from running around after the children and trying to work, and having too little time to eat.

When I returned to the table I found William also melting down. He had slid off Finney's lap and was standing there screaming for me, arms stiff by his side, cheeks red, face awash with tears. Andrew Bentley was trying to jolly him along, but his initial child friendliness was clearly being stretched to the limit, as indeed was mine.

I gave William a hug – which outraged Hannah even more – and grabbed a plate from the table.

'I'm going to take them outside. The lawn's not mined or anything is it?'

Andrew Bentley looked taken aback, said, 'No, no, no,' and made a very-sorry-to-lose-you face that reached only as far as his lips.

It was not a dignified retreat: Hannah and William competing for ugliest child and clinging to my urine-soaked skirt; me balancing the plate of chips in one hand, clasping their two little hands in the other. The lawn was still wet from the rain, but I found a bench that was almost dry under the canopy of a large beech tree. Gradually the children's sobs subsided sufficiently for chips to be eaten.

I contemplated the parkland that dropped away from me into the valley. I heard a muffled explosion from the woods below and then the rattle of automatic gunfire. I knew that I was not in danger, but that didn't stop my heart rate increasing. My senses were more alive to threats than they had been. Since Adam had been murdered and I was attacked by his killer, I had not been able to regain my sense of safety. The moment I relaxed, my brain played tricks on me. I would go to sleep, then wake well before dawn, my ears straining for the sound of movement, my eyes raking the darkness for intruders. I no longer trusted in security or those who offered it to me.

I knew I'd been giving Finney a hard time. Neither of us have what you would call a traditional family background. My family is almost completely female – it's a long story and not one that inspires confidence in the reliability of men. Finney has nothing by way of family, male or female. Yet it was Finney who seemed to be thinking about permanence and togetherness, Finney who seemed to be offering me security, whereas I felt safer on my own. If I stayed separate, emotionally as well as practically, then I would never have to relearn independence when he left. That, at least, was my logic. But I knew that Finney could sense I was keeping him at arm's length. Perhaps Finney's very lack of family also frightened me. It is one thing to be one of many relationships in someone's life, but it is quite another to be everything to that person. I looked back at the house and saw Finney talking with Bentley. He glanced towards me. I raised my hand in greeting, and he smiled briefly before turning back to the conversation.

People began to emerge from the woods, the group from the seminar room with their instructors. As they came nearer I could see that there were men in full military kit walking slightly apart from the group, talking quietly amongst themselves. One had what appeared to be an automatic rifle slung over his shoulder. Another carried a mesh bag that seemed to be full of grenades. Soldiers and journalists, male to a man, they walked past us, their minds elsewhere. Only one of the group gave me a second look as he passed, then he turned to walk across the lawn towards me.

'Hi, Max.' I stood and greeted him.

'Robin.' His eyes went to the children. 'This is an eccentric choice for a family outing.'

'It's Saturday, I brought them along for the ride. How's it going?'

'A laugh a minute.'

'Any tips?'

'Grenade shrapnel travels up to forty yards in an inverted cone. If you see one coming, hit the ground, feet pointing towards the grenade, legs crossed, hands on your head.'

'I'll remember that.'

Max smiled slightly and nodded.

'Melanie Jacobs's parents wanted me to ask a few questions on their behalf,' I told him. 'They still have no idea why she would have gone missing.'

Max had turned slightly away from me and was gazing out over the valley.

'I don't know if it is relevant . . . I've been away, so I haven't followed the news . . . but has it been suggested that Melanie had met one of the instructors before she came here?'

I shook my head, intrigued. 'I don't think so.'

Behind Max, I could see Finney and Bentley approaching,

deep in conversation. I caught Finney's eye, and he must have got the message that I didn't want to be interrupted just then because he stopped dead in his tracks and Bentley had no choice but to stop too. Finney was doing most of the listening, nodding, interjecting questions that kept Bentley talking.

'I don't know whether it's important,' Max said carefully. 'In the entrance hall there are pictures of all the staff with their names written underneath. When I arrived here yesterday there was no one at reception, so I spent some time kicking my heels there. One of the staff members is called Mike Darling. This took me by surprise because I've seen a photograph of Darling with Melanie.'

I understood why Max seemed unhappy. He was not a journalist given to speculation. He would hate to be the one to give birth to a rumour.

Bentley started walking towards us again. Max watched him approach.

'Ask him,' he said and set off after his colleagues, nodding to Bentley as he passed. I stared after him. Max Amsel doesn't make mistakes.

'Mike Darling was one of Melanie's instructors that day, wasn't he?' I asked Bentley as he reached me. Both men looked at me in surprise.

Bentley frowned.

'I would have to check.'

'I'd have thought,' I said pleasantly, 'you'd know every detail of that day off by heart by now.'

'Why are you interested in Darling?' The words came like bullets.

'Darling and Melanie had met before,' I said. 'Darling did tell you, didn't he?'

Bentley stared. I could see the headlines unfurling behind his eyes.

'My wife is waiting for me. I'll take you to your car now.' The mask of charm was dislodged, the depth of his disquiet revealed, but he forced the words out nevertheless, 'It's been a pleasure.' He turned to walk away.

'I'd like to talk to Mike Darling,' I said. Bentley swung back round, his face tense.

'No.'

'No?' I was startled by the abruptness of the reply.

'I'm afraid that won't be possible,' he said. 'Mike's no longer with us.'

Two

In the Corporation, space is a priority but privacy is the Holy Grail. After Adam's death and my notoriety as a suspect in the investigation, I'd returned to find myself marooned somewhere between the empires of Documentaries and News. Not only did I not have a role, I didn't even have a desk. I'd reconnoitred and discovered what looked at first like a vacant room on the same floor as the newsroom. It was full of stuff, but no human being. So I piled the stuff in a corner and took up residence. Occasionally someone would stick his or her head around the door and there would be a sharp intake of breath as they caught sight of me. But nobody ever turfed me out. My new and unauthorized accommodation had the added advantage that I rarely had to talk to a manager because, for a long and delightful time, the managers hadn't a clue where I was.

Then, a full month after I'd moved in, another face appeared around the door. True to form, there was the sharp intake of breath, but this time the face, chin jutting aggressively, was followed by a substantial body, shoulders thrust forwards.

'What are you doing here?'

'Can I help you?'

'You're sitting at my desk!'

I eyed him. A mass of black hair peppered with white falling over his dark brown eyes, stomach running to a paunch, but a familiar and not unpleasing face with a dimpled chin. He was solid and vast, his skin the colour of honey, his lips almost feminine. Sal Ghosh, back from the Middle East to reclaim his territory. Not a man to take on head to head. He was giving me the same once over and there was recognition in his eyes.

'Hi, I'm Goldilocks,' I extended my hand.

'Sal Ghosh. Get your butt out of my chair, Goldilocks Ballantyne.'

My butt left his chair but not the room, since there was plenty of space for both of our butts – although Sal's was frankly a squeeze – if not for both of our egos. What followed was a couple of weeks of very dirty warfare which ended with a truce when we realized, although we'd rather have died horribly than admit it to each other, that actually we were quite pleased to have the company.

Under the terms of the peace treaty I moved to another desk and Sal and I constructed a wall of newspapers between us that threatened to collapse one day and bury one or the other of us. Occasionally I nudged it in his direction. He moved his producer, Penny, into another corner of the room and then there were three of us. On top of this there was a rotating population of cameramen and women who filled shelves with cameras and cords and mikes and then plastered the shelves with hands-off posters, warning death by disembowelment for anyone nicking camera batteries. There was an editing suite next door, where raw footage could be processed into a logical sequence and a voice recorded over the top in a matter of minutes when necessary. Sal was chronically untidy, and Penny and I rounded off each working day by gathering together the detritus that had found its way onto our desks from his and piling it precariously on his chair. He complained that it was like living with a roomful of cleaning ladies. I think he hadn't noticed that the person who was actually charged with swabbing down our empire was male and called Joe.

Sal was asleep at his desk when I walked in on Monday morning, his leonine head on his plump arms.

'Hi,' I said into his ear, just loudly enough to rouse him. It was cruel, but he'd have done the same to me. He groaned and shuddered. His head reared up and he regarded me balefully through long-lashed eyes.

'I just got in from the airport,' he complained, stretching so that I saw patches of sweat under his arms. 'Foul flight, storms all the way from Jerusalem. Struck by lightning three times, aborted landing, lucky to be alive.'

Sal's ability to create a story out of nothing is legendary in the Corporation. But he does hate to fly. There may, to do him justice, even have been turbulence.

I sat down and logged in. I checked my email and saw that a couple of dozen messages had stacked up over the weekend. I cast an eye down the list and grimaced. A dozen were from family members of people who had, like Melanie, disappeared without trace. Their desperation steamed from the cold face of the monitor.

Sal was watching my face.

'I seem to remember that I warned you,' he said. 'You brought it on yourself. You will be followed by wailing and gnashing of teeth and rending of garments for at least the next decade.'

I ignored him, but I feared he was right. I had even brought the deluge on myself by setting up a website for my series called Missing People. The site featured photographs of the missing people I was following, with some facts about their situations, and invited sightings or other news.

When Melanie disappeared and days and then weeks passed without a body, and with no evidence of murder, I was amazed when DCI Coburn considered the possibility that Melanie had vanished of her own free will. It's not unheard of for people to fake suicide in order to start life afresh. In many cases the people who disappear are mentally ill or emotionally fragile. But once in a while someone vanishes who has no apparent reason to leave his or her life behind. As I read about these cases, I began to realize that the stories of these people who had disappeared would make compelling television. I submitted a proposal to my boss for a series of four programmes following the stories of two men and two women. I wanted to talk to their families and to their friends and colleagues to try to reconstruct what had happened in their lives to make them leave.

My boss is Maeve, who is in turn Head of Current Affairs brackets Documentaries comma Television, close brackets, or HCA (D,TV). She's never made documentaries herself, but she knows a good idea when she hears one. She oversees the commissioning process and is an efficient bureaucrat. Maeve and I have a history. It was Maeve who had failed to stand up for me after Adam's death and I hadn't really forgiven her for that. But she'd done her best to make it up to me and we worked well together. Anyway, Maeve liked the idea and I'd been working on it for the past two months, with the result that families of several of those who had disappeared now saw me as their one best hope of finding their missing loved one.

I looked up. Sal hated it when I didn't talk to him. He was watching me balefully, puppy-dog eyes waiting for a pat and a kind word.

'I want you to come with me,' I told him.

'All right,' he said and hauled himself obediently to his feet.

We made our way through miles of corridor. We did not discuss Melanie on the way, or indeed why we were making this trip. Sal, I suspect, rather liked the idea of a mystery tour, but he never likes to stay silent for long, so we analysed the various colours of carpet that we encountered on our journey.

'It's all political,' he said. 'Look how faded the reds are, the way the blues seep out of the management offices and leak down towards the editors. Look, it's purple there, where the blue is murdering the red.'

'Or the other way round.'

I spotted a yellow and that had him floored.

'Perhaps it was on special offer,' I suggested.

Sal looked disgruntled.

'So where are we going?' he asked at last.

I took him to the East Wing, following the instructions Max Amsel had given me when I'd spoken to him on the telephone the night before. We came to a halt next to a publicity board. A section of wall about a metre square had been given over to publicity photographs, a montage of correspondents all over the world and a little blurb about how selfless and noble was the Corporation's pursuit of news.

'Look,' I ordered Sal. 'Although God knows why Max was over here, let alone why he was staring at this.'

'That's why he stopped to take a look.' Sal pointed to a photograph. There was Max in Red Square with the spires of the Kremlin behind him. A nice shot. Max five years younger and somehow five years taller.

'And there she is.'

We both knew who he meant. Melanie, flak-jacketed and helmeted, hair drawn back behind her head in a ponytail, lying stretched out on the ground in a desert ditch, her camera for an instant removed from her shoulder, her head turned in towards the chest of the man whose body shields her, a man whose stubborn face is contorted in the act, apparently, of shouting orders. The photograph cannot capture bullets, but their presence is taken as read. These two people are taking cover from incoming fire. They are within inches of their lives. The picture silenced us. Was it a snapshot of an instant's tenderness, representative in some way of a relationship between these two people? Or was it a photographic misrepresentation?

We both knew it was Melanie for the simple reason that her name was printed underneath the picture. Otherwise the confusion of the scene, the obfuscation of her face, would have meant that she was unrecognizable.

'So who's Sergeant Mike Darling?' Sal asked after a few moments, peering at the blurb where Melanie's protector was named.

'I don't know,' I answered honestly, 'except that he's now

employed at HazPrep – or he has been, or at least that a man
with the same name has been – and that he may or may not
have been with Melanie that last day.'

'Where was this taken?' Sal was frowning.

I shrugged, then looked around me to check we were on our
own before I removed the photograph carefully from the board.
It was secured by pins, so the only damage to it was a little
perforation. I turned it over, hoping for some identifying mark
on the back. A location, a date, a photographer's name, any of
these would be helpful. There was handwriting, but all it gave
was the name Sergeant Mike Darling, scrawled in pencil.

I removed the slip of paper with the caption that identified
Melanie and Mike Darling by name, and slipped it into my
pocket along with the photograph. Sal rearranged the other
photographs to cover the gap, placing a rather fine, brooding,
portrait of himself at the centre of the board.

I tried the publicity department, but as I'd half suspected the
woman who worked there said she had no record of a board or
photographs in that particular location. She tried so hard to
persuade me that I had been hallucinating that eventually I just
gave up and walked out.

At the picture archive I handed the photograph to a young
man whose name tag identified him as Henry, and who had
elegant wrists and long fingers. He held it under the light to
take a good look, then flipped it over, as I had.

'I can't think where it's come from off the top of my head,'
he told me, 'and without anything to go on, it's going to be like
the needle in the proverbial haystack.'

He saw my pleading expression and rolled his eyes.

'I'll make a copy. Leave it with me,' he said, resigned. I
thanked him, waited while he copied the photograph, and left
my mobile number.

'Did Melanie's boyfriend ever get back to you?' I asked Sal
when I returned to the office.

A couple of years back Sal had briefly pursued Melanie,

apparently challenged by her icy reputation. I knew that had he managed once to bed her, he would have lost interest within a week. But she had not allowed him close. Ironically, her disappearance had aroused in Sal the sort of genuine affection and concern that had not been evident in his over-lusty pursuit of her. Like me, Sal had been trying to put two and two together since Melanie disappeared.

'He told me to get lost. And I quote, "I feel that, in this case, the harsh light of journalistic scrutiny will only serve to blind us to the facts. This is a job for the men of the police force, not for the boys in the press corps."'

'You made that up.'

'I did not. That's what he said. Word for word.'

'Then he sounds as pompous as you,' I told Sal.

I had never met Melanie's boyfriend, Fred Sevi. All I knew was that he was a professor of psychiatry at King's College, that they had known each other for two years, and been together for slightly less than that when she disappeared, and that for a long time after she vanished the police had him in their sights. Sevi told the police that he and Melanie argued before her departure for the War School. On 9 January, Sevi said, he tried to visit Melanie at the school, calling her mobile to tell her he was there, but she refused to see him. Melanie's mother, meanwhile, told the police that her daughter was thinking of breaking off the relationship. But without any proof of wrongdoing, it was difficult for the police even to describe Sevi as a suspect. In any case, if one did view him as a suspect, he had an alibi for the evening of Melanie's disappearance. He had been attending a public lecture on eating disorders in the Institute of Psychiatry's Wolfson Lecture Theatre. He had gone on to a party afterwards near the Elephant and Castle. A minicab driver confirmed he had picked Sevi up at five minutes past midnight and taken him to his home in Greenwich.

My mobile rang. It was Finney sounding busy, lowering his voice and carefully avoiding mentioning any names.

'Yes, he was instructing her group that day and, no, they had no knowledge of any prior relationship,' he told me.

'So what are they going to do about it?' I asked.

'Look, are you sure he didn't make a mistake?'

'I just went and looked. Amsel's right. It's Darling.'

'Still, there's nothing they can do,' Finney said. 'He's left the country.'

'Didn't Bentley make that up?'

'Apparently not. Darling's been in Cambodia clearing landmines for the past four months.'

'Clearing landmines?' I echoed. 'So ... four months ... that means he left just after Melanie disappeared. What a coincidence.'

'There's no reason to think it wasn't.'

'So why did Bentley seem so defensive?'

'Darling annoyed Bentley by leaving at very short notice, as I understand it. But, as you saw, Bentley is defensive about the whole thing. A woman disappeared from his estate and he's already seen customers cancelling because of that. The last thing he wants is to have journalists raising doubts about his staff. Anyway, the police will interview Darling on his return.'

'Which is?'

'In another two months.'

'Oh, come on. He's never coming back.'

'There's something else. He was seen talking to her just before she disappeared. In the bar. He was the last one to speak to her. So they've already questioned him and they were satisfied he had nothing to do with it.'

'Yes, but the fact that they knew each other and he kept quiet about it changes all that, surely.' I ignored Finney's instructions not to jump to conclusions. I hung up. Then I went to find Ivor Collins and sweet-talked my way past his secretary and into his office.

'So,' he said, tipping his head in what I was coming to recognize as his way of asking a question.

'Melanie knew one of her instructors,' I replied, placing the photograph on the desk in front of him. 'His name's Mike Darling. He was chatting to her in the bar before she disappeared. He's lied to the police. He told them he'd never met her before, but look at this.'

Collins was gazing at the photograph where it lay. He had not touched it. He looked concerned.

'I see,' he said in the rasp that always made me think he was ill, frowning up at me. 'Have you told the police?'

'I have, but Darling is abroad for two months and they say they can't do anything until he comes back.'

'It's certainly an interesting development. I would like to have something to tell Melanie's parents.' He spoke slowly, as though he was running through the options. 'Where is he now?'

'He's clearing landmines in Cambodia.'

'Really?' Collins's eyebrows rose. 'Well, I'll give it some thought, but I don't see what we can do except wait, do you?' he said.

I returned to the office impatient that the first clue Melanie's disappearance had given up led to the other end of the earth, and exasperated that neither the police nor the Corporation seemed willing to pursue it. Sal was looking at me expectantly, and I told him what I'd learned from Finney, and of Collins's unsatisfactory response. He shook his head in irritation.

'I can't believe no one's prepared just to get on a plane to Cambodia and go and see what Darling has to say for himself,' I complained. 'Everyone seems to be content to cross their fingers and wait for her to turn up.'

'So go,' Sal said.

I stared at him.

'Stop whining and go to Cambodia,' he repeated.

Three

Route Five, Pursat, Cambodia

The jungle is livid, the air solid with moisture from the monsoon rain. I feel as though I am breathing steam. Our Toyota Land Cruiser kicks up the yellow dust and it falls limply back down to the ground. My knowledge of this country's history imposes an air of menace. When I stop the car to pee, I don't wander off into the undergrowth because it is strewn with landmines. I have no intention of getting blown up with my knickers down.

For hours we've been driving on a road that is one vast pothole. We set out later than we intended and then lost an hour changing a tyre, an operation that took all three of us: Dave, our local driver and myself. Dave, my cameraman, is the perfect travelling companion. He never gets ruffled, never notices discomfort, takes everything in through cinematic eyes. We listen to Dave's choice of audio book, Herodotus's history of the Persian Wars.

'Have you been to this part of the world before?' Dave asks me. Dave is prematurely grey, bespectacled, with a small goatee beard. He has worked all over the world, but recently my Missing People series has taken us to rather less exotic locations, like Salford and Middlesbrough.

I shake my head, pull a face.

'Nope.'

'It's not your kind of thing, is it?' Dave ventures. 'Something that takes you away from your kids.'

For a moment I consider telling Dave to keep his nose out of my personal life, but I know I'm overreacting. He's right. Every time I go away I have to steel myself.

'Earning us a living means I have to go away sometimes,' I say eventually. 'I just like to keep it quick.'

My itinerary doesn't allow for much slippage. Hannah and William are waiting for me in London, and every day the invisible elastic band between us seems to stretch further. The twins are not impressed by professional ambition, particularly in their mother. And to them a week feels like a year, a month like a lifetime.

All this means that, unlike Melanie and Sal, I won't make a career out of trouble spots. I gaze out the window at this land formed by monsoon and heat, with the history of genocide hanging over it like a cloud. Despite all that I have read, when we pass close to villages I am still shocked by the number of people, adults and children, who are missing limbs. It is a landscape that has existed all my life and that I have never before seen, and that I would not have seen now if it were not for Melanie, who is now my work, my 'story'. How much of the world is that 'other' place, the unknown, strange, threatening or exotic, heavenly or hellish? Melanie had seen it all, bumping across roads like this one, seeing worlds from the window that a tourist would never see, sharing terrain with the people who work the land and on occasion with the soldiers who come to protect or plunder.

In between the fighting and the famines there must have been hours of companionship on the road, and beautiful vistas, and the joy of unexpected friendship from strangers. And for the first time I think of her in a different way. For the first time I don't ask myself why on earth she chose this life. For the first time, instead, I think what an immensely rich life she chose.

'Does Maeve know what you're up to?'

'I sent her an email the day we left, so she knows I'm in

Cambodia,' I said slowly, 'and she knows I'm following up on a
missing person. I just didn't happen to tell her that the missing
person is Melanie.'

'I think,' Dave said wearily, 'that she might not like it.'

'Why do you think I haven't told her?'

'Brilliant.' His voice was heavily sarcastic.

'I'll tell her when I get back.'

'Fucking brilliant.'

'I'm making a series on people who just disappear and that's
what Melanie did. I see no need to explain myself to anyone.'
I sounded defensive, even to my own ears.

Dave mulled this over. After a moment he got to the problem
that had struck me about thirty seconds after Sal suggested I go
to Cambodia.

'Where did you get the budget?'

'Well . . . Originally I budgeted for a trip to Russia to follow
up a student who disappeared, but then he turned up at his
sister's wedding, so . . .'

'You had wriggle room.'

'I had wriggle room.'

There was silence in the car for a moment. Then he said,
'Even the Corporation's given up on her. You'd think they'd
want everyone to keep looking.'

In the early days after Melanie's disappearance, the assumption in the press was that she had been murdered. When no
body was found, and rumours began to circulate about her
stressed mental state and the possibility that she had simply
chosen to vanish, the Corporation began to come in for flak.
Had her editors pushed her too hard? Had Melanie been given
sufficient support? Had she been offered counselling for the
many horrors she had seen? The speculation was, of course, no
more than speculation. Pressure, stress, support: these things
were almost impossible to measure objectively. And the Corporation had chosen not to engage in the debate.

'Melanie Jacobs is still missing,' one Corporation spokesman said. 'At a time like this we feel it is irresponsible to whip up a storm of rumour and innuendo.'

The speculation had gradually died down and I suspected that behind the Corporation's decision to let Melanie's name slip quietly out of the news was a desire to let sleeping dogs lie. I couldn't, however, understand why. In my case, the Corporation had failed to support me when it looked as though I was going to be arrested on a murder charge. No such notoriety stained Melanie's reputation.

'Darling may even have done a runner,' I told Dave. He must know we're on our way, I had to make a dozen calls to track him down, so someone will have got word to him.'

Dave remained silent, and the silence was less enthusiastic than ever.

'Do you know Melanie well?' Carefully, I avoided the miserable past tense.

'I worked alongside her once. In Sierra Leone.'

'And?'

'And she's a crazy lady.'

'How's that?'

'She's fearless, nothing stops her. She gets herself into situations, any situation if she'll get pictures out of it. I wasn't there, but I heard. She was with a stills guy from one of the wires. They were on the road to Masiaka. They went through one rebel roadblock. Just kept going. Then another roadblock. At the second one they opened fire on her. She and the photographer got out and ran for it. They didn't get back till the next day. We all thought she was dead then.'

It was a variation on a story I'd heard before. Dave was probably right that it was Sierra Leone. I'd heard a similar story from Sudan.

'There's a point where tough turns into stupid. Maybe,' Dave mused, 'she thought she had to show she was tough because she's a woman.'

I looked at him. Men either think women aren't trying hard enough, or else they think they're trying too hard.

'Maybe she was just tough,' I said.

The track broadened out to become a clearing in the trees, a dusty open space, with what looked like a string of market stalls and a dozen ramshackle houses high on stilts. Dave checked the map.

'OK, we're here.'

We pulled in next to a Subaru SUV parked outside a hut that looked vaguely official. It had a signboard outside and a poster tacked to the wall illustrating the various shapes and sizes of landmine. I opened the car door and stepped out, groaning with the pleasure of stretching my legs. The sun was lower in the sky than I had expected. I looked at my watch and grimaced. Evening was drawing in, the light was going. I didn't want to have to come back the next day to film. It would be hard enough to get Mike Darling to agree to an interview at all, without asking him to put it on hold for twelve hours. Dave was thinking the same thoughts.

'It's going to be a rabbit in the headlights job,' he muttered.

From nowhere, dusty children appeared, crowding around the car. I reached into the back for my bag, dug out some Corporation pencils, and distributed them to eager hands, wishing I'd brought more. Several of the children were missing limbs.

A figure eased his way through the throng. He was dressed in military fatigues. He had wiry, sand-coloured hair, broad shoulders on a lean body, and a leathery, freckled face. His jaw was set. I had seen this face before, in the photograph. I had even seen the expression before, obstinacy under fire, determination that he would not be beaten.

'So you found me,' he said.

A point in his favour already then. He had known I was on my way and he had not run.

'I'm Robin Ballantyne.' I extended my hand, but he did not take it and after a moment I let it drop. 'Could you spare us some time?'

Darling opened his mouth as if to retort, but then his eyes went to the crowd that had gathered and instead he jerked his head and led the way inside the wooden shack. We sat at a simple table. In the centre was a tray that bore a glass pot of clear, leafy tea and several glasses. Darling took a chair opposite us and for a moment he just sat, tipping his chair on its back legs and staring at us in unfriendly silence. Then he seemed to come to an unspoken decision. The chair legs hit the floor sharply as he sat forward, reached for the pot and poured tea into glasses for us. It was a courteous gesture, but his face was dark with displeasure.

'Well?' he demanded. 'What's all this about?'

I cleared my throat, 'I'm making a documentary series about people who disappear. People like Melanie, who vanish. We want to look into their state of mind, what might have made them run away. And since you were the last person to talk to Melanie, we would really appreciate it if you would answer a few questions. I know this is short notice—'

'It's not short notice, it's no notice,' Darling pointed out, his irritation barely in check. 'You arrive out of nowhere, uninvited.'

'If we do an interview now, we can be on our way right away. We'll drive on to town tonight. We won't have to bother you after that.'

'I've got nothing to say to you.'

'Then it shouldn't take long.'

Darling didn't want us there, but he was savvy enough to know that Dave could film him sending us away and then it would look very bad for him. I don't exactly like the idea of shaming people into talking on film, but I've honed my persuasive forces pretty well over the years. Sometimes you just can't walk away empty-handed. Like everything else, it's a judgement call. There are times when I've wished I'd pushed harder as some lowlife escapes the camera. And I'm afraid to say there are times when I've spent a sleepless night wishing I hadn't pushed my way into something that should have remained private.

Darling's eyes caught movement at the door and he made a half-hearted attempt at social niceties.

'Justin, say hello to Robin and Dave from the Corporation.'

Justin had pushed open the door and was half inside, half out, embarrassed to find us there. He was slightly built, with a white face like a moon, and fine white-blond hair that he wore to his shoulders. He was handsome in a pale way, even beautiful. He wore jeans and a pale blue T-shirt. He also had a handgun in a holster strapped under his arm.

'Sorry,' he said, 'very sorry,' and partly withdrew so that only his head remained visible in the doorway.

'This is Justin,' Darling repeated, 'our resident big kid.'

Justin forced a smile. He must have been about eighteen. His baby-faced looks made him appear placid, but there was a flicker of what looked like real irritation in his huge grey eyes at Darling's teasing. Still, if there was anger, he sat on it.

'I just came to say food's ready,' he said. He turned to us and spoke again, and his voice was precise and light. 'There's plenty to go round. Although we're not up to much in the way of domestic comfort, I'm afraid.'

'Thank you, but we really have to film before the light goes.' I tried to move things along, but Darling was still trying to delay.

'Or should I say Justin's our resident big girl,' he muttered and rose from his chair. Again the tone was bantering, but the words were hostile, pushing the boundaries of teasing. 'Let's eat. I'm not going to let my food go cold just to talk to you.'

Outside the hut, at the back, another simple table and chairs had been placed on a wooden veranda. The air was thick with the haze of blackening mosquito coils. Beyond the dirt yard the countryside turned into scrubland, with patches of elephant grass and bamboo, and beyond that again the hill was forested. Through the dirt there ran a path that led to a small bridge over what looked like a ditch and had once perhaps been a river.

Another man was sitting at the table, one ankle propped on his knee, and a glass of beer in his hand. He stood up and reached out to shake our hands, introducing himself as Alan Hudder and passing me a business card that described him as a security specialist. This man was Darling's age, and he too carried himself like a soldier, although he was thicker around the middle. A few questions, as Alan poured us Anchor beer, gathered the information that he and Mike had been in the SAS together, and that they had learned their mine-clearance skills in Africa and Afghanistan. They had left the army to go into the private sector and now worked on short-term contracts.

The mine-clearance project came from an international security consultancy, a subcontract of a subcontract of a subcontract of a UN-funded programme.

'And why not?' Alan asked rhetorically. 'The beer's cheap.'

I glanced at Dave. He shrugged. We couldn't hurry this along. We'd just have to settle for an interview in the black of a rural Cambodian night. We'd be lucky if Darling agreed to an interview at all.

A local woman brought a bowl of rice to the table and some plates of wok-fried vegetables and meat. Dave was talking to Alan about Cambodian liquor and, since I was sitting next to him, I talked to Justin, aware all the time that Mike Darling was listening. I learned that Justin was at Warwick University, that he had completed his second year studying geography and that this was his summer holiday.

'Kes – his dad – wanted us to make a man of him,' Darling said, his voice rising above Justin's. Justin fell silent, his face contorted in humiliation. But Alan was now on his case.

'I thought I told you to lose the gun.' His tone was hectoring.

'You've got one,' Justin retorted.

'Everybody's bloody got one around here. The difference is I don't flaunt it. This isn't *Indiana Jones and the Temple of Doom*.'

A red flush of embarrassment infused Justin's face.

Dave, whom I had never seen speak unkindly, attempted to change the subject. He asked Justin how it was going.

'I can't bear the heat,' Justin muttered.

'Or the shits, or the mosquitoes,' Mike added, these things to him mere pinpricks.

Abruptly, Justin stood up and excused himself.

'Gone to drink himself silly,' Alan commented

I watched Justin's retreating back, his shoulders slouched in defeat. As he reached the shack, he stopped to kick it hard, then walked on. His lips were moving, as though he was talking to himself. I became aware, after a moment, that Mike Darling was watching my face.

'What's on your mind?' he asked, pouring more beer.

'That we could give Justin a ride back to Phnom Penh and put him on a plane home.'

Mike grinned.

'You think we've got him clearing mines, but we're not stupid. He came out a month ago to help out at the local school, teach English to the kids. That was the deal with Kes. And I'm not kidding. He looks like a girl, but he's stubborn as a mule. He wanted to come along and he came, we didn't force him.'

I was unconvinced.

'He's twenty years old,' Mike protested at my expression. 'He's not as much of a baby as he looks. He's got to learn that the world's not all about getting up at lunchtime and slopping around in student bars.'

'He wants to be here,' Alan insisted. 'He fancies Mike's daughter and this is his way of showing Jacqui he's not a wuss, that he's as hard as her dad.'

'Leave Jacqui out of it,' Mike said sharply. 'They've known each other since they were kids. They're like brother and sister. That's an end to it.'

Alan said nothing, but he made a face that suggested Mike was deluding himself. When he spoke again, he didn't mention Jacqui's name.

'Justin's going a bit doolally, don't you think? I don't know what Kes would think.'

'He's not much like his dad, that's true,' Mike said tightly.

We talked a little more, about landmines and the surrounding area, which was still thick with them. The priority was to clear farming land and the land around villages where the children played.

Mike pointed out the areas where the mine-clearance teams had been operating. 'We started over there, behind the school,' he told me, 'but here we back right onto the worst of it. You see the bridge on the track over there – that was once the way into the village. It's heavily mined.'

In the dark it was impossible to see the markers, the skulls and crossbones that defined the area that was still off-limits. It was like knowing there was an animal out there in the dark, waiting to prey on you if you stepped outside your pool of light. It made me eager to be gone.

'Can we film our interview now?' I asked.

If it had not been for the garrulous Alan, I think that even then Mike might just have sent us on our way.

'Why not, Mikey?' Alan joked. 'Have you got something to hide?'

Mike puffed out his cheeks. His arms were folded defensively in front of his chest and he glared at his friend, but Alan had given him no way out. I was eager to seize the moment.

I glanced around for Dave, but he was already setting up the lighting. Our driver had gone off to eat his supper, so Dave was moving the car round to the side of the shack and adjusting the strength of the headlamps. They threw a ghastly light into the darkness. It wasn't ideal, but we didn't have time for big lights. And we probably didn't have the electricity for them either. Dave put a tape in the DigiBeta and raised it to his shoulder. At last we were ready to film. Alan was eager to be in on this too, and I knew Mike would split if I tried to exclude Alan, so I let him tell me stuff I already knew about HazPrep.

Alan couldn't stop talking, nor could he stop glancing directly at the camera. I didn't bother to tell him not to. I wouldn't be using the film.

I asked about Melanie.

'Mike was the last person to see Melanie alive. You should ask him,' Alan said helpfully. Silently, I gave thanks for this man. Nevertheless, hearing that phrase again, 'the last person to see Melanie alive', made my skin crawl.

'The police soon realized I had nothing to do with it,' Mike said, goaded into speaking, his face as white as chalk in the light, his voice defensive. That wasn't proof of anything, I told myself. In the cold light of the headlamps it must have felt like an interrogation. 'I scarcely knew her. We exchanged a few words in the bar. She said she had to go and off she went. Everyone in the bar saw her leave. Last I saw of her. Next morning she wasn't at class, wasn't in her room, wasn't any-where.'

'Why did she go outside? Why didn't she walk through the building to her room?'

Mike shrugged. 'I have no idea. Should I have?'

'What did she talk about that night?' I asked.

Mike shrugged again, but unlike Alan's his eyes never left mine. It was almost as though he was trying to outstare me, as though I'd give in and go away if he looked at me hard enough. On film it would look menacing. He wasn't doing himself any favours.

'Same stuff we all talk about all the time. About how easy it is to get killed. How she sometimes felt like getting out of the profession, leaving it behind.'

'She talked about leaving her job?' I echoed him. 'I thought you said you exchanged a few words.'

'We had a few conversations over the three days.'

'Did she say where she was going if she left her job?'

'She wasn't speaking in those terms.' Mike had become icily exact. 'Perhaps I've overstated it. She simply said that there were times when she didn't want to see another war. She'd seen several of her colleagues killed.'

'On the day of Melanie's disappearance you practised a hostage-taking situation,' I said. 'She was hooded, pushed to the ground, then taken to what she was told was an execution ground. She was expected to talk herself out of trouble. It must have been a frightening experience.'

'Melanie was a good talker from what I hear. She knew how to talk her way into things and she knew how to talk herself out of them. She'd been in bad situations before. She'd have had a fighting chance. Not like some of them.'

'But you think she'd had enough of her job.' I tried to pin him down, but he just looked at me as though he was seeing me in the cross hairs of his rifle sights. So I left the question hanging and moved on.

'Melanie's belongings were still in her room,' I said, 'which suggested to the police that she didn't go by choice.'

'Or that she did go by choice and left her stuff behind.' Mike shrugged. 'People do strange things.'

'Do you believe Melanie Jacobs is dead or alive?'

'How should I know?'

'I'm asking what you think.'

He considered. He passed both palms slowly over his face and drew in a great breath.

'I think she's alive,' he said at last. He made it sound like an article of faith. I let the silence lengthen.

'You knew Melanie,' I said. 'She's been gone for six months and none of her family or friends has heard anything from her. Does that sound like Melanie to you?'

'I hardly know the woman.'

I could feel that he was willing me not to say what I said next.

'But you had met before,' I said.

He didn't reply at once and what started out as hesitation grew into a gulf of silence. His eyes pleaded with me.

'Wasn't that so?' I prompted him.

'No . . . yes . . . we may have met. I don't remember.'

I had the photograph in my pocket but to pull it out, hey presto, would be the kind of sensationalist journalism that one tries one's best not to stoop to. Besides, what did it prove? It was just a play of light on film, Melanie's face hidden. It would be too easy for Mike to say simply that it wasn't Melanie at all, that the caption was wrong. He might even be right there. Until I'd tracked down the photographer, I couldn't be one hundred per cent sure myself that it was Melanie. But the expression on his face told me there was something there.

'Where did you meet?'

'I can't tell you that.'

'When?'

'Three years ago.'

'How?'

'I'm not at liberty to discuss special operations.'

We stared at each other.

'What was the nature of your relationship with Melanie?'

'Relationship? We were in the middle of a bloody war.'

Suddenly, in the distance, a slurred, argumentative voice was raised, complaining. It was Justin. He was fed up with being made fun of, fed up with this hellhole.

Mike, enraged by my questioning, stood up and yelled in the general direction of the voice. 'Go home then, if you're such a baby. Go on, get out of here. I've had enough of your whining.'

A single shot was fired into the night.

'Fuck,' Mike muttered, as anxious as he was angry. 'Where's the stupid bugger gone?'

He was peering into the night when there was another shot and the sound of a voice, ranting.

'Justin.' Mike shouted the boy's name. 'Justin.'

About thirty yards away from us a figure emerged into the light thrown by the car's headlights. He was walking backwards, gun raised above his head, yelling. A child ran up to him, fascinated by the spectacle, and Justin waved him away with the gun. An adult grabbed the child and picked him up, swinging him away from Justin. The boy was crying, his voice rising into the night air and mingling with Justin's.

'Stop, you idiot,' Mike shouted out, moving forward so that his voice reached Justin. But Justin wasn't listening. And I realized, in that moment, what it was that had Mike so panicked. It wasn't the gun. Or not only the gun. It was that Justin was wandering drunkenly and witlessly into the minefield.

I started to run towards him, calling out, adding my voice to Mike's. In the dark it was hard to get my footing, and I stumbled but regained my balance. Still Justin was not listening. Drunkenly, he thought we were shouting to argue with him, not that we were trying to stop him. I was only yards from Justin now and he was waving his gun around. Next to me a villager suddenly stopped and grabbed my arm, bringing me to an abrupt halt too. He pointed at the ground. I could not see what he was alerting me to, but I understood that I was about to step inside the skull and crossbones markers that defined the minefield. I stopped short of the minefield and yelled at Justin again. At last, illuminated in headlamps, he seemed to hear us.

Confusion crossed his face, then panic. He took another step backwards. He did not see that he was moving towards the small bridge over the gully. I would learn later that no one had dared to walk there for years. And then, as he put his left foot behind him, a tremendous blast hit us, staggering backwards, temporarily deafening us, spraying debris that reached to our faces, forcing us to close our eyes.

Already my memory of that night-time drive exists only in snatches. We drive through the night across the potholes towards Phnom Penh. I'm in the passenger seat, my eye swollen closed, the whole of that side of my face bandaged, blood leaking through the dressing. I'm dimly aware that our driver is casting worried looks at me. Dave is on the back seat, huddled in the corner. Justin lies across the back seat of the car, what remains of his left leg bandaged by Mike, who stopped the bleeding with a tourniquet, who gave Justin a shot of diamorphine for the screaming pain, and who now holds Justin's head on his lap.

'Jesus, Kes, what have I done? I didn't mean this, not this,' I hear Mike mutter under his breath, not once but a hundred times, pleading with Jesus and with Justin's father, the two entangled, judge and jury who will condemn him for what he has allowed to happen. In my muddy brain, I hallucinate that it is Melanie blown apart on the back seat there with Mike, and that we are at the War School, driving through the bomb-strewn woods.

Four

Hong Kong

When I awoke, it was not fear that immediately enveloped me but confusion. I could feel the cool clean sheets of a hospital bed on my skin. I raised my hand to my face and felt bandage. I turned my head and peered as well as I could with one sleepy eye at the view from the window. Dense jungle-like vegetation, a precipitous cliff, distant blue sea. The door opened and a middle-aged man entered wearing a white coat and a smile somewhat less bright.

'Miss Ballantyne, I am Dr Kerry.' I stared at him. Dr Kerry had an Irish accent and to say I was disoriented would be an understatement.

'You've been medevacked to Hong Kong,' he said, with another of those half-smiles, 'and I'm glad to be able to tell you that we were worried, but you'll be fine. Or, at least, I'm assuming you can remember who you are . . .'

I nodded. My name, date of birth, my children, their birthday. Name of husband? I shook my head and he smiled and shrugged.

He handed me a mirror and peeled off a dressing to show me a rude red weal that stretched from the edge of my eye almost to my ear. The wound had been stitched neatly. It seemed a ridiculously small injury to have caused so much blood and pain. I had been hit by a flying shard of metal.

Landmines can be packed with objects intended to cause maximum damage to bystanders and many landmine victims spend
the rest of their lives with tiny pellets of metal peppered across
their faces and their eyes. I was lucky. A small piece of metal,
most likely a nail, had struck my face just at the outer edge of
my eye. Half an inch less lucky and it would have gouged my
eye out. As it was, the wound was healing, the bruising would
recede and the scarring would be covered by my hair if I grew
it a little longer.

'When can I go home?'

'Forty-eight hours. With a history of head injury like yours
we don't want to put you straight on a long-haul flight.'

I couldn't argue. Forty-eight hours was nothing, of course. I
understood that in the greater scheme of things, but I wanted to
be gone that very minute. I felt fine. A little woozy perhaps, but
basically fine. I was alive, after all. So I felt as though I'd been
told my plane would sit on the tarmac for the next forty-eight
hours, with me on board.

'You can help to cheer up the boy who lost his leg.'

I stared at Dr Kerry. Somehow, ridiculously, it came as a
shock to hear that Justin was still without his leg. The scene,
Justin staggering backwards, shouting drunkenly, came back to
me, then the blast. The awful car ride, Mike in desperation on
the back seat cradling Justin. I remembered Mike arguing with
doctors, fighting to clamber aboard the small aircraft at the
Phnom Penh airfield, being gently pulled away, airport officials
explaining the plane was full.

'Justin really wasn't himself,' Dr Kerry was saying. 'He'd
drunk an astonishing quantity of vodka, and on top of that it
seems the poor lad may have had a little bit of a psychotic
episode.'

'How can you be a "little bit" psychotic?'

'He was taking anti-malarial drugs, which can bring on
temporary psychosis in a small number of cases. He's lucky to
be alive, but he doesn't feel lucky. And although he's stopped

taking the drugs, they're still in his system, so he doesn't feel himself at all.'

'What about his parents?' I clutched at straws. I was sorry for Justin, but I was pretty sorry for myself too.

'I understand his mother died several years ago and the father has telephoned to say he'll meet his son at the airport on his return.'

After Dr Kerry had gone, I practised getting out of bed a few times and in between I practised lying down a few times. I could not work out why I was so exhausted. Then I tottered pathetically along the corridors until I found Justin in a private room. He lay on the bed, his face turned towards the window. He was hooked up to an intravenous drip. His left leg, what remained of it, was in some type of cast. When I went into the room, he turned his face and looked at me, but he didn't say anything, and after a moment he turned his face to the window again. I went and stood by the bed.

'How are you feeling?'

He didn't reply, so I sat in the chair next to his bed and read the newspaper to myself. A doctor came in, introducing himself as Dr Lam and I got up to leave, but he waved me back into a chair and pulled a face at me.

'You don't have to go,' he said. 'She doesn't have to go, Justin, does she? I just want to give you a rundown on how you're doing. Usually when I do this, there is some family or a friend here. She can remember the bits you forget, so you don't have to bother me to say it all over again tomorrow. What do you think? Can the young lady stay?'

There was a moment's silence and then a low, cold voice from the bed. 'She's old enough to be my mother.'

I stood up to go, but as I pulled the door open Justin spoke again, this time in the childishly courteous voice I remembered from before the accident. 'I'm sorry. She can stay.'

'Biologically,' I told him, settling back into my chair, 'I am barely old enough to be your mother. For practical purposes, I'm at most an elder sister.'

'Don't flatter yourself, Aunty,' the doctor said and Justin gave a small grunt of appreciation. Now he had Justin's attention, the doctor continued. 'OK, now let me tell you what's going on here. Justin, I want you to look at me and see where I am pointing. OK. Your leg was blown off here, mid-calf. Look, here. Originally, there was more leg, but the wound was very untidy, the bone was shredded above the ankle. Landmines are designed to tear people up, so I had to neaten the wound for you. Look, Justin, look where I'm pointing, don't keep looking away. At the moment you have a rigid cast on your leg, which helps control the swelling. Of course, it won't always be bandaged like this. We'll change the dressings soon, but we have to control the swelling for some time, so we will use elastic bandages, perhaps, or a compression sleeve. I had to cut off more of the bone also because it must be shorter than the skin, because the skin has to be stretched over the stump and sewn together, as if I'm wrapping a parcel. Do you understand?'

I glanced at Justin's face, but there was such raw shock there that I looked away. Instead I watched Dr Lam. It was clear he had done this before and that he had perfected this blunt, upbeat, style in order to bring his patients face to face with their new reality.

'The good news is that you still have your knee joint, and that will make things much easier when you have your new leg and you start to have physiotherapy. Soon we will give you a cast designed to take a simple training prosthesis called a pylon, so that you can learn to stand and walk. They will make your new leg for you in England. There's no point in fitting it until the healing is done because the leg will change shape a bit, the muscle will wither, the swelling will subside. You can go home as soon as your wound is healed a little more and when you are comfortable in a wheelchair. Most important over the next few weeks is hygiene for the wound and making sure the dressings are clean because what we do not want is infection. Any questions? No? OK, you are wondering what there is in your drip. These are antibiotics to guard against infection. We are also giving you painkillers. And these will continue for some time. Right now, if we didn't give you painkillers, your leg would hurt all over. You might even feel hurt from the part of the leg that is not there. It is called phantom pain. We have to find ways to control this.'

'Is there anything he won't be able to do?' I asked, embracing Dr Lam's principle of learning the worst.

'Did you have plans to play football for England, Justin?' he asked.

Justin was by this point incapable of speech, incapable of even shaking his head, but Dr Lam assumed a negative.

'That's OK then, you will have a normal life,' and on this airy assurance, Dr Lam took his leave.

I sat there for a while after he had gone. I couldn't think of anything to say, comforting or otherwise. And Justin was silent likewise. After a while I heard him clear his throat. Then he said, 'When's my dad going to get here?'

I got up and went over to the bed. His face looked waxen, his blond hair a sickly yellow against the stark white of the pillowcase, his pale grey eyes silver with pain.

'Did they tell you he's coming?' I asked.

'No. I just thought—'

'I don't know,' I said quickly. 'I thought he was waiting for you to come back home, but maybe I'm wrong. I can check. It's just a few days.'

Justin closed his eyes and later I left, hoping that he would sleep.

That night I called home. My mother was worried and tearful. Dave had already told her what had happened, but I had to go through everything again and only when she knew every detail did she seem to feel better. I spoke to the children, who had no idea anything was wrong, and I spoke to Carol, who lives with us and looks after the children while I work. I cried a little when I hung up, but that hurt so I had to stop.

Then I called Finney, who had heard the basics from my mother. He sounded exasperated.

'What on earth is going on?' he demanded.

'I was in the wrong place at the wrong time.'

'What were you doing in a minefield?'

'I wasn't in a minefield. I was at the edge of it. These things spit out shrapnel.'

There was silence from his end.

'Does it hurt?'

'Well – ' I tried to jolly him along – 'I'm not going to have a facelift if this is how it feels.'

That night the telephone beside my bed rang. It was Maeve, spluttering more with frustration than condolence. Why couldn't she reach me on my mobile? Was I in pain? When would I be back? Would I need time off work? But once I'd reassured her that I was not at death's door, the cloak of concern was rapidly shed.

'Robin.' Her voice was tense. 'It occurs to me that I can't quite remember what you're up to out there. I'm sure you've run it past me, but could you just remind me?'

I took a deep breath. The time for keeping Maeve out of the loop was past.

'I'm putting Melanie Jacobs into my series on missing people,' I told her, 'and I discovered that the last man to speak to her had met her before, which the police weren't aware of. He left England after Melanie disappeared and came to Cambodia.'

There was a terribly long silence as my words bounced off some distant satellite and found their way to Maeve, and she absorbed them then exploded back into the stratosphere.

'But you can't. You simply can't do something like that without informing me!'

'Why not?'

'You know as well as I do,' Maeve retorted, 'that Melanie Jacobs is not just anybody. She's a Corporation employee and as such there are procedures that must be respected.'

'OK, I respect the procedures.'

'You do?'

'I'm informing you, aren't I?'

'Robin, I know that you have never, ever, respected any procedure in your life. At times I have even admired that lack of respect. But in this case it's not that simple.'

'Why not?'

There was a knock on my door and a nurse peered into the room, looking concerned at my raised voice. From the other end of the line came a sigh of exasperation.

'Do nothing,' she told me. 'Speak to no one, arrange no further interviews, don't even think about Melanie Jacobs until you have talked to me. Do you understand?'

I told her that I understood, but of course I didn't. I had expected a slapped wrist, not a gagging order.

When Dave came to visit, he brought my laptop. I rigged up a connection through the hospital telephone and found an email from Finney.

Saw Veronica Mann at a meeting today. Haven't seen her in ages now she's transferred. She sends her best wishes. She said I probably hadn't been properly sympathetic. Sorry about that. She also said I should try and make you laugh. I said I'd feel more like telling jokes if you could find a way to steer clear of major head injury in the near future.

I read through the email a few times, hoping to find a smidgeon of comfort somewhere, but if it was there I couldn't see it. He hadn't even put my name at the beginning of the email or signed off at the end. I wasn't expecting a row of hugs and kisses, but a simple 'love from' wouldn't have gone amiss. A message from my mother, however, disclosed the newsworthy fact that Finney had dropped by my house while she was there. This was the first known instance of Finney seeking out my family when I was absent. He had even been persuaded by Carol to read a bedtime story to Hannah and William, which he had done, my mother wrote, 'in the same Tone of Voice he'd use if he was giving Evidence in court'.

When I went to visit Justin the next day, I found him seated, out of bed, and more animated than he had been. He was, however, extremely upset. Once he started talking, he couldn't stop. It was as though all the pent-up emotion of the past days, and perhaps even of the past few weeks, was pouring out of him.

It was the thought of going home that sparked the outburst.

'Who's going to look after me? Dad's not a nursemaid.'

'You'll look after yourself,' I kept telling him. But it seemed as if Justin felt he had no choice but to be dependent from now on. He could not see things getting better. In his mind's eye, he would be lying flat on his back or sitting in a chair for years to come.

He talked and talked about the time he had spent with Mike, seeming to blame him for the catastrophe that had ripped his leg off. Justin, it emerged, felt that Mike had bullied him mercilessly. When I asked him for specifics, the bullying he described was not so much cruel as insensitive, as much about Justin's own sense of inadequacy as about Mike's urge to rub his nose in it. He talked about Mike's friendship with his father, Kes, a friendship that to Justin embodied an overwhelming weight of machismo.

'I can't compete,' he told me. 'Even my dad's name – his real name's Kevin, but everyone calls him Kes, short for Kestrel. Dad says it's because he's done more parachute jumps into enemy territory than anyone ever. There were always four of them. Mike and Alan, and then there's my dad and Ray Jackson. When Ray died, that was when they all decided to get out the army.

They're like blood brothers. I haven't been to war and I don't want to go. Dad was like ... born to go to war. That's the way his brain works. Mike is straight down the line, black and white, friend or foe, everything has a right way and a wrong way. And Dad's like forget the rules, let's play it by ear. They always joke that Mike's the one who wrote the book and Dad's the one who tore it up. But they'll both think I'm an idiot. And I'll be living with both of them like the resident bloody cripple.'

I stopped him and got him to back up and explain what he was talking about. Once he started to pour it all out, he couldn't stop. He hated his stepmother, Sheryl, who had married his father only a year after his mother died of leukaemia. Now his dad had left the army and gone into the private security sector, there was serious cash coming in for the first time. He'd been earning £250 a week with the SAS, but he could quadruple that doing contract security work in Saudi, and make thousands as a bodyguard in Afghanistan or Iraq. When Sheryl was left a part share in a decrepit house near Sydenham Hill Wood, she had insisted that Justin's father move out of their modest Norwood flat, and had persuaded Mike's wife Anita that they should go into partnership. Anita and Mike would buy the other share of the house, and they would renovate it, turning the ground floor into a gallery for Anita's paintings. The first floor would be a flat for Kes and Sheryl, and the second floor a flat for Mike and Anita.

I caught myself looking somewhat dispassionately at Justin. Of course I was sympathetic, but I have to say that what interested me more than Justin's misery was the fact that he was going to share a house with the family of Mike Darling, the last man known to have seen Melanie before her disappearance.

'Dad's there about one month in three and Mike just upped and left four months ago.'

'So I heard,' I said. 'Why did he do that?'

Justin shrugged.

'He just flipped. Around the time that woman disappeared.

He was questioned by the police because he'd been having a drink with her before she vanished, and he was so pissed off he completely lost it. Not with the police, but at home he was yelling and screaming – they had no right to interrogate him, he was being treated like a criminal. Then he said he needed to get away. That's what Jacqui says, anyway. Jacqui's mum, Anita, she'd just had a new baby, so she didn't want Mike to go, she was begging and pleading and crying, saying Mike had promised he wouldn't go away again, but he went anyway. So Jacqui's gone to live with her mum to look after the baby because she can't cope. She's got some kind of post-natal thing.'

'Post-natal depression?'

'Yeah. That's it.'

'What about you and Jacqui then?' I asked unthinkingly. Every time he mentioned the name of Mike's daughter, his voice took on a worshipful tone. And the two of them had clearly kept in touch somehow while Justin was in Cambodia. It sounded to me as though when Justin had left Britain their childhood friendship had been hovering on the brink of an entirely new and hormonally driven relationship. If Justin had gone to Cambodia to prove himself a man to Jacqui, however, things had not gone as he would have hoped.

'What about it? ' his voice had become flat again. 'She's a dancer. She's not going to be interested in a one-legged freak.'

'You'll have to ask her about that,' I said. Justin sank into a sulky silence and I kicked myself. It wasn't exactly a sympathetic response. But what else was I supposed to say? I can't even guarantee myself love. I can't go around guaranteeing it for other people.

Five

London

I returned home to my haunted house. The wailing and the bumps in the night have nothing to do with anything supernatural. Hannah and William do the wailing and the bumping. It's Adam, who willed us his flat, who is therefore both ghost and patron of our home. We saw next to nothing of Adam when he was alive. He's there now, though. Not in chilly blasts, thank God, or I'd have moved out long ago and left him to haunt himself. He's a rather warmer presence than that. Sometimes I find myself talking to him – I get on better with him now he's dead. But usually I can't even hear myself think, let alone listen out for ghostly voices.

Arriving from the airport, I let myself in through the basement door. The house is large and semi-detached, and once upon a time a medium-grand family would have occupied the whole place. Nowadays, unless you're a millionaire, you only get part of a house. This one had been split and Adam had bought the basement – which gave us the garden – and the ground floor. This means that from the street we either had to go down steps to the basement door, which is ours alone, or we could take the steps up to the red-painted door, which was originally the main door to the house and which we share with the flats above. The basement resonated only to the breathing of sleeping children. Their bedroom and mine are both downstairs, along with a big kitchen and dining room, which have been knocked into one. Carol had retired to her room upstairs. During my working day Carol looks after Hannah and William in our flat, along with one other child, a three-year-old boy whose single mother is my neighbour and works as a legal assistant in the city. The arrangement suits all of us. My neighbour gets a childminder next door. She can drop off and pick up in an instant. The kids have a playmate. And because my neighbour pays a portion of Carol's salary the financial pressure on me is relieved slightly. Once in a while the system breaks down and we all get ratty, but for the most part it works.

I could hear Carol's television whispering and the occasional burst of studio laughter. She always retreats to her room when the children go to bed and she hates to be disturbed, unless she's babysitting and a child wakes up. Usually she's out on a Friday night, but my travelling had put paid to that this week. I would have to make it up to her. Carol had become so indispensable that even the slightest chance that she might go is enough to make me quiver with anxiety.

I think I would know if she was unhappy because she's not the type to fake it. I know that we have diametrically opposed views on a vast range of issues. But the only reason I know that is because she likes nothing better than to get a good political argument going. At least I know that she appreciates me as a sparring partner. But I have to live with the knowledge that if she finds someone she disagrees with more, she may end up leaving me for them. Of course, I didn't pay her a fortune either, although it felt as though I did.

I went straight to the twins' room and kissed them on their smooth foreheads, pale in the sliver of light from the hallway. I gazed down at them. I was tempted to wake them to say hello, but it wouldn't have been wise. In less than two weeks they seemed to have grown, their plump little legs reaching further down in their beds, arms longer. They share a room because we need a room for Carol, but I wish I could separate them because bedtime every night is a riot. At three years old they are like puppies, their bodies like bundles of industrial springs. The commandments of later childhood – thou shalt not launch thyself head first off the bed, thou shalt not beat thy twin into a pulp, thou shalt not lob food at thy mother – are still just the stuff of nightmare, a glimpse into a bleak future.

I went to the kitchen and dug in the fridge. There seemed to be a lot of rather excellent food in the there, and I assumed that was thanks to Carol's boyfriend, Antonio, who runs an Italian deli. My head was throbbing. I was too tired for anything but a tub of pumpkin soup, which I opened and warmed in a saucepan. I drank the soup, and tore a crust from a loaf of bread, loving the feeling of sitting at my own table in my own home, gazing around me and recognizing with pleasure the familiar things, the toybox full to overflowing, the two pairs of tiny Wellingtons standing by the door into the garden, the rainbow-coloured plastic cutlery draining next to the sink. Then I called Finney. When we were first introduced in a police interrogation room we weren't on first-name terms, so Finney has stuck, and he professes not to mind. Sometimes, just to wind me up, he calls me Ballantyne, which makes my skin turn cold. I called him at home, but there was no answer. I looked at my watch. It was nearly midnight. I tried his mobile and he answered sleepily.

'Where are you?' I demanded.

'I'm in front of your telly. Where do you bloody think I am? Where have you been, more to the point? I got here two hours ago with food.'

I told him about the delayed flight, and all the time I was talking I was walking up the stairs, and then I opened the door to the sitting room, where I found Finney stretched out on the sofa, mobile to his ear. He'd kicked his shoes off, and his shirt and tie were all over the place from being asleep. The television was on, sound muted. I grinned, he grinned back. I turned off my mobile and he did the same.

'How did you get in? You didn't disturb Carol, did you?'

He pulled me down on top of him. He took my face gently between his hands, and examined my wound.

'You gave me a key.'

And even as I was kissing him I was thinking, I can't believe I did that.

The next day Dave and I drove to King's College. I sent Dave off to get coffee in the student canteen and caught Fred Sevi between lectures in his office. He wore his dark hair to his ears, and his jeans and hooded fleece were indistinguishable from his students', but he did not appear to be playing at youth. It seemed to me, rather, that Sevi had simply absorbed the informality of the air around him, that he did not want to exist anywhere but here. I could not imagine him donning a bow tie to woo the media. Quietly polite, he rose to greet me, shook my hand unsmilingly, and sat back down at a table so overwhelmed by paper that his desktop's flat-screen monitor was buried. His eyes observed me coolly.

'I think my colleague, Sal, wanted to meet you,' I told him, 'but it didn't work out.'

'I was not eager to get involved in a media circus,' he said. 'I thought I should leave this up to DCI Coburn. I thought the police would have found Melanie by now. I'm beginning to give up on them . . . But hope is tenacious. You've heard there's been a sighting.'

I had seen it on the agency wire before I left the office. In Cumbria a group of walkers had seen a woman answering Melanie's description, with a rucksack and long dark hair, buying groceries in a village shop. Later a separate caller had contacted the police, reporting that a woman who looked like Melanie Jacobs had come on her own into his bar, just three miles from the village shop, and had drunk a lager before leaving, also on her own. None of the witnesses could really explain why Melanie Jacobs had leapt to their minds when her photograph had scarcely touched the newspapers or the television for the past five months. Nevertheless, to have two such calls, and in such close geographical proximity, meant that the police could not ignore them. Moreover, the barman assured them that he had gone home and Googled Melanie's picture to test it against his memory. I was glad that I had decided to ignore Maeve and pursue Melanie's story.

'Do you think it's Melanie?' I asked Sevi.

He gave a dismissive grimace and shook his head.

'I don't think Melanie is the Lake District type,' he said. 'If she's run, she's gone to chase hellfire and damnation.'

I risked a smile – he had captured Melanie perfectly in that image – and his mouth moved in what might have been a response.

'You must miss her,' I said, emboldened by my progress through his reserve.

'I hardly ever saw her,' he said. 'I'm used to missing her.'

When Melanie disappeared, one of the things that had excited DCI Coburn about Sevi was that he had refused to give interviews to the media. Coburn felt that this might be indicative of a sense of guilt, a fear that he might give himself away in the glare of the spotlight. I understood from Finney that even in his meetings with the police Sevi had been awkward and uneasy. So it was with little hope of success that I told him now that I wanted to interview him on film and that I had Dave on hand to do so, if he would agree.

Sevi gave a funny little laugh, just a twitch of the lips and an exhalation of air.

'You lot don't give up, do you?'

'You never know when something's going to spark someone's memory,' I said. 'Maybe if someone is moved by seeing you talk about Melanie they'll share some information they've been keeping from the police.'

'And if not I can console myself that I made touching television. And now, in our newest reality show, the grieving boyfriend speaks.'

'You would just be doing your best for Melanie,' I told him.

Sevi's eyes rested on my face, a small smile on his lips.

'What efforts have you made to find her?' I asked him. It came out as a challenge, but I always get snippy when academics start sneering at the media.

The small smile disappeared.

'If she went of her own free will,' he said slowly, 'then she will come back of her own free will. If she did not go of her own free will, then there is nothing that any of us can do. By now she is dead.'

The only sound was the clock ticking on his bookshelf.

'Very well,' he said after a moment. 'If the police can't manage it, I suppose we'll have to depend on their poor cousins in the investigative media.' He fell silent, aware perhaps that he was overdoing his contempt for me. 'I don't mean to be unhelpful, but our lives were private. It's not in my nature to bare them to public scrutiny and it wasn't in Melanie's. I don't think she would like it . . .' For the first time, I saw a spasm of loss cross his face. 'But you're right. It might help. I will do your interview for you.'

'I'll call Dave,' I told him. 'I'm afraid there will be some messing around with lights, but we'll try and make it as painless as possible.'

Sevi waited while we set up. He must have had a million other things to do, but he showed no impatience. He didn't even busy himself with email or paperwork, and when his telephone rang he cut short the conversation, telling whoever had called that he was in the middle of something and would call back. My first question, to make him relax, was to ask how he and Melanie had met. He answered me shortly that it had been at the party of a mutual friend. Then he just carried right on speaking. He did not relax in front of the camera, but talked more quickly than he would have done normally, and rarely stopped.

'As you know, I'm a psychiatrist. I have had some experience working with the military. One of the points we had in common was this fascination with the psychology of the warrior. What happens to a man in battle? Why choose war? How does a soldier feel about the fact that he is allowed to kill a man in war but not in his front room? It was part of her fascination to me, of course, too. She was, in a way, a fieldworker for me. Look out for this, I would say to her. And when she returned she would report back. She would tell me about the interplay of journalism and war, the growth of trust, the sudden volte-face when, on occasion, she filmed something the military didn't want made public and she became untrustworthy in their eyes. We debated the moral difficulty of reporting on the wrongness of a war when you are dependent on those who are fighting it for your protection. We were,' he paused, searching for the right words, 'intellectually, entirely complementary.'

'You moved in together,' I prompted when he stopped for breath.

'For what it was worth,' he agreed. 'She was away more than she was around. But I can't switch off the part of me that's a psychiatrist. I'm trained to read the signs, and when the signs are displayed, well – ' he made a little gesture with his hands – 'I read them. So when Melanie started to display symptoms of post-traumatic stress I couldn't not point it out to her. She was a woman who loved her work—'

'I'm sorry.' I couldn't help interrupting him. 'You've used the past tense repeatedly . . .'

'Have I?' Fred Sevi frowned. 'Surely, linguistically, I'm not implying that she's dead by deploying the past tense. I'm simply describing our history, which was necessarily in the past at this point.'

'I'm sorry. Please go on.'

He stared at me for a moment, apparently unable to continue.

'You say she exhibited specific symptoms of post-traumatic stress.' I tried again, and this time he gathered himself to respond.

'Yes, well, the first time it happened a car backfired and she hit the pavement. It was hard to miss, a classic case. She was depressed, she had trouble sleeping, she had nightmares, she hated crowds, she started at loud noises, she had flashbacks, she no longer enjoyed sex.'

Interviewees who volunteer details of their own sex lives on film are usually exhibitionists, but Sevi, I think, was simply so used to looking at sex as a measure of psychological wellbeing, that he saw no shame or awkwardness in it.

'Did you ask Melanie how this post-traumatic stress started?'

'She blew up at me on the half a dozen occasions I asked her about it. She would not communicate with me and not just about that. Gradually she grew more withdrawn and our relationship deteriorated. She said she just needed more rest. She continued to report from war zones, despite my explicit request that she should not go. She was inevitably sleepless the night before she left. And irritable, unpleasant to live with. She became almost obsessive about the weights of relative body armours – she was already overloaded with her camera.'

'You've told the police all this?'

'Certainly. It seems absolutely pertinent to her disappearance. And I think I can say that the police are beginning to think, like me, that Melanie has disappeared of her own accord.'

'If you're right, and she was suffering from post-traumatic stress, do you think she might have panicked at HazPrep, that the staged situations might have set off some uncontrollable fear?'

'It's possible,' he said slowly. 'You must understand, these panic attacks are unpredictable. No matter how much she knew, intellectually, that these events were not real, it is possible . . .

yes, it's certainly possible that she might have felt uncontrollable and unreasonable fear.'

'Might she have run?'

'Run where?'

'There's been a sighting of a woman in Cumbria,' I reminded him. We had already talked about it, of course, but now I wanted his reaction on film.

'If she felt, as you are suggesting, that her state of mind was causing her to lose her ability to do her job,' he said slowly, 'then I think she would run to somewhere she could test herself, where she could force herself to confront her fears. I think she would pursue danger.'

'You don't think she would seek out safety?'

He thought for a minute.

'I thought, as I've said, that when we met she was doing that, seeking me out, seeking out safety, security, as an antidote to the conditions she worked under. But in fact she paid no more than lip service to the idea of settling comfortably. She was a woman who needed danger to feel alive.'

'The night before Melanie disappeared – ' I started the sentence carefully. Now we were at the end of the interview, I could afford to ask the questions that might annoy him – 'I believe you went to the HazPrep compound to try to see her.'

There was the minutest of hesitations before he answered. 'I did.'

'Could you tell me why?'

He gave a snort of irritation, but after a minute he said, 'Before Melanie went on the training course, we'd had a disagreement. A couple of days after she left I became upset ... I drank more than I should have. I drove out there to see her, to smooth things over. I rang her on my mobile. She refused to speak to me or see me. I realized that I'd gone too far and went home again.'

'The next night was the night that Melanie disappeared.'

'That is so. I was at a public lecture.'

'You didn't try to ring her?'

Sevi shifted uncomfortably on his seat.

'Actually, I think I do remember trying to get hold of her after the lecture. It had slipped my mind.'

'It slipped your mind,' I repeated. 'It must have been the last time you spoke to her.'

'Yes,' he said, 'yes, it must have been. Although the conversation was so brief that it scarcely counted. She just told me how bad the reception was and I told her I'd try the next day. Look, I think it's really lunchtime.'

I nodded at Dave and he stopped filming.

'Did you ever hear Melanie refer to a man called Mike Darling?' I asked Sevi as Dave cleared the equipment away.

Sevi pulled a face.

'Who is he?'

'A former special forces soldier and one of the instructors on her course. They'd met once before.'

'No.' Sevi looked surprised. 'I didn't think she knew anyone at HazPrep – but then she wouldn't have been aware of it herself before she went there. And I haven't, of course, seen her since.'

He gathered some papers into a backpack and stood up.

'Can I offer you some lunch?' I asked. 'Unless you have plans.'

'I have no plans,' he said slowly. He thought for a moment, his mouth twisting in indecision. I wondered whether he was regretting his earlier hostility. 'Yes, I suppose so,' he said at last. 'Let me show you my favourite eatery.'

When we were seated in a Middle Eastern restaurant, dipping pitta bread into a plate of hummus, it became clear that Sevi wanted to say more about his relationship with Melanie. 'I think that when she met me,' he said, 'she was looking for a way to have a normal life, with a man and perhaps a family. She knew, of course, as people generally do, that she was in psychological trouble, and she was casting around for a way to fix it. I'm emotionally stable, inasmuch as any of us are. I'm psychologically solid. In hard terms, I appealed as a potential mate. But people are who they are. She had chosen a lonely, dangerous job which pushed her to the limit because actually that was what she wanted. She was willing to talk about the stresses of war in an objective way. But when I told her that I thought *she* was suffering, she didn't want to hear it. I was becoming an irritation to her. That was what we rowed about – and not for the first time.'

'How did she feel about the HazPrep training course?' I asked. 'Was that making her anxious?'

'Anxious?' Sevi considered this, chewing on a piece of bread. 'I would describe her mood the day before she left as profoundly fed up. She wouldn't talk to me about her work because it had become such a big point of contention between us. From what little I could gather, there was some problem at work. Maybe it was just logistics – the amount of time taken up just by arranging flights and visas, and the eternally changing diary was a constant frustration. It was, I think, symptomatic of her condition that she was increasingly irritated, not only by me but by last-minute changes of plan and the demands of editors. She saw HazPrep as a distraction. She knew she should go, but she just wanted to get away from it all and be her own master again.'

It was not a long lunch. Sevi had to rush off to teach and I stayed for a couple of minutes after he had left to settle the bill and finish my coffee. Sevi, I thought, had been remarkably open with me about the state of his relationship with Melanie. I wondered how much of it he had shared with the police. And yet, despite my sense that he had been very frank with me, I couldn't help feeling that he was hiding something. But perhaps I was just becoming chronically suspicious.

*

That night I had an early dinner with Sal, who wanted to hear what I had learned from Sevi. I'd been reluctant, but then he'd said, 'Don't tell me you've got a date with PC Plod,' and I realized afterwards that Sal had actually antagonized me into eating with him. He smiled at me sweetly and bent to kiss my cheek as he arrived, pulling off his coat and shaking raindrops from his shaggy hair.

'You see,' he said, 'I'm almost punctual.'

'There's no such thing as almost punctual.'

'Well – ' he threw up his hands – 'it's a long story, but if you insist.'

He proceeded to regale me with a tale that involved a watch still set on foreign time, a taxi, a prostitute from Bristol, and a government minister from somewhere Nordic. I took a slug of wine.

'Maeve thinks you're losing it, chasing after Melanie like this when she's warned you off.' He must have finished the story without my even noticing and now he was sitting hunched over. When he is on television his size fills the screen, dominates whatever the scene. His size is less solid in real life. If you prod Sal, your fingers encounter flesh, not muscle.

I gazed at him.

'Well, I think Maeve's losing it.'

He didn't grace my weedy comeback with a response. Instead, he pretended not to hear, greeting the waiter, who arrived carrying a salad for me and something deep-fried and garlicky for Sal.

'Fred Sevi told me that Melanie had symptoms of post-traumatic stress. That she had nightmares and flashbacks, and startled reactions to sudden noise. It started about a year before she disappeared, but she wouldn't talk to him about it.'

'You know,' Sal said, when the waiter had gone, 'I remember . . .' he paused in order to fill his mouth with food, and this time he forgot to finish his sentence, and carried on eating. I picked at my salad until, after a few minutes, Sal re-emerged. I don't know what had prompted it, but his story seemed to be a litany of the most inhumanly cruel things Sal had seen: civilians dead because their organs had been shaken loose in the shock wave of a bomb; soldiers in a variety of awful deaths – their wounds infected with the atomized flesh of their comrades, or clutching armfuls of their own guts as they collapsed, or burning, trapped inside tanks or buildings, and strung up from bridges or dragged along roads. For the past decade Sal had flown from one beleaguered country to the next, and had been disgorged from the plane always clutching his microphone and his satellite phone to jog from one murderous scene to another. Yet he told it with the same sort of cynical, world-weary finesse. Here a narrow escape, a friendly hand extended by a local, there a moment of quick thinking that saved the day.

'What,' I interrupted eventually, 'are you trying to say? I mean, you act like a buffoon – you know you do. And you ooze cynicism, if you don't mind me saying. But the things you see are awful beyond words. How can you bear it?'

He shot me a look from under long-lashed eyes.

'Perhaps you're not really a buffoon at all,' I said.

He scowled, as if he found my suggestion offensive.

'It falls to us to spread the word,' he said slowly. 'No greater honour is there than that truth is heard because of us. A bit of sleeplessness, irritation, jumpiness, who doesn't have that? Melanie carried on filming – well, of course she did, we all do.'

Sal's pomposity and his tongue-in-cheek delivery meant that it was impossible to know how much of any given sentiment was genuine and how much simply theatre. It made this conversation impossible. Sal saw this on my face and made another effort.

'Adrenalin's the thing,' he continued. 'War is life in the raw. You sleep in dirt, you shit in a hole in the ground, your body stinks. Here you think your body fails you, but out there it seems indestructible, set on continuing to draw breath. Life inside of you, optimistic, looking forward, death and dirt and evil all around, not touching you. It's . . . exquisite!'

I stared at him for a moment, shaken by that last word. Was it just another unreliable verbal flourish? Sal, it appeared, had even shocked himself. He stared down at the table.

'I'm not sure Melanie was finding it exquisite.'

I spoke quietly, aware that our conversational matter was drawing glances from the next table.

In one move, Sal licked some sauce from his sleeve, wiped his mouth with his napkin and shook his head. Then he made a very pertinent point.

'You have only Fred Sevi's word that she was in a state at all. Now, if she's dead, he'll be one of the very first people DCI Coburn looks at. How convenient, then, that he has already been telling people about her confused state of mind.'

I thought of Fred Sevi's permanently pained expression, his hurt eyes. I thought of his comment that, if Melanie had run, she had gone to find hellfire and damnation.

Sal returned to his theme. 'You have to learn to focus on the job, be detached. You can't go crusading around because you don't know enough. You don't know who to trust because you don't know anything. Turn around and they'll likely stab you in the back. And I mean your fellow hacks. I land and I'm clutching a bundle of printouts. History, culture, religion, useful phrases in Tajik, or Tagalog, or whatever, a couple of maps, and the last twenty-four hours of wires, which might at least tell me where the front line is. Insta-expert. And I am. Expert. I mean it. Question me at the airport on the way out and I'm word perfect. And the whole bloody bundle of paper is in my head because by then I've seen it with my own eyes. By the time I'm on my way out I know who to trust, and I've seen the front line, and I've made one lifelong friend and lost another. And – ' here he held up a plump finger to instruct me that this was an important point – 'and you have to leave behind any illusion that you can change anything or you might as well be dead. You have to be able to say this is bigger than me, this is beyond me. Then you can relax, you are no longer torn by moral anxiety. When I was in Rwanda I saw a mother and child hacked . . .'

'For Christ's sake!' The exclamation came from the next table. Sal and I both turned to look. A man and a woman were gazing at us, annoyed, but they were struck dumb as soon as they had our attention. The man made a gesture that said, 'We're trying to eat.' Sal gave a ghoulish smile that was, I think, intended to be apologetic and the man looked away, still angry.

'This is why we don't fuck up,' Sal murmured, still slightly too loudly, indicating the rest of the clientele with a jerk of his head that took in the whole room. 'This is why we don't get grounded. This is why we don't piss off Maeve or Ivor or any one of them. You asked if I have nightmares. This is it, this is my nightmare. This is complacent bloody PC Plodland. Put any one of them where I've been, and they'd be mincemeat.'

'OK, that's enough,' I interjected, but Sal was on a roll.

'Look, I like Finney.' Sal had met him once at a party and I remember they had nothing to talk about. 'But you and he are different animals, Robin. He's a fucking elephant.'

I told Sal to shut up again and, realizing that he had gone too far, he set about smothering me in the balm of his boozy good humour, but I'd lost whatever taste I'd had for his company. I drove him home. As we pulled up outside his door, he invited me in.

'Can I offer you brandy and an adrenalin surge?'

'You're seeing someone, Sal.'

'I'm resting. No strings, no illusions, just friendship and sex. It's all there is at the end of the day.'

'That's what you've learned in the face of death, is it?'

'Fuck off,' he said cheerfully.

'Sal, who in their right minds wouldn't be tempted? But we share an office.'

'So? We can save time, fuck on the desk. It would be superbly efficient. You can tell Maeve it's therapeutic. She can put it in a time-management study. Ten minutes of aerobic exercise.'

'Ten minutes? I can't wait.'

'Best not to hang round when it's in public.'

'You're going to regret this in the morning,' I muttered. I leaned over to open the door for him and pushed him gently out. He landed like a cat on the pavement.

I waved and drove off, my car feeling strangely empty. When I got back home it felt empty too. I thought of our fellow diners, and how Sal had probably ruined their evening. And then I thought of Sal arriving home to his empty flat and his memories and his alcohol. I had never heard Sal talk like that before about the carnage he'd witnessed. It was rare to hear him sounding earnest about anything, unless he was on air. But that evening it was as though, once he'd started, he couldn't stop.

Carol had gone to bed, the children were fast asleep. I went around switching on lights. I turned on the TV, then turned it off again. I sat on the sofa and thought of Melanie and what Sevi had said. He'd made her sound so alone. I felt like phoning Finney. I wanted to hear his voice. But I mustn't start thinking about him like that, I told myself, I must not depend on him even for comfort. I must resist, I must get by on my own. People have so many ways of vanishing.

Six

The twins were playing with the contents of my mother's underwear drawer. Hannah had a pair of my mother's underpants on her head and William had wrapped a greying bra around his neck.

'Look at me, look at me,' he shouted, bouncing up and down.

I was sitting on the bed, watching my mother pack. Into the suitcase she dropped several very worthy books, a selection of legal journals, cotton shirts and skirts in pastel shades, trousers, a digital camera still in its box, sunglasses still with a price tag attached, a new swimming costume, goggles, an unopened bottle of sun cream. My mother has long white-grey hair and a dowdy-grey wardrobe. She had never, as long as I remember, exposed her white skin to the sun.

'I thought this was supposed to be a spiritual retreat,' I said. 'They have a pool?'

'They have a pool,' my mother answered firmly. 'There's no rule that says Buddhists can't swim.'

'I'm sure they're wonderful swimmers,' I agreed and my mother gave me a look. The look was not unamused – she was aware that this was a very New Age expedition for a very middle-aged person – but nor did the look invite me to poke further fun.

She started to battle good-naturedly with Hannah. 'I need them, darling. People still have to wear underpants in California,' she told her. 'It's the law.'

My mother was going to California to find herself. Or to lose her family, which probably amounted to the same thing. Her life has not been easy since she met my father more than forty years ago. He left her six years later, but somehow he'd left such a mess behind him – not to mention three daughters – that things didn't get much easier.

The past couple of years have been particularly tough. She works full-time as a lawyer. On top of that she had to nurse my sister Lorna through chronic fatigue syndrome, a debilitating condition that is what it sounds like, an almost perpetual state of physical exhaustion. In Lorna's case, she was almost bed-bound for two years. Her recovery over recent months has been of the two steps forward, one step back variety. She is no good at pacing herself, she never has been. She rushes forward and then she is brought up short by a wall of fatigue. But she rarely needs nursing now and she has a part-time job, although she is frustrated by the limitations her body imposes on her.

My mother was seeing Lorna through all this, and then came Adam's death and the attack on me, and she ended up playing nurse to me and babysitter to my twins through long months while I recovered. It was hardly surprising that she needed a rest, and perfectly natural that she should at long last decide to accept a standing invitation to her friend Nancy's place in Santa Barbara. But she had an open ticket and she wouldn't say when she was coming back. She was practically going into exile.

The doorbell rang. My sisters Lorna and Tanya stood at the door. Tanya's husband, Patrick, was getting their three girls out of the car.

I kissed Lorna's porcelain cheek.

'You're looking well,' I told her. She'd tied her red-gold ringlets on top of her head, so that they cascaded down, and she was wearing a brown suede jacket, tailored into her neat waist.

'Why wouldn't I?' she asked, as though she had never had a day of illness in her life. She likes to pretend that there is nothing wrong with her and never has been, which drives my mother up the wall.

Tanya has a pretty blonde look that is softer than Lorna's dramatic beauty. She wears pinks to Lorna's purples, and big baggy sweaters in pastel colours that swamp a figure she thinks is too plump.

My mother was to fly in the middle of the week, so we were having Sunday lunch together. Even Finney had submitted to the family mealtime, so momentous was the occasion. He turned up just as we were about to eat, cutting it close, as he always does on such occasions. He was looking weary. He'd been at work on a case until the early hours and he grumbled that there had been precious little progress to show for it.

'We should go away too,' he told me, as he stepped inside. 'Don't you want a holiday?'

'Uhuh,' I said, kissing him, not paying attention. Finney hadn't taken any time off as long as I'd known him, but he liked to talk about holidays.

My mother had produced an unconventional lunch, a strange vegetable risotto with a vast but wilting salad and a thick, un-identifiable soup. We all looked at it warily, and Tanya's eldest, Chloë, grimaced and rolled her eyes.

'I needed to use up the food in the house,' my mother explained. 'I've been trying all week to wean myself off meat. I just can't make myself like tofu.'

Lorna had brought a bottle of champagne, which she poured into tumblers, the only glasses my mother had.

'To welcome you back in one piece – just,' Lorna said, handing me one, 'and launch Ma on her way to California.'

My mother gave her oldest daughter a look which said – confirming what I suspected – that she would not be going to California at all if it were not for the fact that Lorna had made her too angry to stay. Lorna is the one who has embraced the return of my father after more than thirty years' absence. Embracing my father means offending my mother. Gilbert, my father, scuttled out when I was four years old, his pockets filled with a substantial amount of money that did not belong to him. For more than thirty years we thought he was dead. Or at least, Tanya and I did. It had emerged that Lorna kept in touch with him secretly all that time. When he'd turned up again nearly two years earlier, as if from a crack in the wall, he'd churned up a third of a century of trouble.

My mother raised her glass, then replied to Lorna's toast.

'How sweet of you, Lorna, to wish me so happily on my way to the far ends of the earth. Would that you had done so with your other parent.'

Lorna opened her mouth to respond, but thought better of it. The rest of us raised our glasses with our mother and drank to her rapier slash of a toast. Finney fought to control an evil grin. There was silence as we shovelled the rice busily into our mouths.

It was my mother who eventually broke the silence, asking after my friend Jane, who is hugely pregnant. Jane, I said, was terrified of childbirth.

'Well, she's a control freak,' Lorna commented. 'Control freaks hate the unpredictability of childbirth.'

'Takes one to know one,' Patrick muttered under his breath.

For the rest of the afternoon, none of us mentioned Gilbert, my father. There are other taboos too, of course. No one asks Lorna how Father Joe is, because she's touchy about her relationship with the American priest I introduced her to. Although anyone who has seen them together knows that they are in love. No one asks Lorna how she's feeling, because she likes to pretend she's not sick any more. No one asks Tanya or Patrick about work because their jobs nursing at the hospital leave them exhausted, underpaid and disillusioned. I had a sense, that afternoon, that sometimes my family's hearth is as alien as any foreign country.

I left the children at my mother's house for the evening while I took Finney out. He had to be dragged.

'Do we really have to go to the ballet?' He looked mournful.

'It's modern dance, not ballet,' I told him. 'It may even be contemporary dance. I'm not sure I know the difference. You'll enjoy it anyway.'

Half an hour later, seated in a small theatre in Islington, I was still confused, but I thought the fact that the dancers were all-but naked would at least cheer Finney. I'd seen the choreography reviewed as 'witty', although I wasn't sure what the joke was. At the intermission I elbowed Finney awake and came clean, pointing at Jacqui Darling's name in the programme.

'You see?' I said. 'Mike Darling's daughter.'

He squinted dozily down at the photographs in the programme.

'Which one is she?

'This one.' She was a small girlish woman with pale, tea-coloured skin, long dark hair in rows of tight plaits and a body like flexible steel. You could see the rest of them working as though it was heavy labour, all this jumping and pounding and twisting. But she had a natural grace and she was flirtatious too.

Finney shook his head.

'You made me sit through this because of her?'

Around us, the audience were filtering back to their seats. A woman squeezing past looked with disgust at Finney.

'I'm just curious,' I said in a low voice. 'Justin told me she's dancing with this company, and I've heard so much about her. Her father was the last—'

'For God's sake, just stay out of it.' He was irritated and spoke more loudly than was strictly necessary. 'Will you just for once, for me, stay home and look after your kids, and—'

The lights dimmed, and the theatre fell suddenly silent. His voice trailed off.

'And look after you?' I finished for him, whispering in his ear.

'I was going to say and look after yourself,' he murmured back.

'Oh,' I mouthed in the dark.

I reached for his hand and we sat there, our fingers entwined, and watched as the dancers trotted back on stage. I have never had a relationship with a man that lasted, from my father onwards. I could see the attraction of waking up in the same bed as Finney every day and retiring to the same bed at night. But I wasn't sure how these things were supposed to work. Did one live in the expectation of betrayal? Was every day a succession of compromises and concessions? Finney once saved my life. When we talk about it I pretend, of course, that I'd have survived without him, that he was simply incidental. But the fact is that without him I probably would be dead and my children orphans, which is a hefty debt, and one that I'm not sure how to repay. I know I can't hand over my independence. Of course, I'm not sure that he requires it.

Within moments I felt the grip of Finney's hand relax and I knew he was asleep.

Seven

I scoured the building for films that Melanie had made. It was a scattershot approach, no method to it. I raided the archives and came back with an armful of tapes. Dave frowned at me as I half dropped, half dumped, the mountain of videos on his desk.

'What are you looking for?'

'I'm looking for the film that goes with the photograph,' I told him.

He touched his hand to his goatee and scanned the labels on the video boxes: Kosovo, Macedonia, Congo, Liberia, Rwanda, Iraq, Afghanistan.

'For Christ's sake, Robin, you'll slit your wrists if you watch all that straight off.'

'Want to help?'

He shook his head.

'Dave, no one else has done this.'

'All right,' he said slowly. 'I suppose I can run through some video for you. Off the top of my head I'd say it looked like a desert environment, but a ditch is a ditch. There's not much to go on.'

'Can you think of anyone else who'd watch through a couple of hours of film for me? Like you said, there's an awful lot of it.'

'Some of Melanie's friends might help out.'

That afternoon I sat in the editing suite. Three times there was a knock on the door and three times it was a colleague of Melanie's. Each time I parcelled out a video or two and a copy of the photograph which I'd run off on a colour copier, and each time it was I who received thanks, as though they were grateful someone had given them something to do to help.

'So you think this Mike Darling killed her,' one of Melanie's colleagues said, as he was about to leave.

'I doubt it,' I replied, trying to sound cool. 'But he may be able to help answer some questions about Melanie's last hours.'

After that exchange I began to worry about how widely Dave had been advertising this exercise. It might be best, I thought, not to shout about the fact that I was pursuing the investigation of one man, Mike Darling, when I had no evidence that he was involved in Melanie's disappearance. Except, of course, that he had lied to everyone, including the police.

The next time there was a knock at the door I reached for a videotape from my stack, ready to dole it out, but it was Maeve who walked in.

'Robin.' Her tone was icy. I'd been ignoring her instructions, hoping she'd just let it go. She perched her bottom – or the bony surface that passed for her bottom – on top of the desk. She stretched out a manicured hand complete with red talons to pick up a videotape from the stack, glanced at its spine, then replaced it. I thought how terribly thin she had become. Her ankles looked as though they might snap just from the stress of standing. The lines across her forehead had become so deep that she looked permanently worried, and when she ran her hand anxiously through her helmet of black hair I saw that the roots were almost white. I was suddenly concerned about her. Only illness or extreme stress, surely, could take this toll.

'If you choose to ignore my warning that is, of course, your business,' she said. Her tone was controlled but furious. 'But please do me the courtesy of acknowledging that I work in your best interests. You are making me look ridiculous and it doesn't seem to have occurred to you that I may actually have been trying to spare you from getting involved in something you really don't want to be involved in.'

'I don't,' I told her slowly, 'know what you're talking about.'

'I mean that you are trying to help Melanie, if she can still be helped, but you might not be doing that.'

My face must have betrayed my confusion.

'Let me get this clear. You think in some way I'm harming Melanie?'

'Well, I'm not the one who's going to explain it to you. You've effectively gone over my head. And so,' and here her tone of voice said, 'Now your father will deal with you', but she actually said, 'now Ivor Collins wants to see you.'

Maeve as good as frogmarched me to Collins's office, although I told her I knew the way perfectly well. I had the feeling she was determined to be in on whatever conversation took place.

'Robin, thank you for coming to talk to me again. I do appreciate it.' The long, narrow face peered up at me from his desk, the snowy hair and blue eyes striking me afresh.

I nodded and glanced across at Maeve, who was leaning lightly against the wall. Indeed, she would have been incapable of leaning heavily.

'Conversation, I always find, is worth more than a mountain of memos. Maeve,' he turned to my boss, 'would you like to leave us on our own for a minute?'

Maeve, without thinking, shook her head violently.

'No,' she said, the hurt painfully obvious. 'No. I think it would be useful for me to sit in.'

A little smile crossed Collins's face, and for once I felt like jumping to her defence. Maeve might as well have come to him to beg for a plaster for her finger. She didn't want to be left out, she wanted to be in the loop. The survival of her career depended on it.

'That's fine by me,' I said.

'I think, Maeve,' Collins said slowly with what was almost a hiss, 'that it might be a good idea to find something else to do, don't you?'

Maeve flinched.

'Of course.' She fled like a will-o'-the-wisp through the door. She scarcely had to open it.

'Maeve told me about the plans for your series on missing people.' Collins started to speak the moment she was gone. 'As you know, my respect for Maeve is profound. And my respect for Melanie. Do you understand all this?'

'No,' I said, 'I don't.'

Collins gazed at my face and smiled. 'Very well,' he said, still speaking in a low, dry voice. 'In stark terms, I've brought you here to tell you you'll be pulling the Melanie Jacobs content from your series.'

I stared at him, speechless. I had never been expressly forbidden to cover a story.

He continued. 'There are simply elements of the story that you do not know and that you will inevitably have to report if you do your job properly. To do so, in fact, would be to invade the privacy of Melanie Jacobs if she is still alive. Believe me, she would not thank you.'

'So you're appointing yourself her guardian.'

'Yes.' He leaned back in his chair and it swung round with his weight. 'Yes, I am. Within the Corporation, at least. I think that is legitimate. She is not here to defend herself . . .'

'Defend . . .?'

'You don't think you are attacking her,' he said, 'but you are going at this like a bull in a china shop.'

'What are we talking about?'

'Would you choose to have all your personal and professional information shared if you went missing?'

'Isn't that what journalists do? Dig up things people don't choose to make public?'

Collins didn't answer. Instead, he got up from his seat and went and opened the door for me.

'I'm sure I have your cooperation,' he said.

I didn't reply. I didn't move. And when he saw the expression on my face, Collins changed his mind and pushed the door closed again.

'You misunderstand,' he said softly, turning back towards me. 'You simply won't make the programme. I'm speaking on behalf of Melanie Jacobs. Regard it as an instruction from beyond . . .'

He broke off and, for the first time in the conversation, looked genuinely shaken.

'Beyond what?'

'From Melanie, that's all I meant.'

I returned to the office feeling physically sick. I didn't want to hurt Melanie. But I thought it was also entirely possible that Collins had his own agenda. Without more information, I found it impossible to know what to do. Sal wasn't in the office. The darkness of the afternoon had worked its way inside the room. I turned on the light and went over to gaze out of the window. The Corporation offices look out over the shops and restaurants of London's West End. It was pouring with mid-summer rain again, but the streets were busy, and there weren't many umbrellas in evidence. It had been such a wet summer that people seemed to have got used to it. They hardly even ran for cover any more. It was as though the entire population had turned into mermaids and mermen, swimming through the streets as naturally as they walked. There were a couple of girls on the corner eating out of fast-food wrappers in the rain, apparently perfectly happy to eat chips that were slopping around in half a gallon of water. I felt as though I was looking through the glass of a goldfish bowl. I turned away. One surefire way to tell you'd got too mashed up in Corporation politics was when the outside world began to look like an alternative universe.

I sat at my desk and checked through my inbox. Guiltily, I opened some of my dozens of missing people emails. There was one from a woman whose husband left for work one morning and hadn't been seen since. She and her sons were still reeling. There was a second email from the police in Salford. Another of my missing people had been found dead and his family wanted to withdraw from the documentary. I had already done several interviews with them and I hoped they would change their minds, but I would understand if they did not.

I would be kidding myself if I thought anyone had agreed to take part in the making of this series if it was not in the hopes that they would be reunited. There's a whole world of television that specializes in fairy-tale endings, even if they have to pay the fairies. So it's hard to explain to people that I can't change anything. There are people who simply don't want to be found and there are people who walk away from everything for a good reason. It's not my job to decide who deserves to be reunited and who does not.

I checked the website that had been set up by Melanie's mother. There was a photograph of Melanie, a full description and the details of when she had gone missing and where. Nothing new.

My mobile rang. It was Q, short for Quentin, the Corporation's political editor and my friend Jane's husband-to-be (Jane had resisted marriage until Quentin could prove that he was willing and able to father a child for her).

'We've got a little girl,' he said breathlessly, 'She's perfect. Six pounds, brown eyes, bald as a golf ball. Jane says you're to come and see her now.'

At St Thomas's, I found Jane and Quentin, both exhausted, and a little scrap of a girl wrapped in soft cotton and placed in a crib at the end of the bed.

'She's gorgeous,' I exclaimed. 'So tiny.'

'We're calling her Rosemary, it's just such a pretty name we couldn't resist.'

I had never heard Q talk like this. I handed Jane the package I'd stopped off to buy on the way.

'She's such a wee thing.' Jane was fretting. 'I should have eaten more carbohydrates.'

'She's going to be fine,' Q comforted her. He was waving a champagne bottle at me and a paper cup. 'It was an easy birth. It might have been harder if she was bigger.'

'Q,' Jane said sharply, jabbing my present in his direction, 'doesn't know what he's talking about and missed every pre-natal class he signed up for, and should shut up if he knows what's good for him.'

It was a pleasure to see two professional giants shrunk to human size by one baby. Jane is the editor of *Controversies*, a late-night news analysis programme that she has managed to turn into an institution – no easy matter in an era of rolling twenty-four-hour news, and insta-analysis on the web. The programme could have been named for her. She was born with the urge to stir, and she's still doing it nearly forty years later, only now she's getting paid for it. She looked pale against the pillows. Her dramatic black hair, which is usually sculpted and pinned, had fanned out around her head. Her lips were almost white, and her Chinese skin opalescent. Jane grew up in Perth-shire, and has the accent to match, but her parents fled north China to escape Mao.

She opened the gift wrapping and soon little pink and lilac suits lay scattered around her on the white sheets.

'They're gorgeous, but will she really need so many?' she asked faintly, then added uncertainly, 'They're very pink. I'm not sure I want a pink sort of a girl.'

'You've called her Rosemary – what do you expect? Any-way, little girls are all pink, it's just the way they are,' I told her. 'You just have to go with the flow. Can I hold her?'

I lifted Rosemary in my arms. She was as light as a feather compared with Hannah and William. Her eyes were tight shut, but her little face was in constant motion as though delightful

memories of the womb were alternating with shocked realization that things now could only get worse.

'They didn't bathe her,' Jane was saying behind me. 'I hope
that's the right thing . . . all very Chinese. My mother would be
pleased.'

Jane fussed a little more and then she drifted off to sleep.
I had no desire to return to the office. The hospital room was
cosy, little Rosemary was snuggled against my tummy and Q
kept replenishing my paper cup with champagne. Q is as much
of a political animal as the men and women he covers. He has
an ear to every Corporation keyhole, a finger in every Corporation pie. There is nothing he loves more than intrigue.

It wasn't long before we'd run out of baby talk and I found
myself somewhat boozily relating to him my pursuit of Melanie
and describing that morning's conversation with Ivor Collins.

I told Q how the conversation with Collins had ended.

'He was going to say "beyond the grave".'

'You think Collins knows Melanie's dead? You're not lining
him up as a murderer?' He smiled with the slightly supercilious
expression that sometimes rubs me up the wrong way. 'I've
never found him that sinister. Surely we all assume that she's
dead. I know I do.'

I pulled a face, unwilling to agree, and changed tack.

'Maybe he's right, I'm just blithely marching into something
I know nothing about,' I said. 'It's the same with all these people
who've disappeared. Once you begin to dig a little under the
surface nothing's as simple as it looks.'

'Collins's concerns about Melanie aren't of the same nature,
are they? He's not worried about skeletons in the closet?'

'Wouldn't fear of exposure make her want to disappear?'

Q pulled a face.

'Exposure of what?'

'Well, exactly. It's all smoke and mirrors. Maybe Collins just
has a guilty conscience so he's trying to frighten me off.'

'A conscience? Collins? I don't think so.'

We both fell silent. Q reached for the bottle again, and all I could hear was the dribble of champagne into his cup, and a newborn baby crying in the next room.

'I'll keep my ear to the ground,' he said.

Eight

I read *Goodnight Moon* to the children determinedly through a chorus of giggles and shrieks. The house in *Goodnight Moon*, with its high ceilings and its fireplace and its rich paint-work, warm carpet and striped heavy curtains is not unlike our flat. The rooms are cavernous and I sometimes look up from the book and half-expect to see a little old lady sitting in a rocking chair by the fireplace, whispering 'hush'. I close the book, switch on a tape of nursery songs, lean over to kiss twin foreheads, spend a few moments begging them to be quiet, then make my way to the kitchen, holding my breath in case one of them hears my footsteps and calls out to me. I can still hear flurries of laughter, and Hannah shouting out, 'Goodnight toilet!' to a squeal of delight from William, and there is even the thump of a foot on the floor, but I ignore it.

I toast a piece of bread and grill a tomato on top with garlic, chopped basil and butter, which is all the cooking I have the energy for. Then I collapse on the sofa and put in a videotape, turning the volume down low so that the sound of gunfire doesn't disturb the children. After a few minutes, I put my supper aside, unable to carry on eating.

These are images of hell on earth, a pendulum of violence that Melanie clings to as it swings from continent to continent. In Gaza she runs with the camera, filming, through a cloud of tear gas. I can hear it catching in her throat, hear those who are running alongside her crying out, see them falling to their knees, clutching at their eyes.

In Kosovo she tours sites of mass graves on open green hills. She is handed a white paper suit to cover her clothes in order to enter a bullet-riddled house, the site of a massacre, which is full of rotting bodies. She is handed a mask because inside investigators are piecing bodies together like jigsaws. She stops filming to put on the protective gear. She and her fellow journalists process in, walk from room to room, pausing here and there, as if they were looking to buy a property. In the village, a group of women wail for a son whose body is exhumed from a mass grave and transferred, in a sheet, to a coffin.

In Falluja she films body parts in the streets, patrolling troops, burned flesh. She is there when a roadside bomb goes off and four soldiers are felled in an instant, quivering on the ground, waiting for help, blood spilling from them. It is the sound that makes my flesh ice over, the high-pitched cries of pain. They are the cries of grown men, but their screams sound like a newborn demanding help to stay alive.

In several of the film clips, especially in Rwanda and Iraq, there are images which would never have made it onto television even in the middle of the night when no one is watching. Images so evil that they would leave a bloody stain on the television screen. Men, women and children turned into gaping wounds, fly-crawling orifices, brains liquified, entrails raw, flesh pierced and punctured, eyes open with the spirit fled. She must have known these images would never be shown, so I wonder why she films them. Is it because she wants to campaign, back in headquarters, for a more bloody telling of the story? There are journalists who believe that to report war in the way it arrives, sanitized, on the evening news, is essentially to misrepresent the truth. Is it because she feels these things must be documented, whether or not they are ever shown? Or could it be a morbid fascination born of being too long around the dead?

Suddenly it seems ridiculous to me to suspect Mike Darling

of anything when all at once the accepted version of Melanie's disappearance seems to make perfect sense. Which horror of all these was the worst? What one thing makes a person break who has already seen so very much? Because, it seems to me as the images flicker across the scene, that to break is inevitable.

When the telephone rings, I am relieved of the obligation to watch, and I find myself filling my lungs with air as though I have been drowning. It is Q, Rosemary crying in the background.

'Are you free at one for lunch tomorrow?' the new father asks. 'I may have something for you.'

The day Lieutenant Sean Howie died in Kabul, three years ago, his parents were not there. Nor were the superior officers who would later try to determine how exactly he had died. At least the commanding officers had access to evidence, to witness reports, to forensic clues. His parents, however, had only the little that they could glean from talking to their son's friends, and they had little enough to say. Some could not bring themselves to talk about Sean's death, and others were intimidated by the cloak of secrecy the Ministry of Defence had thrown over the events of that night. The little information his parents had they transcribed, and that meagre record of their son's last minutes they sent to Ivor Collins and to the army because they blamed both the army and Melanie for his death.

I don't know how Q got hold of the dossier, but he passed it to me over a hurried lunch the next day.

'It's a photocopy,' he said in a low voice, 'but I'm assuming it's the information that matters. As you can see, the Corporation received it a year ago, long after the boy died.'

I thanked him.

'Though I'm not sure how far I can go with this,' I said. 'Can I ask how you got hold of it?'

'I have a friend in personnel,' he said and winked.

Back at home in the evening, I thumbed through the pages of printout. The complaints against the army were fairly well documented. Sean Howie's parents had a letter from their son complaining about the communications equipment his unit had been issued with. It had a tendency to go off-frequency, as indeed it had done on the night he died.

This claim was backed up by photocopies of other soldiers' letters home, letters that had been passed on by friends. One soldier sent a wish list of equipment to his mother, including a walkie-talkie, and asked her to buy them on the Internet and get them sent to him, but Lieutenant Sean Howie asked for nothing. He just joked about his vulnerability.

'I suppose it gives the enemy a fighting chance,' he wrote once, 'which otherwise they wouldn't have, given as how they're not what you'd call crack troops. I never thought I'd be fighting a war without good comms. What next? Hey, lads, you're way too good to fight people this badly trained, so we're going to take away your body armour. Maybe we should pretend to be crap so they don't take away our guns.'

There was a photocopy, in the dossier, of a brief note from the army, saying that the issue of the failed communications equipment was being looked into. The note was dated two months after Sean Howie's death. I looked for a subsequent document that might give the findings of this investigation, but there was nothing.

There was, however, an extract from a letter Sean Howie had written to his girlfriend, dated just one day before he was to die. The rest of the letter was blacked out.

'We've got a camerawoman with us,' Howie wrote. 'She's a bit stand-offish, keeps herself to herself. Still, she likes the action – her camera's never off her shoulder. The only thing she's ever interested in is where the shooting is, and whether that's where we're going, and if not why not.'

That was the last word from Sean Howie. If he wrote again there was no record of it among the papers I had been given.

The next transcript in the dossier came from a fellow soldier, Taylor Sullivan, describing the ambush in which Howie was killed.

We were on the road out of town when we realized we couldn't raise anyone on the comms. We carried on and out of the town, thinking we'd catch up with the others. We didn't think we were lost, just that we'd got a bit behind. It's so hot, we're all boiled up and we're all on the lookout for trouble, a bit on edge. Mel the camerawoman's with us, we're all crammed up, and she's always got her head stuck out because she wants to see what's going on, and she says, 'Look, there's a bridge. Wasn't there a bridge on the route?' And Sean, who's driving, says, 'You must be crazy, I'm not going over there without any cover.' I thought Sean was right. Melanie wants us to engage with the enemy because that's how she gets her pictures. But we just wanted to get home safe. But Phil mutters something about Sean being too scared to move – it's like if Melanie said that's the way to go, Phil thinks she must be right. He was a bit soft on her, although I didn't see the attraction. Sean gets all fired up, and they have a bit of an argument. Sean asks Phil to repeat what he said, and Phil says, 'What's the point? You heard me. First you get us lost, then we're going to get shot at while we sit here dithering.' Sean is really pissed off, and he's got to show he's up for anything, and he drives towards the bridge. There's this whacking great pipe on the road, and we have to drive around it at an angle to get onto the bridge. I know we should have thought about it, but it all happened so fast. Once we're on the bridge we realize – the pipe blocks off a retreat because we can't reverse at that angle. Sean, who has sixth sense, says something about how it's too quiet. Then he says 'Fuck,' and something explodes at the front of the vehicle, knocking us sideways, and the Land Rover collapses and tips onto its side, and we fall on top of each other, and the engine's groaning and smoking, and we pile out, and someone's screaming, and Phil's wetting himself, and we're under fire, and we're sheltering under the Land Rover, returning fire where we can, and then up rolls the Land Rover that was behind us in the patrol, and I know they can get us out of there. But I don't see Sean anywhere, and when I go and open the door of our Land Rover, he falls out, and you can see he's dead. I'm not going to go into details, obviously, but I want you to know that he must have died instantly. The rest of us got out in one piece, but Sean didn't, and I want you to know that he died because of his bravery in the service of his country.

Taylor Sullivan had printed his telephone number at the top of the page, but when I called, it was a woman's voice that answered. I explained who I was and that I would like to speak to Taylor. But that, it seemed, was a problem.

'I'm terribly sorry,' she said in a voice so quiet I had to strain to hear her, 'but my son was asked not to speak to anyone about what happened, and although the investigation's over it's probably better for us if he doesn't go over it all again in his head. He should never really have written to Sean's parents at all, although of course he felt he had to. Anyway, it's all there. If you've seen the letter, you've seen all there is. He goes over it again and again, and it's always just as he wrote it.'

I tried to persuade her, but in her quiet and polite way she was unmovable.

I called Finney. I just wanted to talk. The misery of last night's videos and today's dossier lay heavy on me. I was trying not to rely on Finney for moral support, of course, trying to maintain my independence. But that all seemed trivial in comparison with the world as I was seeing it through Melanie's eyes. How, I wondered, could she not have needed Sevi to comfort her? Finney sounded cheerful enough, but something in his voice made me realize I had no idea what he was doing, or who he was with. I pictured him at the other end of the line, in jeans and a sweater, dark, greying curls in need of a cut. Finney's wife left him even before Adam left me.

Finney is self-sufficient. He grew up in a children's home. It was a kind place, but still he had to learn to look out for himself. No one ever expected him to go to university and so he never expected to go. Instead he went from one institution to another, from orphanage to police force. I once met the woman who ran Finney's orphanage – she had since retired – and she told me that Finney was remarkably self-contained. She said that he spoke very little, and yet he possessed a clarity of purpose which led the other children to accept him as their leader even when he ignored them.

He is entirely familiar with the selection of ready-to-cook meals at his local supermarket and has mastered the art of the two-for-the-price-of-one shop. He's hardly ever at home, so he saves his washing up for a once-a-week extravaganza of suds and loud music. He hates watching television. He reads rapidly and for information, not for pleasure.

I imagine him, the sitting-room window thrown wide onto his tiny yard to let in the sun, lying on his oversized sofa, remote control within arm's reach on the carpet, his eyes closed. He listens to a small selection of music that he loves. He has a soft spot for gospel music – something I only know because I walked in on him one day and found him singing an improvised bass harmony. He stopped as soon as he saw that I was there and neither of us has mentioned it since.

He listens to the radio for hours, in particular to the news and current affairs programmes, although he is scathing about journalists. And he likes silence.

When I telephoned there was a woman's voice in the background, and I didn't know whether it was the television, the radio, or a live woman.

'Do you want to come over?' I offered.

He sighed.

'I've got a couple of things I have to do here.'

'OK. I'm going to take a trip down to Mike Darling's house on Saturday. Do you want to come? No kids. We could have a pub lunch on the way.'

Adam's parents, Norma and Harold, were scheduled to come and take the children out for the day. There was a pause, and I fancied I could hear Finney thinking. I guessed he wanted to warn me off Mike Darling again, but that he didn't dare.

'Can I let you know in the morning? I'm sorry, I'm just busy with things . . .' his voice was low and distracted.

I assured him that was fine. I put the phone down and stared at it, as though it could tell me more. It wasn't like Finney to play hard to get.

Nine

Sydenham Hill Wood has absorbed the gardens of grand Victorian villas, so that amid the sycamores and the dog violets there are small ponds and a ruined folly. The address Justin had given me was on the edge of the wood. I pulled up outside and peered out at the house.

'Oh my,' I murmured. I was beginning to see why Justin was dreading his homecoming. Once upon a time – a hundred and thirty years ago – this would have been an impressive home, tall, imposing, detached from its neighbours and surrounded by lawns. Now it looked like the shaky survivor of an earthquake, its red-brick walls propped up by scaffolding, windows gaping darkly on the second floor, a slip of fabric taking the place of curtains on the first. On the ground floor the original windows had gone altogether, to be replaced by much larger panes of glass.

What I could see of the garden was crying with neglect. Much of the gravel drive was eaten up by weeds, and a large patch had disappeared under a heap of building materials, bags of cement casting a powdery pall over the spiky grass. A battered green Mini was parked outside, alongside a purple Polo. A pot of white paint was sitting open to receive rain and flies alike. I observed all this and shrank from it. And this was in the kind light of a sunny summer's day.

The house backed onto the wood, indeed it seemed to be almost part of it, as though, if it were only allowed to crumble further, the house would happily collapse into the earth and be digested by it. Already one side was covered in ivy, as though the process of absorption had begun.

I got out of the car and approached the front door. There was a hand-painted plaque announcing that this was the 'Tree House Gallery' and more realistically, in small lettering, 'Under Construction'.

There was no doorbell and actually no door, just a sheet of plywood shielding an unlit space. I shouted hello, but there was no reply. So I walked around the edge of the house, and was surprised to find that the garden behind, although wild, was pleasant. Pleasant enough, indeed, to be inhabited.

I could see a woman sitting in a deckchair, her head thrown back so that her face was warmed by the sun. Her hands lay in her lap, her fingers touching the edges of what looked like a blue airmail letter. Her long black hair twisted in heavy curls over her shoulders. I knew her from Justin's description. Anita, her skin the colour of wheat, the inheritance from a Sri Lankan mother. She had a soft fullness to her, no longer the lean lines of youth, but she was beautiful.

Cross-legged in a yoga pose, the soles of her feet facing upwards, head bent over a book, was the girl I had last seen on stage as Finney dozed beside me. Jacqui, the twenty-year-old dancer, Mike and Anita's daughter. She was tickling Christopher, her baby brother, who crawled around on a blanket on the grass next to her. He was one of those babies who would have the same face at forty as he had at ten months. There was no baby fat on him. He scarcely seemed to notice his sister's attempts to make him laugh. But he kept butting her with his head and crawling onto her, and curling up against her as though he craved contact.

Jacqui looked up and watched as I approached Anita, who opened her eyes but made no attempt to emerge from the deckchair. I wasn't sure that her eyes were focusing.

'I'm Robin Ballantyne. I came to see Justin.'

Anita nodded at me, her eyelids barely lifting. Then she seemed to doze off again. Her face was sad even in sleep. She looked fragile, as though if we woke her again she would burst into tears.

Jacqui scrambled to her bare feet and came over, and immediately the baby boy crawled after her and wrapped his arms around her leg.

'I saw you dance last week,' I told her.

'Yeah?' She smiled. 'It went OK, or so I was told.'

I told her that I had enjoyed the evening, which was true up to a point.

'Christopher was in the wings,' she told me, bending to touch the baby's nose with the tip of her finger. 'We sneaked him in in his pushchair and he was good as gold. He loves to have music around him.'

Jacqui's hair was plaited and beaded, and there were flashes of metal at her nose and her belly, which was bare between low-slung trousers and a high-cut sweatshirt. She had her mother's bone structure, and it was that which made her more than pretty. There was something about the set of the jaw and the cheekbone that would, for the rest of her life, send men like Justin to the ends of the earth for her. Her eyes were her father's, observant and restless, never still.

I glanced back at Anita and Jacqui's eyes followed mine.

'Mum's a bit strung out,' she said defensively. As she spoke, she stroked Christopher's head. 'She's not sleeping at night, so she dozes off during the day.'

'I was hoping to see Justin.'

'He's still at the hospital, his physio got delayed. He asked me to look after you until he got back. I don't know . . .' Her voice trailed off and her eyes went to her mother again. 'Do you want to look around?'

I bit back what I felt like saying, which was that I was happy to wait in the car. Instead I followed her as she picked her way through the long grass in bare feet. Her toenails were painted a deep gold. She had swept Christopher up in her arms, and he was clinging to her like a koala bear. I glanced back, but Anita was still sound asleep and her mouth had fallen open. She looked twenty years older, like the grandmother rather than the mother of the child sitting so comfortably on his big sister's hip.

'Is your dad back from Cambodia yet?' I asked.

She shook her head and looked sideways at me.

'He's keeping out the way,' she said. 'It's what he does best.'

So much, I thought, for a man trained to face any enemy.

'He's good at schedules, and equipment and expeditions and orienteering, and all that stuff, but he's crap when it comes to his wife being pissed off at him. Or his friend. Or me, actually.'

'So you're all pissed off with him.'

Mike's daughter gave me a hard look that, had she but known it, mirrored her father's almost exactly. I found myself wishing I had a camera with me now. The rules about the use of hidden filming are strict – there's got to be a clearly demonstrable reason to invade people's privacy, but it's the only way truly to be a fly on the wall. As soon as you lug a full-size news camera into any situation, you might as well be directing a Broadway musical for all the reality you're going to get on film.

'I mean hypothetically,' she said.

'Has your father talked about me?' I knew I was pushing her on the subject of Mike, and it didn't surprise me when she just gave me a cool glance and shook her head.

There were more building materials piled outside the back door, including a heap of bricks. Jacqui pushed open the glass door and we stepped into a large, light space that had been opened up so that it was no longer rooms but a series of spaces defined by partitions.

I saw that the alcoves, which would eventually be exhibition galleries, were doubling for now as living space.

'Mum's flat on the second floor isn't really ready yet,' Jacqui explained. 'Sheryl and Kes have moved into the first floor, but Justin can't do stairs yet. Mum and Christopher have been using this area downstairs anyway, so Justin's got a bed down here too.'

At Jacqui's invitation I peered into one of the spaces, which was transformed by its only furniture, a bed, long and low and beautiful, with a tan leather headboard that curved in elegant Italian lines. The white sheets were twisted, tumbled to the floor. There was something about the careless beauty of that bed that arrested my eyes.

'They've knocked down lots of the original internal walls, as you can see. Not all of them, though, so the place feels open, but there are lots of alcoves, which means lots of wall space to hang pictures. And they've enlarged the windows to let more natural light in. They haven't painted yet, so it still looks a bit rough.

'These are Mum's,' Jacqui went on, with a hint of pride in her voice, and I dragged my eyes from the beautiful bed and looked where she was pointing, at a row of tiny oils hung on the unplastered brick walls, each a miniature explosion of colour. I stepped up to look at the pictures more carefully, and saw on examination that each was an exquisitely rendered still life, a classic arrangement, vase and flowers and fruit. There was another canvas on an easel, the painting scarcely begun, no more than a few tentative strokes. I went over to look at it. Even in these early stages, it was clear that this was to be a painting of the bed, the twist of the sheet already outlined in brown ink.

'The paintings are beautiful,' I told Jacqui. I bent down to pick up a brush where it had fallen on the floor. I handed it to her and she smiled.

'Do you know what this brush is made from?' she asked me.

I shook my head. I knew nothing about painting.

'It's called Kolinsky,' she told me. 'It's mink. This one isn't so romantic.' She held up a second brush. 'It's weasel hair.'

There were bottles of turpentine and linseed oils, and tubes of oil, their names as gorgeous as their colours: burnt umber, Chinese vermilion.

'Luckily Mum does big ones too,' she said, smiling wryly

and nodding at a stack of canvases in the corner, 'or we'd never fill all the wall space.'

'Is the bed your mum's too?' I couldn't help asking.

She nodded.

'Whatever else you say about her, you can't say she doesn't have a good eye. And that's Christopher's room.' She gestured at the neighbouring space, with a baby's crib and a camp bed. 'Mine too at the moment.'

'You live here then?'

Jacqui pulled a face.

'No. Definitely not. I share a house with friends off the Caledonian Road. I'm just here temporarily. That's the theory, anyway.' She broke off and gave a shake of her head, then considered me. I had the strong impression that she really wanted to talk, and when she spoke again it was as though she was sharing a confidence. 'For years Mum's been worried sick about Dad and all the places he goes to and the things he has to do. She's not the world's most independent person. So without him she's like a shadow of herself. She was so happy when he said he'd leave the army and come and be at home, and that he wouldn't go away again. There's plenty of security work not too far from here. So Mum started painting again and then she got pregnant right away, which they said was an accident, and they decided to go in together with Sheryl and Kes on this place. And then Christopher was born and Mum got post-natal depression, and Dad buggered off to the other side of the world, and she's like a zombie all over again.'

'Is your mum on medication?'

'I don't know. She went to see the doctor, but I don't know if he did anything for her. She must be taking something – she's not herself.'

'So you've been left holding the baby,' I said.

'I don't mind that,' she said. 'Well, I do. That sounds terrible. He's my little brother. But I can't be his mother. And to tell you the truth that's what I'm doing right now, being his mum because his own mum isn't up to it.'

'How can you look after Christopher and rehearse for a show?'

'Yeah, well, that's the question.'

Jacqui turned and led me around the rest of the space. In the corner, as far as it was possible to be from Anita's bedroom, Justin had set up camp in another alcove.

Justin's lodgings seemed to consist of a mattress on the floor, with a duvet crumpled into a mound on top of it. The bedding looked too hot and heavy for summer nights. Jacqui stared at Justin's bed.

'He's been saying he might as well have died,' she said.

'I think I'd be pretty depressed too,' I told her. 'It doesn't mean it will last.'

'He doesn't think he's going to be able to do anything,' she said quietly, 'like walk and run and have a job and a girlfriend.'

Confusion clouded her face.

'He'll do all those things,' I told her. 'Justin doesn't strike me as the gung-ho type. It'll take him a while, but he'll get there.'

'If he can do one of those things, he'll believe he can do the others.' She sounded as though she was thinking aloud.

'It's going to take him a while to find his way through it.'

'Yes, but other people can help him,' she said with determination, and I thought that in that moment she had reached a decision.

We heard movement from the staircase, and from the shadows first a woman and then a man emerged. The woman extended a large-boned hand. She had a disconcerting smile that turned her mouth down, not up. She was of indeterminate age, with long, uniformly black hair. She wore a Lycra T-shirt and leather trousers that followed exactly the line of her too-thin legs, rising to a large flat bottom and a layer of thickening waist. Her fingernails were glossed. She looked down a narrow nose at me as I told her my name. Her face, I felt, would once have been pretty and responsive, but it had hardened and become aloof, every feature coated in foundation, powder, the mascara on the lashes grating onto the loose skin beneath. Her eyes had a skimming, quick-moving quality to them that suggested she did not want to dwell too long or look too deep.

'Sheryl.' Justin's stepmother gave me her name. 'Who are you?'

The man who had followed her, elderly, with pronounced cheekbones and thin white hair, pushed past and extended towards me a hand that was covered in age spots.

'I know who you are, Miss Ballantyne.' He spoke slowly and smiled an enormously friendly smile. 'I'm Ronald Evans, I recognize your face from the television.'

I smiled tightly. People who saw my face in the newspaper and on television at the time of Adam's death do sometimes recognize me. I never react well.

Sheryl's eyes went to Justin's mattress.

'I didn't know we were having press here. We're not usually in this state.'

She looked around her impatiently, wanting to tidy us all up. But Ronald was talking enthusiastically, his head nodding slightly, beyond his control.

'I'm Sheryl's next-door neighbour. Don't you find it impressive what they are doing? My dear – ' and here he turned to her and seized her hand in his – 'you won't regret it, despite the temporary difficulties. Discomfort is a little thing weighed against the success of your project.'

'Ronald,' Sheryl told me, 'says that our surroundings are expressions of our inner landscape. He's a man of great vision.'

Ronald Evans made an embarrassed noise and turned away slightly.

'Sheryl's too kind,' he said. 'She asked my opinion about one or two things, and I gave it. I don't think I've quite reached the

status of a visionary. Has anyone offered Miss Ballantyne a cup
of tea?'

Nobody answered him. Sheryl had started straightening
Justin's bed and Jacqui was watching her, scowling. Ronald took
me by the hand and led me into another alcove, where a kettle,
a toaster and a microwave seemed to constitute the kitchen. He
looked around, then hissed at me, 'I don't know how long they
can all camp like this. Let's go up to Sheryl's, it's much more
comfortable. Sheryl.' He turned and spoke over his shoulder,
'I'm going to take Miss Ballantyne upstairs, if you don't mind.'

She waved her hand in agreement and went on gathering
up Justin's dirty clothes from the floor. Ronald led the way
upstairs slowly and shakily, speaking as he went. 'It's a terrible
strain to have everyone on top of each other like this. I don't
mean . . . oh no, I don't mean it like that at all.'

We got to the top of the stairs, and Ronald came to a halt
and gathered breath. I looked around me and found it difficult
to believe that I was in the same house.

The overwhelming style was what I believe some magazines
would describe as 'contemporary'. A sofa was covered in leop-
ard-print fabric and at the windows the scraps of fabric I'd seen
from the outside turned out to be draped gauze. The dining
chairs were moulded metal against a glass table. A great deal of
effort – never mind money – had clearly gone into all this, but
the overall effect was unfortunate. There were incongruous
touches that suggested flounces rather than moulded metal
formed the landscape of Sheryl's soul. There were embroidered
cushions on the leopard-skin sofa, and the fabric at the windows
was secured with vast pink bows. I followed Ronald into a small
but well-equipped kitchen. He filled the kettle with water and
turned to me. 'It's been such a stressful time. The news of
Justin's injury. You can imagine, it was devastating for Kes.'

He said the name Kes with a certain amount of awkwardness, as though it required some concentration to pronounce.

'I haven't met Kes.'

'Ah, well.' He stopped for a moment, a teabag between finger and thumb. 'Mike and Kes are very good friends.'

'So I've heard.'

'But Justin is Kes's son. He blamed Mike, of course. It should never have been allowed to happen.'

I made a non-committal noise.

'I was here for dinner the night they heard – I do so admire Sheryl.' He paused and his voice dropped to a whisper, 'Sheryl's the only cheerful thing around here at the moment. She often comes over to me in the evening to watch television, just for the company, her husband's away so much. Anyway, as I was saying, we were all having dinner in the garden. Sheryl is a wonderful cook and she always wants to to look after people, so she'd cooked a pheasant casserole. But Kes was desperately rude about Mike – after a drink or two, you know. And Anita, the poor sweet girl, she's not very with it these days, but she so wanted to defend Mike, and she did her best, but Kes was very cruel to her. I couldn't blame him, his son had been so horribly hurt. Anyway, Anita left the table in tears and rushed off inside, and Kes had to go after her and apologize. It was awful, quite awful.'

At that moment, a man appeared at the entrance to the kitchen. He was tall and thin, and his blond hair had faded and receded from his long face, but it was not hard to identify him as Justin's father, Kes. He looked white with exhaustion. I was not sure how much of Ronald Evans's gossip he could have heard.

'Kes,' Ronald said, looking embarrassed, 'I'm sorry. I asked Sheryl if we might make ourselves some tea.'

Kes ignored him. His eyes were on me.

I held out my hand. 'I'm Robin Ballantyne.'

'And why are you in my kitchen?' The directness of the questioned was softened by the fact that he took my hand briefly.

'I came to see Justin,' I said, smiling. 'I did ring, but I understand you were delayed.'

'You came to see Justin,' Kes echoed with a note of sarcasm. 'You don't happen to have a hidden camera on you?'

'Excuse me?'

'Mike told me all about you,' Kes said, his tone more mocking than aggressive. 'How you pitched up in Pursat, how you started asking Mike questions about the woman who disappeared. What's your game? '

'There's no game,' I said, no longer smiling. 'I came to see Justin.'

Kes looked from me to Ronald, then back again. But as he opened his mouth to respond, he was interrupted by the arrival of Anita and Sheryl. Anita's eyes were still puffy from sleep. It was Sheryl who looked excited, but as she spoke I realized that she was reporting Anita's news.

'Mike just rang Anita,' she said, 'He's coming back. Isn't that wonderful?' She held a mobile phone in her hand and she waved it high, like a victory flag.

Anita looked from Sheryl to Kes and then to me, in growing confusion. Her eyes welled with tears, and she sat down hard on a kitchen chair and started to sob. Sheryl bent solicitously over her friend.

'Perhaps you could have your cup of tea another time,' Kes said to me.

I nodded, turned away from Anita's distress, and walked downstairs, followed by a flustered and apologetic Ronald. Justin was waiting, looking anxiously up the stairs.

'You're looking much better,' I told him. 'I'll see you some other time. I think I should be off.'

'I'm sorry about all this.' He was flushed with humiliation and frustration as he fumbled his crutches awkwardly back under him so that he could walk me to the door. 'I wish I could walk away like you.'

Ten

I spent all morning trying to get hold of Finney to tell him that Mike Darling was on his way back to Britain. It wasn't my place to tell DCI Coburn what his job was, but his ability to conduct a criminal investigation far outshone mine, and my priority was to find out what had happened to Melanie. When I eventually got hold of Finney, he heard me out, but he was reluctant to get involved.

'I'm not going to tell them what to do,' he told me in a low voice. 'They'll find out soon enough that he's back. Coburn's a professional. He knows what he's doing.'

I dragged Sal to the canteen for coffee. He hated any place that didn't serve alcohol and sneered around him at anyone who dared to come close.

'I've seen an allegation that Melanie led a patrol into danger just to get the pictures. Is that possible?'

'It sounds unlikely.' Sal's eyelids were still heavy and he looked as though he was sleep-talking, but I knew his brain was wide awake. 'But Robin, you know the line between truth and finessed truth doesn't actually exist.'

'Doesn't it?'

'All right.' Sal hunched his shoulders and appeared to warm to the subject. 'Just for argument's sake, you understand. If you see a correspondent reporting from Moscow, with a window onto Red Square behind him, is he in Moscow?'

'Yes.'

'Correct. Is there a window onto Red Square behind him?'

'Probably not. There's most likely a screen, with pre-recorded film of Red Square that loops round and round. Watch long enough and the same clouds scud across the same bit of sky.'

'Is that faking it?' Sal is great on rhetorical questions, and he answered himself. 'Not at all, it's just misleading.'

'It's faking it,' I disagreed.

'Call it what you will. Faking it, being creative, that's my point.' Sal made an expansive gesture. 'How about this? You're making a documentary about Arizona. You need some filler shots, you've got so much sand it's pouring out of your ears. You have some great film you shot in New Mexico with wheeling birds in the sky. Vultures, eagles, parrots, I don't know one bloody bird from the next. You edit them in. Hey presto, New Mexican parrots in the sky above Arizona deserts. Faked, misleading? Does it matter unless you're a bird?'

'Or an ornithologist,' I said. 'Here's one. An anchor in the studio in London. He's just read a news report about a shoot-out in Atlanta. The correspondent in the USA is on the screen. He describes the shooting in dramatic detail as though he was there, or had at least interviewed a witness. But actually he just watched it on CNN. It happens all the time. But all of these are trivial, you're right.'

'Trivial.' Sal savoured the word. 'OK. You're on top of a hill in Afghanistan in a lull in the fighting, Northern Alliance fighters with a few dug-in tanks on your hilltop, Taliban opposite, everyone just sitting and waiting. So peaceful you could hear a pin drop. Down below is a village, women and children going about their business. On top of the hill, the men with the guns see you arrive with a bloody big camera, and they say hey-ho, here we go, helpful as anything. Shall we take a potshot to make your trip worthwhile? Set up your camera over there, maybe you'd like to stand in that trench we've helpfully dug.'

Sal broke off. Reached for his coffee and pulled a disapproving face as the cold liquid hit his throat.

'And?'

He shook his head, shrugged.

'Well, they'd probably have fired the guns sometime. If not that day, maybe the next. If not then, maybe in a week's time. You might as well get it on film while you're there.'

When Lorna called and reminded me it was time for our weekly lunch, I tried to back out of it. In the end I couldn't say no. By the evening my big sister is exhausted. She's returned to work on a part-time basis and her office is around the corner from mine, so we grab what we can when we can.

She suggested we meet in a café called La Dolce Vita and I agreed. There's never any point in disagreeing with Lorna. When I got there she waved me over to the window, where she'd secured a table, and greeted me as she often did with an imperative rather than a hello.

'Sit,' she ordered, 'and relax.'

It was hot outside and like a greenhouse by the window, but Lorna always feels cold, so I put up with it. I found myself almost blinded by the sunlight, so I dug my sunglasses out of my bag.

'Did I miss something? You've won an Oscar?' Lorna enquired. I glared at her.

'Seriously, how's your face?'

She reached out across the table and I allowed her to remove my sunglasses and lift my hair back from my scar.

'I can hardly see it,' she said. 'I don't know what all the fuss was about. OK, let's order or we'll never get our food.' She beckoned a waiter and ordered, on my behalf as well as hers, two grilled vegetable salads. 'That is what you want, isn't it?' she checked as he turned to go.

'That's fine.'

She's my sister, so my expression immediately alerted her to the fact that my mind was not on grilled vegetables and when I said nothing, she persisted.

'It's nothing,' I told her and refused to budge. Lorna sticks her nose into everyone's business. You have to give her the verbal equivalent of a light smack to keep her out of it.

Lorna was annoyed, but there was also something eating her up, something making her excited and jumpy.

'Joe is coming over,' she told me.

I had introduced Lorna to Father Joe Riberra nearly two years ago, and it was difficult to forget the bolt of electricity that seemed to pass between them as they shook hands that first time. I knew they'd been in email contact since, but I didn't know whether sexual energy of that sort could flourish in the ether. Had she converted him to lust or had he converted her to the Lord?

It soon emerged that Lorna had seen a programme a couple of days before about the celibacy of the priesthood and it was now obsessing her. Did I realize that celibacy was not a dogma of the church, but a regulation – that the pope could change it at will? she asked. Did I realize that many priests had left the official Catholic church in order to marry, but continued in a breakaway church? Did I realize that in the early church priests had married and had defied calls to abstain from sex, that they had had children, and that some popes were even the sons of popes, and that it was not until the year 1139 that Pope Innocent II finally decreed that priests must not marry?

'It sounds as though you made notes.'

'I just remember because it's so interesting,' she retorted. 'Don't you think it's interesting? We've all grown up thinking Catholic priests have to be celibate, but they don't, not really.'

'Lorna,' I said gently, 'you'd have to convince him, not me, and I would think he knows most of this already.'

She stared at me.

'I have to have him,' she said, tears rising to her huge eyes.

I gazed at her and my heart went out to her. When we were young, she was the dominating force, the stunning beauty, the razor-sharp mind. For the past few years she had been physically incapable of taking control of her life. Now, as she recovered her energy, she seemed to want to grab hold of everything and bend it to her will, as though all of this – a hunger for love, the need for sex – had roared back to her full throttle.

There were many times, when we were young, when Lorna had comforted me. But it has always been impossible for me to comfort her. When I started to speak she waved me off the subject. I waited, as always, on her whim. When she spoke again it was in a conversational tone.

'Gilbert,' she said, and as soon as she uttered his name I knew this topic might be easier for her, but not for me. 'Gilbert ran into trouble in France.'

'What kind of trouble?' My voice sounded heavy.

'I dread to think – business trouble, I suppose. He's not very forthcoming, but he needed a place to stay, so I've let him stay at Ma's. Well, Ma's not there.' She was immediately on the defensive and with good reason. 'The place is empty. It might as well be used or it's just going to waste.'

My jaw had dropped. I was appalled.

'She'll kill you,' I said. Which was not, in my view, an exaggeration. What Ma would do when she returned to find her former husband and anti-Christ installed in her home was too horrible to contemplate.

Lorna had that obstinate look in her eye that we had all missed so much while she was ill, and which now irritated me beyond reason.

'She'll never know – he'll be gone long before she gets back. He understands it's just temporary, but he's so grateful. He's got nowhere else to go.'

'And why is it he has no friends?' I challenged her. 'Could it be that he is untrustworthy and dishonest, and takes advantage.'

'He has me.' Lorna was gruffly defensive.

'You're mad,' I told her and I was really angry. Angry that she was unable to let well alone, angry that she was wilfully antagonizing our mother, angry that she was getting me involved.

For an hour I tried to talk Lorna out of installing Gilbert in Ma's house, but either she didn't see it or she relished the prospect of baiting Ma. I suspected the latter and by the time I left the restaurant we were scarcely speaking.

When I got back to my desk, I found an email waiting from my mother.

It's all very pretty, obviously. But what is the Point? What am I supposed to be Doing with myself? I'm Bored. I think I will be back later this week. I'm going to ring up and find out about planes. I haven't unpacked, I don't think I belong here. Nancy seemed quite Normal in London, but I can't get the hang of her here.

It was as well she had not overheard my conversation with Lorna, or she would indeed be on the next plane. I replied.

You're scarcely off the plane, Ma, give it a chance. For heaven's sake RELAX.

And then I remembered that was exactly what Lorna had told me to do before she sent my blood pressure rocketing.

That afternoon several things fell into place. Henry from the photo archive finally rang me and gave me the name of the photographer who had taken the picture of Mike and Melanie.

Edwin Rochester. I had never heard the name, but I called around and learned that he was a young freelancer. I rang around some more – by now I was calling way beyond the circle of my immediate acquaintances – and within another hour I had a cellphone number for him. When I finally got through to him, it felt a little like tracking down Father Christmas. Except that he had a New Zealand accent. He was at Heathrow, he told me, about to fly off to Chechnya. How could he help me? I could hear him scratching his head at first, when I described the photograph. But then he got it. Afghanistan, he told me: the photograph had been taken on the road from Kabul to Mazar-e-Sharif in late October three years earlier, just before the launch of the air war. I got to my feet and fired questions at him while I paced the room. This new piece of information was a revelation. Afghanistan, between Kabul and Mazar-e-Sharif, north of the Salang Pass, on a road of stark, arid beauty with minefields to right and left and the bright fertility of an irrigated valley in the distance. That was where Mike Darling and Melanie had met for the first time. And immediately my brain made the connection with Sean Howie, who had died in an ambush in Kabul. Melanie had been there, too, weeks later.

'What happened?' I asked over the sounds of the tannoy at his end.

'Melanie and I were driving north to join the Northern Alliance. It was a pretty hellish journey. We spotted this patrol stuck a couple of hundred metres away in a little valley. They'd been following a jeep track off the main road – God knows where they were heading – and we saw them from the road and drove down out of curiosity. We might even have offered to give them a tug. But as soon as we got there we came under fire from the ridge. A couple of them were out of the vehicle trying to move some rocks, and we'd just got out of our jeep to go and talk to them, so when they started firing we were all way out in the open and we hit the ground. That's when I took the photo.'

'What happened then?'

'Well, there was some shooting back and forth, and after a while they scarpered and we got out of there. Melanie stayed with the patrol – she'd been trying to get film of special forces.'

'They asked her along?'

Edwin gave a bark of laughter.

'You must be kidding. Those guys can't stand journalists. Melanie was muttering to me that she wanted to stick around, but I wasn't interested. I had to get on to Mazar-e-Sharif. So Melanie told me to drive on and leave her there, and that she'd catch up with me later. So that's pretty much what I did. The next time those guys turned around, they'd have just found her there with her backpack and her camera.'

'You just left her there? In the middle of Afghanistan?'

'Hey.' He sounded defensive. 'You can't argue with Melanie when she's got an idea in her head.'

I shook my head in disbelief. But the fact was that she had survived. Besides, something else was nagging at me.

'So how did the photo get to have Darling's name on it if the SAS are so publicity shy?'

'I showed the photos to Melanie later when we were both back in London. She must have told me his name and I must have written it on the print and forgotten about it. I was in a hurry when I gave those prints to the publicity department, didn't really look at what was in the envelope, just dropped it off and ran. I guess someone in the publicity department didn't realize Darling's name shouldn't have been used. Actually his face shouldn't have been used either, but there you go. You say you found the picture on a publicity board? It must have been up there for years.'

'Nothing went on between Mike and Melanie did it?' I felt I had to ask, although it sounded ridiculous. From what Edwin had just told me, the photograph was taken as they met under fire. No tenderness, then, just a rude introduction.

'Between the guy in the picture and Melanie?' Edwin repeated the question incredulously, as though it sounded as

ridiculous to him as it did to me. 'If so, she didn't tell me about
it.'

I could hear, from his breathing that he was walking through
the terminal.

'Hey, that's my flight they're calling. Darling and Melanie?'
he repeated again, wonderingly, as though he might need a few
hours to think it over. 'Nah,' he said, eventually. 'What could
have gone on out there? Although anything could have happened after I left. She stayed on with them. Can't help you with
that.' In the background I could hear a woman's voice asking
for his boarding pass. 'Sorry, gotta go.'

I said goodbye, but the phone had already gone dead.

As I hung up, I realized I'd failed to ask him all the questions
a producer should ask: what is your schedule? Could you make
some time to answer some questions on film for me? I didn't
beat myself up about it. I knew Edwin would have said no
anyway. Trying to get any journalist on the receiving end of an
interview is like persuading a pig to fly. They're not attracted
by the moment of fame: they know that what goes up comes
down.

Finney called me to say he'd passed on my message about
Mike's return.

'Did you know, incidentally,' he asked, 'that Veronica Mann
is now working down there?'

Veronica Mann had worked with Finney when he was
investigating Adam's death. I had seen them both as the enemy
then, but Finney had become my lover and Veronica my friend.
Not that we had seen much of each other in the past year.

'You told me she got transferred. What was that about?'

'Some jerk making trouble for her. I dealt with him. But she
wanted a change of air.'

'Will she have anything to do with the investigation of Mike
Darling?'

'I don't even know if there's going to be an investigation of
Mike Darling,' he warned me. 'Don't hold your breath.'

I hung up, frustrated and in need of coffee. So I took a walk
to the canteen, and then to thank Henry in the picture library.
He reached under the counter and brought out a buff envelope,
full of still photographs taken by Edwin Rochester in Afghanistan. I thanked him again and took the photos back to the office.

Edwin Rochester operated on that spot where journalism
meets art and history. I thumbed through the black-and-white
prints. I was familiar with news photographs. But the play of
light and the careful composition of the frame lent these photographs an almost spiritual dimension in Edwin's hands. This is
what stills photography can do which the movie camera rarely
achieves. The movie camera appears to offer more: a continuous
flow of images, no danger of boredom, nothing missing, no gaps
and the energy, the flow, of real life. And yet it is the still
photograph that forces the viewer's eye to dwell and examine
life minutely, to confront the expression on the face, the twist of
a limb, the stance of victor or defeated.

Mostly these were pictures of combatants and civilians
caught in the crossfire. But there were pictures of village boys
leading jeeps through the shallows of a river and of donkey
convoys. There were photographs of Melanie, too, in cafes, in
hotel rooms, on her own, with other journalists. Two pictures
were of a picnic on an unidentified hillside in an unidentified
country, a blanket spread on the ground, Melanie smiling, with
a hunk of bread and cheese in her hand, and then, presumably
having eaten her fill, lying on her back in the deep grass, eyes
closed in sleep. I don't know why they were there, in the
envelope with the other pictures. They were surely of no use to
the Corporation. I rang up Henry and asked him why these
photographs were stored in the photo archive, but all he could
suggest was that Edwin Rochester had forgotten that they were
in the envelope, which tallied with what Edwin had told me on
the phone.

In several of these images, Melanie looked exhausted. Typi-
cally, she had a slight smile on her face and she was holding a

cigarette between her fingers. She dressed for comfort – T-shirts and jeans, and her hair was loose over her shoulders. She allowed the grey to show in among the brown. She was tall and strong, born to carry a camera. In one photograph she wore a sleeveless shirt, and the muscles on her arms were defined and powerful.

I flicked through the collection and it occurred to me how very many photographs there were, and how sympathetic they were, catching her in different lights, in different moods, her eyes always distant, watching, full of knowledge.

That night I went back to the videotapes. I went straight to the Afghanistan film, fast-forwarding, stopping only to check faces. At last I found it, a night-time scene in a narrow street of mud houses, four men who had adopted local dress, gathering together. I recognized Mike Darling, his face only partially swathed in a scarf.

I froze the image.

I had discounted Afghanistan after reading the account of Sean Howie's death. The whole story there was something and nothing, Melanie's involvement so minimal that I couldn't believe it had anything to do with her death. But something else had happened in Afghanistan.

I gazed at the screen, and slowly, out of context, I thought I recognized two other partially covered faces. There was Alan Hudder, whom I hadn't seen since we met in Cambodia. In Afghanistan he had looked less fleshy, more focused. The other face I recognized was that of Kes. He stood talking with the group in a low voice, as though he was giving instructions. He was gesturing with his hands. The fourth face was so heavily swathed in cloth I could not see it. The screen went blank. I frowned, suspecting mischief, then I glanced at the digital readout, which had stopped at forty-two minutes, and I realized that this at least was not a mystery. Melanie had simply run out of tape.

Eleven

The next morning, before I'd left for work, I dug out the business card that Alan Hudder had given me shortly before Justin stepped on a mine and blew his leg off. I rang his number and a woman answered.

'Yes, yes, I'm Alan's wife, Kay.' She introduced herself cheerfully. 'I'm afraid he's abroad still. Who is this?'

I introduced myself, then told her that I'd filmed an interview with her husband in Pursat and that I just wanted to follow up on a couple of things he'd said. She did not appear to have heard of me.

'I'm sure he'd be delighted to speak to you,' she said, 'but he is actually in Saudi and will be for some time.'

'Would it be possible for me to speak to him on the phone, do you think?'

'Well . . .' There was the first indication of hesitation.

'Or I don't know if you could help me with this. I know that Alan was in Afghanistan with Kes Laver and Mike Darling, and there was one other man. I wonder if you know how I can get in touch with him.'

For a moment there was complete silence on the line.

'Oh dear, no, that would be Ray Jackson,' she told me. 'He died out there.'

'Oh, I see.' Soldiers die in wartime of course, and now that she had said it I remembered Justin saying something about Ray

Jackson, and how his death had galvanized his father to leave the army. 'What happened?'

'Well, it was sniper fire, I think. Alan's never really said what sort of mission they were on.' In the background, I heard a doorbell. 'I'm sorry, I have people coming round, so I'll have to get off the phone now. But let me give you the number for Ray's wife. Her name's Alice and she lives in London. She'll be able to tell you more than I can.'

Alice Jackson sounded harried and unenthusiastic about meeting me.

'Look,' she said, 'I work in Boots at Piccadilly Circus. Come to the pharmacy counter at twelve-thirty, and I'll try to take my lunch then.'

I thanked her, and at half-past twelve made my way through aisles of shampoo and toothpaste and found a small, solid blonde woman with shoulder-length hair clipped back behind her ears wearing a badge on her chest that identified her as Alice Jackson. She had a wide mouth and large eyes, and a polite but weary look about her that was tried to its limits as she attempted to answer a series of questions from an obese woman who was asking for a tonic for her daughter.

Eventually the woman heaved herself off to look at the shelves of alternative medicines and Alice turned to me with a sigh.

'OK,' she said. 'I've got an hour for you.'

'Can I take you to lunch?'

Alice looked me up and down. I was wearing a skirt and for once my T-shirt was of the tailored, expensive kind, rather than the baggy food-stained kind.

'You know . . .?' Alice said, 'I really don't want to sit in some crowded restaurant, and if it's not crowded then I'm not dressed for it. Would it be all right if we bought some sandwiches and took them to the park?'

She went to take off her white coat and pick up her bag, then we queued at the food section to pay for sandwiches and bottles of water. We headed out of the store and into throngs of shoppers. Eros sat on top of his plinth. With the best will in the world he'd have hit the wrong man and woman if he tried to take aim on a pair of lovers in that crowd. We elbowed our way towards Green Park.

'You must get tired of hearing everyone's problems,' I said.

'Oh, it's all right,' she said. 'It takes my mind off my own problems. And it makes me thankful for my good health and for Olivia's.'

'Olivia's your daughter?'

'Yes, she's ten now. She was seven when her father died. Look, I don't know what you want to know. I try not to dwell on Ray's death. It upsets me too much and I don't have time to be upset.'

Ahead of us a Japanese couple vacated a park bench and we sat down, a fat grey squirrel immediately approaching to sniff around us. We unwrapped our sandwiches.

'Did you hear about Melanie Jacobs, the camerawoman who disappeared?' I asked.

She didn't remember the details, but anyway they weren't the most important thing. I explained that I was tracing Melanie's life back through the film that she'd taken, and that I'd seen her husband's face on the tape from Afghanistan, along with the faces of Alan, Mike and Kes. I described the scene to her, the small group of men in local dress about to enter a small town of earthen dwellings at night. She asked me about the date on the tape, and I told her it was October three years earlier.

Alice went pale. She placed the sandwich on its plastic wrapper and stared down at it.

'I think the film was taken in a village somewhere south of Mazar-e-Sharif,' I said, 'and that small special forces patrols like Ray's were being sent on missions to make contact with local militia chiefs.'

'So that was her, then, the camerawoman who was with them that night. She's the one who disappeared.' She frowned. 'The film must have been taken the night Ray died.'

I didn't want to press her, so I sat and waited, sipping from my water bottle. The sun beat down on us.

'The night Ray died,' she repeated slowly. 'Well, it's all supposed to be secret, but I can't see how it matters now. I don't know all the details myself. But from what I've been told, the men were going behind enemy lines on a routine reconnaissance patrol. That's one of the things they were trained to do, to go in small groups behind enemy lines and see what was there, so everyone knew what they were getting themselves into. Anyway, the way I know that it must be the night Ray died is because I know there was a camerawoman there when he died. And that was the only time they had a journalist with them. I know it was a bit controversial.' She glanced at me, as though I would object to her describing Melanie's presence as controversial.

'Of course they never recovered his body – he was officially missing in action. So there was a lot of investigation into what went wrong. They couldn't get it straight for a long time; at least, they couldn't tell me exactly how he died, or why. In the end, I was told they were ambushed, and Ray was shot in the eye at short range by a sniper, and died instantly. End,' she said slowly and deliberately, 'of story. I'm sorry, I know that sounds heartless, but it nearly destroyed me to have everything picked over. I have Olivia. I have to move on. I told . . .'

She stopped short, and picked up her sandwich and took a bite.

'Who did you tell?'

She gave me a look, chewed and swallowed. 'I told the others: Mike and Kes and Alan.'

'What did you tell them?'

'That I can't keep going over it. I have to move on. The men were all so close, and Sheryl and Anita and Kay, they were so supportive. Sheryl and Kes took such good care of me after Ray's death. Sheryl especially – she used to bring me food, and help with Olivia's homework and, oh, she was so kind. Kes too. So kind.'

She chewed her lip, her eyes fixed on some distant point in the past, then shook her head.

'I know they were only trying to help, but it wasn't helpful to have Kes or any of them going over everything time and time again. What had gone wrong and so on, reliving that night, how so and so shouldn't have done this and that and maybe this, and if only that, on and on and on. I dropped a few hints that we couldn't keep living in the past, and ... anyway, after a while, I suppose we really did move on because I haven't seen much of anyone recently. I mean, we all keep in contact, we speak on the phone now and again.'

We sat and ate in silence.

'How about Anita?' I asked eventually.

'I used to talk to Anita all the time.' She nodded. 'And we used to meet up sometimes and go for a meal. But I haven't spoken to her for months. Well, it must be nearly a year now because the last time I saw her she was about six months gone, and the baby must be nine months old now.'

'Ten,' I told her and she smiled.

'Anita's got a lot on her plate,' she said. 'When the husbands are gone, when you've got a baby, it's just awful. Such hard work and no one to back you up. Anita never coped well. She was always so eaten up with anxiety about Mike, it was like she was living on another planet. She just lived for word from him. She used to paint beautifully in the early days, but she let that slide. She didn't join in with us. We used to joke about it, but if she didn't have a nervous breakdown she came very close to it. Still, look at her. She's got her husband, and it's me who lost mine. Maybe I should have worried more.' She shook her head.

'I don't mean to be unsympathetic. Anita's mum and sisters are in Sri Lanka, so she's got no support network except for her daughter, who's got her own life to lead.'

She looked at her watch.

'Look,' she said, 'I don't know if I've been any help, but I've got to go.'

I walked back with her to Boots, and when I said goodbye, I gave her one of my cards and asked her to call me if I could help her with anything. She nodded and said she doubted that she would need anything. I watched her make her way through the sea of customers. I did not expect to see or hear from her again.

Later that night, when I had put the children to bed, Alice rang me in tears.

'I just had a phone call from Mike Darling,' she said. 'He's just got back from abroad, and he was ringing to tell me not to speak to you. And when I said I already had, he told me that was stupid and that you just wanted to make trouble.'

'That's not true.'

'He said you couldn't be trusted, that you just wanted to stir up rumours.'

'No,' I repeated, 'that's not true.'

'Are you sure? Because I've had enough.' Her voice was still wavering, but her warning was delivered clearly enough. 'Do you understand that? I can't take any more, I'm just beginning to put things back together. If you make trouble for me, I will make sure you pay for it. Do I make myself clear? I don't know what you're up to, but just leave me out of it.'

I tried again to reassure her that I was not intending to make trouble, but she wasn't in a mood to be convinced. She had, after all, known Mike much longer than she had known me. He had been her husband's friend and she had no reason to think he would mislead her. I put the receiver down, worried and

uncomfortable. I had almost nothing to go on. I was just following my nose, digging around to see what turned up. But I was
playing with people's lives. I didn't want to do Alice any harm.

This was the first I had heard that Mike had returned from
Pursat. Alan's wife, I thought, must have told him that I had
been asking about Ray. One way or another, fresh off the plane
from the other side of the world, Mike Darling had made it his
priority to warn his friends not to speak to me. The battle lines
were being drawn.

Twelve

I went to Durham on the train in a child-free carriage. It was unnaturally silent except for the drumming of fingers on laptop keyboards and the hiss of the automatic door every time a shame-faced commuter took a call out in the corridor. I'd come on my own, without Dave, because with Collins' ban ringing in my ears, it would have been a tad antagonistic to go travelling the country with a film crew. Nor could I raise the hopes of Melanie's parents by telling them I was making a documentary on their daughter's disappearance if I wasn't sure that I would be allowed to.

Melanie's mother, Beatrice, had telephoned me.

'We'd like it if you'd come to see us in the next couple of days if it's at all possible,' she'd said. It sounded more like a command than an invitation. Her own pursuit of her vanished daughter had been efficient and energetic, if limited by her situation. But Beatrice's determination that I should visit did not mean there was news. It might just be that they wanted to hear about my visit to HazPrep. I had reported back briefly by email before my trip to Cambodia, but had not since had time to follow it up.

Both Beatrice and Elliot Jacobs received me at the door of their house, as though they had been waiting for my arrival. Of course, I had met them once before, at King's Cross with

Melanie, but this time, without her, I was struck by the echoes of her face in theirs.

'So good of you to come,' Elliot said as he shook my hand, and in an instant I was seated in a sun-bathed sitting room, a cup of tea and a plate of biscuits at my elbow. The room was a jungle of flora, nurtured and allowed to roam, as far as I could see, pretty much at will. Potted ivy had trained itself up over the mantelpiece, and vast ferns filtered the sunlight shining through the bay window. Here and there, there were flowers and buds, but the blooms seemed incidental among the foliage.

'We call this our greenhouse,' Elliot said. 'We've never been much into home decorating, but we love our plants.'

I saw, through the leaves, a piano, and on top of it a selection of photographs, including a large one of Melanie in a graveyard. 'One of her friends, a young man called Edwin Rochester, sent us that a few weeks ago,' Beatrice said, following my eyes. She picked the photograph up and handed it to me. 'It was a lovely gesture,' she said, 'very thoughtful. And I think he's a very good photographer – he's captured Melanie perfectly.'

Melanie was smiling into the lens more cheerfully than I had seen in others of Edwin's photographs, as though she knew this one was destined for her parents' piano. She was, I would have said, putting on a good face.

'She was filming in Bucharest, where Elliot was born, and where his parents are buried,' Beatrice explained, standing next to me, 'so it was very special for us. She was so dedicated to her job.' Beatrice gazed down at the photograph. 'And we are very proud of her, so we can't understand why—'

'You've heard that someone's seen her in Cumbria?' Elliot interrupted.

'We can't be sure, Elliot,' Beatrice warned him.

'It sounds exactly like her,' Elliot told me. 'She loved to camp when she was little. Loved to be outdoors. We went camping two years ago, just Melanie and me, and she said the peace and quiet were like water to her and she was so thirsty for it.'

'Where did you camp? Did she know the Lake District?'

'She knew it,' Beatrice allowed, but her voice carried more doubt than Elliot's.

'We camped at Coniston Water. And for once it didn't rain. Well, there were showers, but no downpours. It was out of season and we took it very easy. We had nothing to rush for. That's what she needs now after all the things she's seen, peace and quiet. We should leave her be until she's had her fill and then she'll come back to us.'

I looked up at Beatrice and saw such agony on her face that the platitute I had been about to voice was silenced. Into the quiet came the ring of the doorbell. Beatrice hurried out, and came back leading by the hand a woman of about my age whom she introduced as Stella Smith.

'Stella was a schoolfriend of Melanie's,' Beatrice said. 'She lives in Germany, but she's back for a couple of weeks to visit her parents, and I wanted you to meet her.' She turned to Elliot. 'We're just going to nip out for a girls' cup of coffee,' she told her husband. He looked surprised and mildly hurt at this abandonment, and I felt embarrassed to leave like that, but Beatrice explained as we got into her car.

'I simply can't talk about Melanie in front of him.' She sounded almost angry at her husband's continued hopefulness. 'He won't let himself see things as they are, and if I forced it on him it would break his heart.'

She drove us into the town, pushing the speed limit and paying little attention to other drivers. Instead she explained to Stella who I was. At which Stella fell silent and sat looking stonily out of the window.

In a tearoom near the castle, Beatrice leaned conspiratorially across the table and explained to me that Stella and she had already talked, and that she wanted me to hear what Stella had to say.

'OK.' I looked expectantly at Stella, but she was holding up her hands defensively. She was small and round and expensively dressed, and I found myself thinking that she was an unlikely friend for Melanie.

'I don't want to make more out of this than it is,' she said nervously. 'I said what I said in confidence to Mrs Jacobs. I didn't mean to involve the press.'

'But Stella,' Beatrice protested, 'I can't see how one could possibly make more out of it than it is.'

Stella shook her head and looked away.

'Well, I'll have to say it then.' Beatrice lowered her voice. 'Stella told me that Fred Sevi had threatened to kill Melanie.'

I leaned back in my chair and addressed Stella.

'Did Melanie tell you this herself?'

Stella nodded wordlessly, her face still turned away from me.

'When was this?'

She looked at me.

'I don't want any of this on television. Or in the newspapers.'

I hate it when people assume that every journalist they meet is a snake in the grass. On the other hand there are indeed plenty of snakes winding through the grass. Frankly, if I met a journalist for the first time, I'd keep my mouth pretty tight shut too. So instead of snapping Stella's head off, I promised I would not quote her.

'I spoke to her two days before she went on the course.'

'In person? I thought you lived in Germany.'

'On the telephone.'

Immediately I was sceptical. Give me an email, give me film, give me paper, a tape recording, anything I can see and feel. A telephone call is nothing, it's a sigh on the breeze, gone with the wind.

'Why was he threatening to kill her?'

'If she left him ... that's what I mean about blowing it out of proportion ... it was said in anger. He would kill himself, he would kill her. People say those things, they don't usually mean them.'

'But then she disappeared,' Beatrice said earnestly. 'It's too much of a coincidence.'

This insistence that Melanie had been murdered was chilling coming from Melanie's own mother, and Stella gave her a keen glance. But I knew Beatrice didn't want her daughter dead. She was simply the kind of person who was determined to take no comfort where there was none. She had insisted in looking in a harsh and unforgiving light at all that had happened since Melanie had disappeared and had decided that her daughter must be dead. She did not want to delude herself.

'Did he say it once, or lots of times?' I tried to pin Stella down.

'I don't know. She didn't say.'

'Did she say how or where?'

'I don't think it got that specific, but I don't know . . . look . . . I know it's your job to ask questions, but I feel as though you're attacking me. All I wanted to tell Beatrice was that I thought the police should take another look at Fred Sevi. I heard what he's been saying: that Melanie had post-traumatic stress, that she was on the edge of a nervous breakdown. I just don't believe it. She never said anything like that to me, about stress or hating her job.'

'Did she talk about having nightmares? Flashbacks? Anything like that?' I tried to sound less aggressive.

'Nothing. Ever.'

'What did you talk about, apart from Fred wanting to kill her?'

I got a sharp glance from Stella for that, but she answered me.

'We were teenagers together, we've always talked about boys . . . men. I got divorced last year. I'm with someone new. We spoke perhaps twice in the year before she disappeared. The first time she was telling me how wonderful Fred was. How he didn't want to tie her down. Then this last time she said he had become unbearably possessive and wouldn't let her do her job, and that he had this horrible habit of psychoanalysing her all the time. It drove her mad.'

'Did she mention any other men?' I asked Stella. I didn't want to mention names in front of Beatrice. She knew Edwin Rochester and she might have known the name Mike Darling. She was in such a state of tension that I believe, had I named them, or said I had any suspicion of them, she would have summoned them to Durham too and asked them to explain themselves.

'I don't remember her mentioning anyone. Melanie wasn't the sort who constantly had a boyfriend on the go. That's why Fred was such a big thing for her. She hadn't had a serious relationship with anyone for a long time. Her lifestyle didn't allow it. She was so disappointed when he turned out like he did.'

'But was she really afraid of Fred?' I still couldn't really believe what Stella was telling me and I knew I wasn't covering it well.

Stella slumped back in her chair, gazing at me.

'I know what you're saying. She didn't seem that scared. It was as though she was giving me another example of how unreasonable he was. She wasn't having hysterics or anything.'

'And of course he has an alibi,' Beatrice pointed out.

'He has an alibi,' I agreed.

'He does? I didn't know that.' Stella sipped her tea, her dark eyes watching us over the rim of her cup.

'So either his alibi is faked,' Beatrice summed up carefully, 'or his threats weren't serious.'

Or, I thought, Stella was making those threats up.

Stella left us in town and on the way back I asked Beatrice what she knew about her. Apparently the two girls had been friends since the age of eleven. They had been in the school choir together and the hockey team.

'Have you ever had reason to doubt Stella's judgement?' I asked Beatrice.

She pursed her lips.

'Only the normal teenage girl things,' she said, 'boys, staying out. I'd have said the same thing about Melanie. Perhaps there was a little bit of tale-telling once or twice and some amateur dramatics, but nothing I would describe as unusual.'

For the rest of the drive she paid little attention to the road and instead talked tirelessly about Melanie. About how proud she had made her parents, but how frightened they had been when she travelled to dangerous places.

'When she was little, Elliot would spend hours telling her how he was born in another country, and how when he was tiny he remembers playing in the snow in Bucharest, and how he always missed his other country. She told him that when she grew up she was going to see all the other countries in the world and we laughed. You spend all this time teaching them to be independent and take the world in their hands,' she told me sadly, 'and then they do it. They go and take the most dangerous job in the world, and you can't say a word. You just have to kiss them goodbye and pray they're OK.' Then, as we arrived back at the house, she said, 'Elliot and I try not to scare each other. We scarcely dare talk about it in case we upset the other one even more. I lie awake in the dark and then I hear him sigh, and I know he's awake too, and . . . we've been married for forty years. We live in each other's heads as much as our own. It doubles the pain.'

At the house Elliot got out an old photograph album for me, and let me thumb through unremarkable pictures of Melanie as a child. I learned that she had three brothers, two of whom lived near Beatrice and Elliot, and who had taken it in turns to visit them each day since Melanie had disappeared.

Then I sat at Beatrice's computer, with yet another cup of tea at my elbow, and I went through the few emails they'd had from Melanie. I had hoped for more, but they were the emails of a woman who knew that her parents were worried, and who was telling them as little as possible in order not to frighten them. She wrote about what food was available, about the weather, the kindliness of the people she had come across. Never about their cruelty.

'Did you get the impression that she'd had enough?' I asked Beatrice, over my shoulder. 'Or that she was having a hard time dealing psychologically with some of the things she'd seen?'

But Beatrice just shook her head.

'She would have told us, wouldn't she?' she asked. But I didn't know the answer to that.

When I told them it was time for me to leave, she took me to the station in her car. As I said goodbye, she leaned across and kissed me on the cheek.

That night I got home late and the children were already in bed. There was a message on my answering machine from Maeve. She was so spitting mad that I thought the answering machine might spontaneously combust. She had received a fax from a lawyer acting on behalf of Mike Darling, requiring that the interview he had given me should not be used, and threatening dire legal consequences if the Corporation failed to comply.

'Shit,' I muttered. Here was another fine mess I'd got Maeve into.

There was a message from Finney too, saying he'd heard through the grapevine that Mike Darling had been asked by DCI Coburn to come in the next morning for questioning about Melanie's disappearance.

And finally a message from Mike Darling himself, his voice low and intense.

'Why are you hounding me? Stay out of it, if you don't want . . . Just stay out of it.'

I stared at the machine. I had never made a secret of my telephone number and it didn't take long for me to work out that Mike could have got it from Justin. But his call, coming late at night into the privacy of my kitchen, shook me badly. He sounded as though he was desperate, trapped in a corner. It was like hearing an echo of my own voice after Adam's murder, and my veins were flooded with shame. I was hounding the man just as I had been hounded. It was Sevi who had made threats against Melanie's life not Mike. I must not pursue the wrong man. And yet his very defensiveness pulled me on, as if I was a fox scenting fear. If he was innocent, a small voice in my head kept asking, why was he so scared?

That night, on the edge of sleep, my head turned into a kaleidoscope of faces and disconnected voices, Beatrice shouting at me in Mike's voice, Elliot Jacobs waving through his window to Fred Sevi, Stella wide-eyed with fear, her mouth sewn shut as she struggled and fought to speak.

Thirteen

Next day I did a Google search on Fred Sevi. Part of our conversation had been nagging at me. He'd told me his background was in military psychology, but I hadn't followed up on it at the time, and to phone him now and ask just that one question would look unfriendly in the extreme. I managed to find his curriculum vitae on a university website. Fred Sevi, born in Istanbul to a Turkish father and a British mother. He had done his first degree there and had served briefly in the armed forces, before moving to Britain to do postgraduate studies and train in psychiatry. His doctoral thesis was a study of the psychological impact of wartime service on the soldier, in particular the experience of shooting to kill enemy combatants. The dissertation itself was not available online.

There was a photograph of Fred Sevi looking darkly handsome, but there were many things I could not find out. It was impossible to tell, from the patchy information afforded by the web, whether Sevi had family in Britain, whether he was liked by his colleagues, or what his romantic history was.

It was the hottest day of the year, with the temperature in the high eighties. Nevertheless, I persisted with my plan, which was to track down Taylor Sullivan. His mother had tried to put me off, but his account of the ambush on the outskirts of Kabul in which Sean Howie had died had taken on extra significance in the light of my discovery that it was also in Afghanistan that Melanie and Mike Darling had met.

The M5 had me tearing my hair out, and when I finally reached Wolverhampton I got lost in an industrial park. For a few horrible minutes I became convinced that I would never find my way out but would live out my days circling nameless roundabouts, glimpsing car parks and prefabricated office buildings at the end of anonymous grass-lined roads, the distant hum of the motorway driving me slowly mad. Eventually, I managed to navigate my way back to the narrow streets of small terraced houses.

I had the advantage of surprise. Taylor Sullivan wasn't expecting me. He answered the door to me in running shorts and nothing else. Even before I introduced myself, he grinned and vanished back indoors to 'get decent' before he reappeared in a T-shirt and running shoes. He heard me out like that, standing on the doorstep.

'I spoke to your mother. Did she tell you?'

Taylor Sullivan gave a lopsided grin and a shake of his head, and waited for me to go on.

'I know you're under pressure not to speak about what happened, but I wanted to hear about the death of Sean Howie.'

He shrugged.

'I'm out,' he said. 'I'm not going back out there for anybody, not queen, not country. Queen wouldn't go, why should I? Come on in. Nah. Let's go out. The house is like a frigging oven. Yo! Ma!' he yelled inside, 'I'm off out. I'll be back for lunch.'

We walked through the streets at high speed, Taylor's long legs eating up the ground.

'So whaddaya want to know?'

'Did you ever meet a man called Mike Darling?'

'Mike Darling, Mike Darling, Mike, Mike, Mike . . . no. Never heard of him.'

'You're sure?' I was disappointed.

'Is that all?'

'No, I also want to know about Melanie, why you seem to

think she had something to do with Sean Howie's death. I looked at what you wrote, but I don't see how she was to blame.'

'Whoa! I thought you wanted to talk about Sean. I never said Melanie was to blame. Nobody's to blame, man, no man left behind, no guilt, no pain, no casualties, just the white glow of victory.' He punched a fist into the air and gave a high-pitched bark of laughter.

'Sean Howie died. His parents are blaming Melanie and they're using your letter as proof.'

'Proof of what?'

'Well, it doesn't seem to me to be proof of anything. But Sean Howie's parents say Melanie pushed the patrol into harm's way because she wanted to attract fire to get better pictures.'

'Yeah, well.'

'Yeah, well, what? Did she or didn't she?'

'Sean Howie was blown in half by a bomb. I'm not kidding. Two halves.'

'But his parents are saying it could have been avoided if she hadn't put the patrol in danger.'

He swung his head to and fro.

'I just wrote what happened,' he said. 'I never wrote that she led the patrol anywhere. How could she do that? Sean made up his own mind, he wasn't a baby. I don't even know if he heard her saying we should go over the bridge.'

'Are you making this up?'

'No. I mean, yeah, she said it, but she didn't mean anything by it. It was like, There's a bridge, guys – weren't we looking for a bridge?'

I was out of breath just walking alongside Taylor. He talked just as fast. Unnaturally fast, as though he couldn't stop. Pedestrians coming the other way were giving him strange looks. Now I stopped short in the middle of the pavement, and he was a good ten yards ahead of me by the time he'd realized and put on the brakes.

'She's getting the blame for the death of this boy,' I told Taylor, 'on the basis of what you wrote.'

Taylor looked to left and right. He had stopped walking, but he wasn't still. His head was bobbing around, his feet shuffling, as though his muscles liked to keep moving.

'Don't you love it?' he said suddenly. He started to dip and pirouette, holding his arms out from his side. He was blocking the pavement, annoying pedestrians who were trying to pass, but he didn't seem to notice. 'After frigging Afghanistan, I thank God every day I was born in Wolverhampton.'

He came to a halt, facing me. 'Look, I didn't want her along. The way I see it, the slightest thing gets fucked up and there's a journalist there, it's all over the fucking world. If she's taking the shit for this, maybe it's like finally she's the one that messed up and now she's got to pay the price.'

Taylor suddenly lost interest in me and wandered off. He stopped in front of a shop, inspecting the trainers in the window, his hands stuffed in his pockets. I went over and stood beside him.

'What would she need to pay the price for?' I asked.

'Don't fucking interrogate me.' He turned and started to shout, his warm breath on my face. 'It's a fucking war, it's not all neat and tidy like a fucking dinner party. Sean's mum and dad need to know he died a hero. Don't you fuck that up.'

He thrust his jaw out and hunched his shoulders forward, and because of his height the pose was aggressive and threatening. I walked away. Shoppers were staring at Taylor, walking around us, keeping well out of range. When I turned back a few moments later, I saw him still standing there, staring once more at the window of the sportswear shop.

I didn't get back to London until nearly five. I was hot and sweaty, and there was nothing I wanted more than to see the children and to have a bath. But I went straight back to the

Corporation and confronted Ivor Collins. His secretary, Bonnie, tried to stop me because I had no appointment. But I was sufficiently riled to raise my voice and argue with her until he came out to see what was happening.

'There is no evidence against Melanie,' I told him as he ushered me into his office. 'I've spoken to Taylor Sullivan. He's just setting Melanie up as some sort of jinx so that Sean Howie's parents have someone to blame.'

Collins looked at me steadily, his narrow head tilted.

'If Taylor Sullivan was the only problem, I would entirely agree with you,' he said, 'but frankly you've just wasted a day on something that wasn't worth your Corporation pay cheque.'

I waited for him to go on, to tell me what was – if Taylor Sullivan was not – the problem. Instead, he bent his cropped white head to his work. I should have contained myself, but instead the suspicions that I'd been harbouring came bubbling to the surface and spewing out of my mouth.

'So what is this about? Have you got a guilty conscience about Melanie? Is that it?' I demanded. 'If it's true that she cracked up, could it be because you put pressure on her to take ever more risky assignments? Did you push her over the edge?'

Still he did not look up.

'Get out now,' he said quietly.

I stood my ground, but still he didn't look up. He just kept on reading through the sheaf of paper on the desk in front of him, and making tiny neat notes in the margin. Still I stood there. Already I was regretting my outburst. I had no evidence for my suspicions, just a visceral distrust of bureaucracy. Perhaps Collins was having second thoughts too.

'See me at ten tomorrow morning,' he said eventually, still without looking up. I turned and left.

I checked my email before I left the Corporation. Sal wasn't around, but he'd sent me a short piece from the wires saying that Mike Darling had spent the morning being questioned about the disappearance of Melanie Jacobs. A police spokeswoman was quoted as saying that the police were grateful to Mr Darling for 'helping with police enquiries', and that the police were not treating him as a suspect 'at this time'. What interested me most about the brief news item was the name of the police spokeswoman, which was Sergeant Veronica Mann.

I called her number and invited her to a takeaway supper at my house that night.

'Robin, I'm desperately touched that you thought of me out of the blue like that,' she said drily, 'but I think you know it's bad timing. For one thing I'm busy. And for another I can't be having supper with a journalist right now. I know you have a job to do, but don't screw me in the process, OK? I know you just want to know about Mike Darling. I know you're involved. But you're going to get nothing from me.'

'All right. But you know I wouldn't create difficulties for you, so anything you can share, think of me. Besides which, I'd really like to catch up.'

'Me too. Sometime, when this is all over, I want to hear about the kids. And I want the scoop on my old boss – have you managed to house-train him?'

'I'm still working on it.'

I heard a chuckle from her end of the line. Finney and Veronica had been good colleagues, almost friends.

'You have my sympathy. I heard his ex is back knocking on his door. That can't be easy for either of you.'

Later that night, once I was at home, and the children were in bed, Finney rang me. I didn't tell him I'd talked to Veronica Mann, didn't tell him I knew about Emma. Back in town, knocking on his door. Whatever that meant.

'Did you hear anything about Mike Darling?' I asked.

'Nothing. And if I had I wouldn't tell you.'

'Thank you.'

'I wanted to know if I could come round for dinner tomorrow night.'

'Sure,' I said lightly. When I'd said goodbye I sat curled on the sofa and stared at the wall. Dinner in the middle of the week? It sounded to me as though I was about to be dumped. So this was it. It was a good thing I hadn't let myself feel safe, then. It had been so tempting to let myself fall for him completely, but I'd always known that he would leave. Well, I had successfully maintained my independence. Mission accomplished. Our parting would be painless. I stood up. I felt vaguely unwell, as though I was sickening for something. My limbs were heavy and there was a dull ache in my head. I locked up and went to bed.

Fourteen

At ten o'clock the next morning I kept my appointment with Ivor Collins. Except that he wasn't even there. Bonnie showed me into a meeting room next to Collins's office, and I found three women facing me. Maeve was there and two women whom I didn't recognize, but who stood to shake my hand and introduced themselves as Lin Pala and Rona Brown from the personnel department. Lin Pala was tiny and skinny, and Rona large all round, but both were turned out in dark-coloured trouser suits with neat shoulders and tailored waists. They each wore modest earrings and discreet necklaces.

I sat down at the table and asked Maeve, 'What's going on?'

'Ivor is eager,' she told me smoothly, 'to correct some mis-understandings that you seem to have developed about the disappearance of Melanie Jacobs. But he felt, if he told you this himself, you might think he was attempting some sort of a cover-up.'

Lin and Rona chuckled politely at the very thought of such a ridiculous thing.

'Ivor was also afraid he might strangle you with his bare hands if he had to speak to you again,' Maeve said and this time Lin and Rona barely cracked a smile. Threats by management to throttle their employees verge on the extremely unfunny in the politically correct world of Human Resources. 'So he's asked us to run you through a few of the personnel issues that we our-selves looked at when Melanie disappeared.'

Maeve turned to Lin.

'OK,' Lin got out a file and put it in front of her on the table, took thick glasses from a box and settled them on her nose, then smiled uncertainly across at me, 'I'm afraid I'm not going to be able to let you see the file, nor can you make notes or record, or pass on to anyone else what is said in this room today. Can you guarantee that you'll treat what I tell you in confidence?'

She looked at me expectantly and I nodded. I could see Maeve, from the corner of my eye, looking suspicious. She got as far as opening her mouth, but Lin thought my nod was good enough and started speaking.

'OK, I'll tell you what you need to know. Which is . . .' She took a deep breath and opened the file.

'Melanie disappeared on January the tenth. When she had not been found by the fifteenth, the Corporation conducted an internal review of her records, partly to see if there was any way in which we could help the police, partly for our own peace of mind.'

'This was Collins's idea?' I interrupted.

Lin glanced enquiringly at Rona, who managed to shrug and nod at the same time.

'Mm-hm,' Lin agreed, but she didn't want to dwell on that. 'First, we looked back at Melanie's history. She's worked for the Corporation for ten years – based in London, but working all over the world, as you know. Remarkably, given the nature of her job, this passed without major incident. On three occasions she sustained minor injuries, and on one occasion she and the correspondent were expelled from a country – Zimbabwe. Five years ago she was sent on her first hazardous environment training course, which also passed without incident. This coincided with the time that we started to require all journalists to get this kind of training.'

Maeve raised her palm to stop Lin. 'I just wanted to add,' she said, 'that we've lost journalists and we're very serious about not losing more. That's why Melanie was on a refresher course, it's why Ivor was upset by your accusations yesterday, and why he wants to give you all the information he can to reassure you on this point.'

She nodded at Lin to continue.

'A year before her disappearance Melanie had some health problems and became very run down. At that point, her line manager suggested that she take some time off. He also suggested stress counselling.'

'Do you know why he did that?'

Lin inspected her notes, then looked up at me. 'We don't have that kind of detail here.'

'Who was her line manager?'

'That would be John Welsh, and I'm sure in normal circumstances he would be happy to speak to you about Melanie, but, as you may know, he's actually in hospital at the moment. He's just had surgery. I don't know when he'll be able to see you.'

'I see, I'm very sorry. I know him slightly.'

'Well,' Lin continued, 'Melanie refused counselling and travelled to Chechnya. On her return, her line manager, Mr Welsh, suggested once more that she talk to someone and again she refused. Mr Welsh was sufficiently concerned that he told her he would not be sending her on further assignments until she had agreed to have counselling. At which point, Melanie agreed.'

'So she saw someone?' I could not contain my surprise. This was not what I had been led to believe by Fred Sevi. 'When was that?'

'That would have been six months before her disappearance. However, she reported no symptoms of stress and the counsellor later confirmed that Melanie had been careful not to let slip any reason to keep her grounded. Indeed, she said that on the basis of what Melanie had told her, she coped well with the stress of her work. Melanie suggested to her that she had been rundown because of relationship problems.'

'Why would Melanie lie?' I interrupted.

'Did she lie?' Lin had a small smile on her face.

'I think so,' I said. 'According to her boyfriend she may have had post-traumatic stress disorder. And obviously John Welsh was worried about her.'

'She loved her job,' Rona said. 'I suppose she just didn't want to be slowed down.'

'Well, can I speak to the counsellor? Who did she see?'

'I'm sorry, there would be a confidentiality issue with that.' Lin looked apologetic. 'Actually we've been very open with you, I'm not sure that you would learn any more.'

Lin consulted her file again.

'After that, Melanie returned to work in a normal way.'

She closed her file and placed her palms on the tabletop. Rona fiddled with her pen. Maeve put her head on one side, as if counting down the seconds to the result of an experiment.

'Thank you,' I said. I'm a born sceptic, but I found myself convinced by their account or at least that Melanie's manager had been concerned, and that he had tried to get her help. The Corporation had not left her out in the cold, nor had they closed their ears to her cries for help; indeed she had uttered none. She had said, time and again, that she was fine. But there was something about that last, sweeping, 'Melanie returned to work in a normal way,' that had me bothered.

'Ivor has implied,' I said, 'that there is something which would be damaging to Melanie if it was made public.'

'Oh, I don't know what that would be,' Rona said, frowning. Lin sat tight, her lips pressed together. Maeve gave a small shake of the head.

'No? Nobody?'

All three of them pulled faces, shook heads.

'Then thank you. That must have been a figment of my imagination.' I stood, shook hands with them each in turn and left the room.

If I'd had to put money on it, I'd have said they were keeping no great secrets from me. But perhaps Ivor Collins was keeping secrets from them.

In the afternoon, Sal threw an *Evening Standard* onto my desk, folded to display an article headlined, 'Police Question Soldier's Statement'.

Sources say the police are looking closely at the account of Mike Darling, a former special forces soldier, who was the last person to see Corporation camerawoman Melanie Jacobs before she disappeared from a training course on 10 January this year. In earlier questioning Sergeant Darling failed to tell police that he and Jacobs had met previously.

Questioned again yesterday, Darling told police that Melanie Jacobs was travelling independently in Afghanistan when they met.

Police sources say there is no evidence linking Darling to Jacobs's disappearance. But Darling has failed fully to explain why, at the time of her disappearance, he did not volunteer information about his previous meeting with Melanie. 'We'll be talking to Mr Darling again tomorrow, and hoping that we make further progress in terms of cooperation,' the police source said.

I called Veronica Mann's number.

'You're talking to the *Standard* and not to me?' I asked her.

'It wasn't me,' she told me shortly, not wanting to discuss it.

'It sounds as though you're treating Darling as a suspect,' I insisted.

'I have no comment,' she said and hung up.

When I got home the children demanded that I get out the hose to water the garden. What they meant was that they wanted me to water them. I was reluctant. My malaise had deepened during the day, and every time I remembered that Finney was coming to dinner, I felt a hollow pit open in my stomach. But the children wanted it so much that they'd already ripped off their clothes and it was very hot. For ten minutes we had a wild time, the two of them soaked to the skin, leaping around and shrieking. Then Hannah slipped on her back and started to roll, giggling hysterically in the mud, and William copied her. For a while I left them to it. Then I spotted a neighbour to our rear looking out of an upstairs window. She had a habit of complaining about everything. She'd ratted on us the year before in the middle of a hosepipe ban. And she'd complained once when I'd let William, then aged two, play naked in my own back yard. What she would make of this display of mud wrestling I had no idea. I waved and decided we'd had quite enough fun for one day. I hosed the mud off the twins. The garden, far from looking refreshed, looked as though a hippo had been wallowing in it.

I carried them back in, first William, then Hannah, because they had become too silly to walk. They are too big to carry round for any length of time. Hannah's feet hung to my thighs. She still liked to play at being baby with me, letting me cradle her. I puffed out my cheeks, and she clapped her hands against them so that my breath exploded in her face and she roared with laughter. Inside, I grabbed towels and draped them over the children. Carol emerged from the sitting room, looking pale.

'You'd left a video in the machine,' she told me. 'It was disgusting.'

I winced. I thought I'd cleared away Melanie's tapes, but I must have forgotten the one in the machine. I didn't like to see Carol like this, her natural good cheer wiped out by what she had seen.

'Journalists are sick,' she said tentatively. I could feel our weekly debate on the morality of journalism coming on.

'We're not the ones who pull the triggers.'

'No, but you make use of all the awfulness.' She warmed to her argument, leaning over to pull William's pyjama trousers over his kicking legs.

'We don't make use of it – people want to know.'

'Why? I mean do they want to be entertained, or do they

really need to know?' Carol stopped, hands on ample hips, to argue this head on, then bent again to pull on William's top before he escaped. 'I mean, once I do know, I don't know what to do about it. Should I care? In which case what can I do? Or shouldn't I care? In which case what kind of person am I? Am I responsible in some way?'

'Of course not.'

'So who is responsible?'

'Well – whoever's responsible. It depends on the situation.'

'Never me, then?'

'That depends . . . on what you . . .'

'Like if I murder someone I'd be responsible?'

'Obviously.'

'But if I vote for someone who kills someone?'

'Well, obviously I . . .' I shrugged and wimped out, tickling Hannah instead of tackling Carol's question. Hannah giggled appreciatively, but Carol ploughed on.

'I mean journalists all act as though everyone else should care because it's everyone's duty to care, but they don't care because they've all been told to be objective, and being objective means being like a robot. But I don't like being messed around. I don't like being shown pictures chosen to make me cry, children with their ribs sticking out, crying because there's nothing to eat, and then having a sit-com shoved in my face a minute later. I mean, am I supposed to care for ten minutes, then stop caring and have a good laugh? I feel manipulated.' She articulated this last word slowly and clearly for maximum effect.

'OK.' If I hadn't been carrying Hannah, I would have raised my hands in defeat. 'I can't tell you what you're supposed to do. We're just the messengers. You decide what you're supposed to do with the information.'

The door bell rang.

'That's a total cop-out,' I heard Carol say as I went to the door.

'It's you who's copping out,' I threw back over my shoulder at her.

It was Finney, early for dinner. For a moment I think I must have just stared at him there. The argument had succeeded where all else had failed. I'd forgotten he was coming to dinner.

'Am I waiting for an appointment?'

'Sorry.' I stood back to let him in. I watched him take off his jacket. He had come straight from the office and was still in his work clothes. I must have been very silent because he glanced at me curiously.

'Are you a hologram?' he asked.

'Sorry.' I smiled at him and he smiled back. And I thought, as if from a great distance, how very much I liked this man, and how very sad I would be if I did not see him again. His gaze lingered on my face for a moment, then moved away, to Hannah.

Hannah looked straight back at him for a moment, then turned away from him and clapped her hands on my cheeks so hard they stung. It was, I thought, an admonishment for having invited this man into her house.

'There's nothing in the fridge,' I told him over her head. 'I haven't had a chance to shop and I haven't got around to ordering in.'

Finney grimaced. Then he spotted Carol at the top of the stairs.

'You're not going out, Carol, are you?' He used the good smile on her, the one that could seduce in an instant. It always annoyed me to be reminded that the smile was his, to use as he pleased, and that it did not belong entirely to me.

Carol and I exchanged a glance. I knew she was waiting for a call from a friend and that they might go out. I knew this was beyond the call of duty. But if Finney was going to tell me that Emma had moved back in, I wanted it done on neutral ground, not in my own living room. My home is my haven. I refuse to soil it with disappointment. Besides, Adam's ghost is here and I can't let him see me weep.

'I'll put the twins to bed first,' I volunteered.

'OK,' Carol agreed, and smiled at Finney, glad to please him. She has her doubts about journalists, but she's fond of a little crime and punishment.

We were too hungry to pick our venue well. The Common Touch used to be a real pub with a real name. Now it's part wine bar, part aspiring fusion restaurant, part club. Which means you can't get to the bar, the menu is bad and expensive, and the music's too loud. Or perhaps we just weren't in the mood. We picked at our food, pushed aside plates piled high with leftovers. I braced myself and launched into it.

'I heard . . . Well, Veronica told me she'd heard . . .'

'That Emma's back.' He finished my sentence for me and reached across the table to take my hand.

'Back where?'

'On my doorstep.'

'Did she – ' I felt ridiculous – 'did she step inside?'

'Look.' He sighed, leaned back in his chair, away from me. 'She turned up out of the blue last week. She's split up with Greg. She was upset. We talked. She wanted us to try again.'

'For God's sake, she walked out on you.'

He gave me a look that told me to butt out of it and I shut up. I withdrew my hand from his.

'She's staying in town,' he said. 'She's got some job interviews. She'll be fine.'

He shook his head and shrugged, as though there was nothing to any of this and the subject should be immediately dismissed.

'I don't much care whether she's fine or not. How do you feel?'

Finney looked uncomfortable.

'What do you mean, how do I feel?'

'What do you think I mean? I mean your ex-wife suddenly reappears and wants you back. How do you feel about that?'

Finney averted his eyes from mine and found something to look at beyond my left shoulder.

'Well . . .' He shrugged again, and screwed his face up. 'It feels strange.'

'Strange good or strange bad?'

He sighed.

'Strange. I don't know. Just strange.'

'And if I hadn't heard it from Veronica?'

'You'd have heard it from me.'

'You've never told me what she's like. I've never even seen a photograph.'

He shrugged.

'What's the point?'

'I want to know, that's the point.'

He shrugged again. 'I don't know.'

'How difficult can it be?' I ran through a few possibilities. Does she look like Catherine Zeta Jones?' He shook his head. 'Nicole Kidman?'

He considered for a moment. 'More Cameron Diaz.'

I groaned and buried my head in my hands.

He reached out and took my hand again. 'Oh, come on, Robin, I'm just kidding around. You started it. What's this about? You don't want my ex-wife to come after me, but you're not sure you want to come after me either. Look . . .' he broke off. 'Recently . . .' He gave up again, then lurched on. 'Maybe you'd prefer it if I just took myself off.'

When I didn't immediately answer, he gave an exasperated grunt and a little shake of the head. How had this happened? I wondered. I'd thought Finney was going to break up with me, but here we were, tables turned.

'It's just that sometimes I don't know how to do this,' I said eventually.

He sat back. Our hands were still clasped, but Finney's jaw was tense, as if he was getting ready to receive a blow.

'Because Adam left you,' he said, 'and you think I'll do the same.'

'You might. My father left us all, your wife left you. Everyone leaves.'

'You're certainly going the right way about it.' He shook his head impatiently. 'What else?'

'Come on, Finney, even your mother abandoned you . . .'

His face froze. We stared at each other, appalled.

'So let's break the habit,' he said slowly.

I had lost all awareness of anyone else in the restaurant. I was aware only of Finney's hand still holding mine. And his mouth, which betrayed his unhappiness. He cleared his throat. 'What else?'

'When I was away, you were so far away. It felt like you didn't exist. But surely, even so far away, I should have been able to, you know, to think of you as close to me.'

He sat back and with the movement his hand slipped away from mine.

'And the twins – did they exist?'

'That's different.'

'And your family, your mother, Lorna, Tanya, are you going to cut them off on the basis that they don't exist either?'

I sat back in my chair, irritated.

'It's not like that. They're there, no matter where I am. If I tried to make them vanish, they'd still be there. If you're there, it's because I choose to be with you . . . or if I choose to be without you. Then you . . . wouldn't be.'

There was a long pause. His voice was hoarse, and so low that I had to strain to hear it. 'Whereas I. By contrast. Do choose to be with you. Entirely.'

I searched his eyes for clues. Was there irony there? Our relationship had been born in a hailstorm of sarcasm and I saw no reason why it should not end the same way. He puffed his cheeks out, then raised his eyebrows in rueful enquiry.

'OK. What else?'

'Nothing else.'

'Thank God for that.'

He sat back and smiled at me, but in a sad, sorry kind of way. I could not help but smile back.

'I thought,' I told him, 'that you'd invited me to dinner to break up with me.'

'Ha!' His face twisted in bitter amusement.

'What?'

'What date is it?'

Realization dawned.

'Oh shit, I'm so sorry,' I said. 'It's your birthday.'

He shook his head, embarrassed to have made anything of it, 'Yeah, well, as you know, it never was much of a birthday.'

Finney doesn't know exactly what day he was born. He was abandoned as a baby by his mother, and he doesn't even know her name. He's never tried to find her. His birthday is a bureaucratic invention, a formula subtracting his estimated age on arrival at the orphanage from the date of arrival.

I reached out and took his hand.

'I'm really sorry.'

But Finney hates pity.

'Come on,' he said, 'let's get out of here.'

If we'd parted outside the restaurant that night, the things I'd said could have ended it forever. I had revealed my lack of trust. We might have walked away and never seen each other again. Instead of which we obstinately returned to my house and went to bed, lying pressed tight together in unhappy silence.

Fifteen

In the morning, Finney left for work looking distracted and hurried. Neither of us was in a mood to revisit the conversation of the night before. I checked my email and found a message from my mother after several days of silence.

The sun is getting to me. It is doing things to me I wouldn't have thought possible. It's Peeling something away, and easing my joints, and Soothing the aches and pains of Old Age, smoothing out the wrinkles like a hot iron. I walk around barefoot and the earth burns through the soles of my feet. Apparently they don't smoke cannabis here as much as they used to, which is a great Pity. Nevertheless, London is receding to the edges of my consciousness, my Daughters and my darling Grandchildren are secure in my Heart of course, but I have to admit that you're not uppermost in my Mind. I am being challenged – so I am told – not to Think, but to Feel.

There is a great change in circumstances here. I've told you all about my friend Nancy. As you might remember, she is married to Nate, but I discovered when I got here that, although they have the same address, they are both with new partners. Nancy has taken a Lesbian lover called DeeDee, and Nate has a Boyfriend – a sixty-year-old boy – called Clark. DeeDee and Clark were previously living together as man and wife, but they have Swapped Partners!!! The two Men live together in the attic, the two Women live in a garden house, and they all get Together for dinner. I have been on the lookout for problems – Surely there must be Problems – but so far I have detected only Peace and Light.

The Subject of your father came up in conversation at lunch the other day. I was asked by Nancy, after I had spoken briefly on the subject, whether he – your father – had any Redeeming Feature. I said No, and she and DeeDee looked at me with Pity. Does he love anything or anyone? DeeDee asked. I told them I didn't know and then I'm afraid I said I didn't really Care. I am sure I set back my Personal Transformation by weeks. But I'm right, aren't I, that he has No redeeming feature?

I read and reread, revelling in the vision of my mother in California. But the bit about my father unsettled me. My mother had never before wavered in her silent contempt for him. It wasn't clear if she was wavering now, but I found her uncertainty disconcerting, and it stayed with me all day long.

I went to the office, where I made arrangements for a trip to Majorca. A sixteen-year-old schoolgirl had last been seen in a nightclub in the early hours of the morning two months earlier. Her three friends only realized the next day that she had gone, and when she failed to turn up for their flight home, they became alarmed. Local police had been looking for her ever since, but her parents seemed to have spent more energy quarrelling than looking for their daughter.

I had a call from reception: Justin was downstairs and did I have a moment to see him?

I glanced around the room. Sal was out of the country, Penny had gone with him, and our usual bevy of camera operators had taken up their cameras and walked off. I wanted very much to speak to Justin and to speak to him in privacy. But to bring him here, into this office, would only remind him that I was a journalist and that he should be discreet.

'OK, I'll come and get him,' I said. He was sitting on a sofa in reception, his crutches propped up next to him. He greeted me with an anxious smile, and I thought how strange it was that he shared his father's pale beauty, but that his facial expressions came from somewhere else. It could only have been his dead mother, I guessed, who had smiled with that worried, lopsided, smile. When he greeted me with an apology, I thought that must have been his mother too. I couldn't imagine Kes apologizing. I had seen Kes's defence of Mike, his refusal to let his friend be harassed by me. Justin, by contrast, seemed to spend his life in a perpetual cower.

'I'm sorry to disturb you,' he said, struggling to his feet.

'No problem. Come on,' I told him, 'I'll show you around.'

He shook his head, frustrated. 'I don't want a tour, I just want to talk.'

I signed him in and suggested coffee from the canteen, but he didn't want that either. So I took him up to the office in the lift, cleared off Sal's comfortable leather chair – there was a pair of socks on it that I assumed belonged to Sal – and Justin sat down awkwardly. I asked about his leg and he said it was still hurting, but it was clear he didn't want to talk about that either. I shouldn't have worried about taking him to the office – he seemed completely unaware of his surroundings.

'I came to apologize for ... well, for the way Dad spoke to you. He just wanted to do things right by Mike. And ... Mike's really angry with you. He thinks it's because of you that the police are questioning him again.'

Justin looked at me questioningly, wanting me to deny it. When I didn't, he pushed some more.

'When Mike came back from the police station he slammed the door and went up to Dad's flat, and I could hear Mike shouting about you and how it's because of you that the police won't let him alone. He was shouting like he wanted to kill you. Dad was telling him to shut up, but once Mike's got something in his head he doesn't let up. Everything is black and white to him: there's wrong and there's right, and what you did was wrong.'

He paused again and again I didn't say anything.

'Is it because of you?' he asked eventually, forced by my silence to state his question bluntly. 'I mean, I'd like to defend you – you're my friend. So if it's got nothing to do with you, I should say that to them. But . . .'

He shook his head slowly. I was touched that he wanted to defend me, but I felt guilty too. If this wounded boy stepped up against Mike and Kes, they would make mincemeat of him. And how real was this friendship Justin was claiming with me? I had befriended him largely because I wanted to get closer to Mike. Justin was a source. It was I who was deriving the net gain from our relationship in terms of knowledge. Even now, hearing how angry Mike was with me, I was glad to have the information, grateful for the insight into Mike's head. To me it indicated a man who was cornered. I deserved nothing from Justin in the way of loyalty.

'Look, I can't tell the police what to do,' I told him. 'When they realized Mike had met Melanie before, they had to find out why he hadn't told them. That's why they're questioning him. If he'd been straight with them in the first place, this wouldn't have happened. But whatever you do don't say that to them. Mike's just angry with me because he doesn't want to be angry with himself. Just stay out of it.'

Justin searched my eyes.

'So it was you who told the police?'

I thought I had finessed this point, but I'm a hopeless liar. I nodded.

Justin shook his head, reached for his crutches and got up.

'Well, all I can say is you should be careful,' he said impatiently, 'because Mike is really really pissed off at you. And he was trained to kill people with his bare hands.'

I couldn't help smiling, it sounded so melodramatic.

'Really.' Justin was hurt. 'Dad's always telling me how Mike was lookout one night and he killed this man who was creeping up on their jeep with a grenade in his hand.'

'OK,' I told him, holding up my hand. 'I'll be careful.'

Justin nodded, satisfied.

'Has Mike talked to you about what happened out there when he met Melanie?'

'You think he talks to me about things like that?'

'Why don't you ask your dad?' I suggested.

'Why should I care what happened?' Justin asked.

'Forget it,' I told him. Which was easier than answering, 'Because you're my source and I want you to do some digging for me.'

Once Justin had gone, moving slowly down the corridor, I stared out of the window until I saw him emerge six storeys below and make his way along the street. It was raining again and the uneven pavement had turned into a delta of pools and puddles. I rang Beatrice.

'Can you remind me what happened to the things Melanie had with her at HazPrep?' I asked.

'I have them here,' she told me. 'The police went through everything, then a woman called Lin from the Corporation packed it all up and Ivor Collins brought it to us here.'

'Lin Pala packed it up?'

'I think so. We talked on the phone. I never met her.'

'Was there anything missing?'

'Well . . . it's difficult to tell since I don't know what she had with her. The only thing I asked Lin about was Melanie's mobile phone . . . I know it sounds silly, but she never went anywhere without it.'

'Then she must have had it with her,' I said. I remembered Bentley and Finney discussing the final electronic signal logged by the transmitter as the phone either ran out of battery or was switched off. It was too dire an image to share with Beatrice.

'Yes,' her mother agreed, sounding suddenly tired, 'she probably did.'

I knew what she was thinking. If Melanie had her phone with her there was even more reason not to vanish. It meant nothing, of course, but one's mind can concoct the most far-fetched scenarios: what if Melanie had forgotten her mobile, got lost in the woods, lost her memory, had no cash for a payphone? Then she might be lost and she might return. But she'd had her mobile with her. Why, then, had she not rung?

I remembered Andrew Bentley at HazPrep suggesting that Melanie had gone outside for a cigarette, or to make a phone call because of the bad reception inside the building. I wondered if the police knew what calls she had made that night or about any she'd received.

'Have you heard any more from Stella?' I asked.

'No,' Beatrice said, 'not since you were here. I think she's gone back to Germany.'

I thought, as I hung up, that would be the last we would hear of Stella's allegations.

For the rest of the day, I tried to put it all out of my mind. I should be leaving Melanie to the police now. I had done what I could – perhaps I had done more than I should. Pointing the police in the direction of Mike Darling might do nothing more than mislead the investigation and harm Darling. The combination of Darling's phone call and Justin's warning made me realize how close to breaking point Darling was. I would, I decided, divert myself. That night I read through my mother's email again and thought about what she had written about my father.

'No,' I murmured to myself, 'he has no Redeeming Feature.'

I felt as though I was betraying my mother, letting her live in happy ignorance on the other side of the world while her former husband with no Redeeming Feature lived in her house. That night, before I fell asleep, I decided I had to put a stop to it. I had booked the next day off. I would spend the morning with my children and in the afternoon I would evict my father.

Sixteen

My mother's doorbell resounded around what should have been her empty house. I had not prepared the way with a phone call. Gilbert had always called on me unannounced and I wanted to return the compliment. I waited. I could sense him on the other side of the door. I glared into the spyhole. Eventually the door opened.

'Robin, how lovely to see you.' A tone of delight. He stood there, in tweed and cotton and polished brogues, welcoming me into what was most emphatically not his home.

'You didn't bring the children!' Said in a tone of disappointment, although on the one or two occasions they had met he had paid them scant attention.

'Gilbert, this is ridiculous.' My father and I did not speak for more than thirty years. Since we were reunited – although I hesitate to put it in terms even vaguely suggestive of a hug – I have not been able to bring myself to call him by anything more familiar than his Christian name. 'I'm not going to bring the children here, to their grandmother's house, to find you . . .' I splutter out of words.

'You think there might be a problem?' He looked taken aback. 'Lorna assured me your mother would come round to the idea.'

'Lorna . . .' I stepped inside, lost for words. 'Lorna . . .' Lorna what? Lorna likes to play with fire. That was what I wanted to say. Lorna wants to sleep with a priest. Lorna wants to deliver a slap in the face to the very mother who nursed her through her illness. Lorna liked to wind up her sister at school and still likes to wind up her sister now. Lorna, the brilliant and confused child of a misbehaving father. Lorna, who looks like an angel.

Lorna, who wanted me and Tanya and my mother to love our father the way we loved her and who would not accept that we could not.

'You cannot stay here,' I told him. Anger was rising inside me again, and I was not sure how much of it was Gilbert and how much my own state of mind. Did this man have a Redeeming Feature? Was I simply not looking hard enough? Unless you count charm as redemption, which I do not. And even then it is charm that comes and goes pragmatically, charm that is employed to effect. Lorna had been gung-ho about putting Gilbert here, but she is not stupid or unfeeling. She is susceptible to Gilbert's charm in a way that I am not, and she is susceptible because she has learned her family history from Gilbert as well as from my mother. In his version of history he is more sinned against than sinning, the victim of the system, and not what I believe him to be, which is a crook.

'Look at you, look at this place, it's all wrong,' I said.

He stood in a corridor that was lined with my mother. Living on her own since we left home years ago, there had been no limiting hand to lie heavy on her style, no conflicting aesthetic. There had been little in the way of money either. This was muddle as interior decoration: a photo of Hannah and William blown up almost to poster size in a clip frame opposite a similar-sized photo of Tanya's three girls; a pile of legal papers that imitated the Tower of Pisa and that had never moved as long as I could remember; a coat stand that had long ago vanished under a vast collection of dark-coloured outer garments almost indistinguishable from each other. Where was Gilbert sleeping? Did I want to know?

'Your mother was always a generous woman,' Gilbert said.

'I can't believe she'd throw me onto the mercy of the capitalist police.'

I looked at him blankly. 'The capitalist police?' I echoed.

'Your mother is a socialist, as am I, whatever our differences. I've done nothing except reallocate capital to the workers. Surely it is in the cause of justice that I should be given shelter.'

This time I told myself not to rise to it. Gilbert is not mad. One could even make the mistake of thinking him quaintly eccentric. But the things he's done haven't been quaintly eccentric. He has stolen from individuals, from small businesses, not from vast institutions that budget for bad luck like him. I've heard this 'all crime is committed by the state' defence before. According to it, theft is natural justice, simply the readjustment of wealth. I knew – because Gilbert is my father, and I know him – that he believes it no more than I do. He believes nothing. If he believed in something, would that count as a redeeming feature?

'Would you like a glass of wine, my dear? You look a little peaky. I have an excellent Pinot Grigio somewhere.'

Glumly I followed him into the kitchen and watched, speechless, as he approached my mother's wine rack with a considerable level of familiarity. He plucked out a bottle of white wine, lifted the corkscrew from the appropriate drawer and opened the bottle with a flourish. I noticed that there were abundant vegetables in the rack. I opened the fridge door, and found it full of dinners for one in silver packaging, steak and Guinness pie, venison with claret, salmon with a lobster sauce. It was scarcely surprising that my father was beginning to show a belly.

'You've been shopping.'

'Not quite,' Gilbert replied, and mentally I winced, because that probably meant he'd been out shoplifting. 'Tesco's has a wonderful delivery service, you know. I ordered online.'

It was just as bad. Had he paid with a stolen credit card?

The only thing I could be sure of was that the wealth of food in the house did not represent an honest transaction. I sat down at the table and rested my head in my hands. If she found out what was happening, Tanya would kill Gilbert and Lorna and me. Probably in that order. As I formulated the thought, the telephone rang. Before I could stop him, Gilbert answered. I noticed that he did not give his name, simply said hello. Even in the midst of charm, you see, he is careful, he watches his back. He listened for a moment, then put down the receiver without comment.

'Who was that?' I asked.

'Perhaps Tanya,' he said, pouring wine into two glasses, although I had said I wanted none. 'Whoever it was hung up.'

I could not think why Tanya would have rung Ma's number since she knew Ma was away. Unless she had got wind of what was happening and was ringing to check it out. In which case she now knew for sure. I felt sick, and angry at Gilbert, and at Lorna, and even at Tanya.

Gilbert put a glass of wine in front of me and sat down happily opposite me, as though expecting an enjoyable chat.

I took a sip and then another. Gilbert was right. It really was a very fine wine.

'What happened in France?'

'Oh.' Gilbert placed his glass carefully on the table and assumed a tone of glib outrage. 'It was quite ridiculous. As you know, I've been teaching English in a school in Paris. The principal became ill last year and I volunteered to take over some of the running of the school. Which I did to the complete satisfaction of the students. You should hear their English – it is delightful.'

I waited. I would not encourage his play-acting.

'And what is the ridiculous part?'

'Well, there was some bad feeling. I left. At my age, I have no need or desire to stay where I'm not wanted.'

'Bad feeling,' I repeated the words. 'You mean the police were involved.'

'Isn't that what it usually means?' Gilbert assumed a wounded air.

'But you didn't hang around to find out.'

'I refuse to be treated in that way. The finances of the school were in a terrible mess when I arrived. All I did was to put them in order. If they are incapable of seeing that, well, I see no need to explain it to them.'

'Where's the cash?'

Gilbert's jaw dropped, and his eyes were wide with hurt.

'Robin,' he scolded. He took a sip of wine and thought for a moment, composing the sentence that followed, his eyes hard. 'I have enriched others, not myself.'

We looked at each other coolly. It was like looking in a distorting mirror. I thought how much I disliked him, and realized with a blinding flash, like lightning, for the very first and most distressing time, that I disliked him precisely because I was afraid that I might be like him. Was it possible that I could be as faithless as him? Could I betray those who tried to love me? Could I be seduced by some other fantastical life and ignore all that was good and solid? It was Finney who came to me in that moment of enlightenment. Why did I fight him off? Why could I not simply embrace him, simply accept his care, negotiate a level of independence that would not alarm him?

I stood up.

'You have to be out of here by the end of the week or I'll telephone the police with this address,' I told him. 'And if they don't extradite you, I will.'

His face dropped and he made to get to his feet too, but stumbled, hitting his thigh hard against the table, and sat back down again with a surprised look on his face.

'Are you all right?' I could not believe I had asked it.

He nodded mutely.

I made for the front door and shut it firmly behind me. Whenever I meet my father, I walk away feeling devastated, as though each encounter takes me through a doorway to a ruined place. Today, my mother's email and my father's final, pathetic, stumble, made it worse.

I needed very badly to hear Finney's voice and when I got home I dialled his number.

It was a woman's voice that said, 'Hello?'

'Hello,' I answered, my heart stopping. 'I think I have a wrong number. I'm looking for Tom Finney.'

'You have the right number, but you haven't caught him at the best of times. Can you ring . . . um . . . tomorrow?'

The voice was not particularly friendly, not particularly cheerful. Nor was it unpleasant. It was a voice that I imagined belonging to a pretty face.

'I'd like to speak to him now.' I found my jaw was set. If he had lied to me, if Emma was moving back in, he had to tell me himself.

For a moment she was gone. If she was consulting someone, she had covered the receiver.

'I'm sorry.' She came back on the line. 'Like I said, now's not a good time.'

I ate my dinner in front of the television, trying to resist the temptation to ring Finney again. He had not called me back and I was beginning to regret saying some of the things I'd said at his disastrous birthday dinner. I tried to console myself with comfort food, bubbling, dribbling cheese on toast and tomato soup.

I was drawn to the news like a fly to a burning bulb. Everyone who works around news becomes a junkie. The focus of a news junkie is narrowed until the detail provides the momentum, every new angle on the story a fascination, a fresh reaction, a new quote, all a cause for analysis, debate, even celebration. And in the detail, of course, is the real history, the minuscule change of angle that mutates into the U-turn, the euphemism that glosses over the lie, the vacillations, the missed possibilities that will all be lost when history macros out. I know people who think it is facile, this obsession with news on the hour. For me, at least, it feels as necessary as eating and drinking.

The top story was about a baby seized from his home. I sat up with a start, spilling crumbs all over myself. There was a picture of the child's distraught mother, her long dark hair spilling over her shoulders, huge eyes welling with tears. It was Anita Darling, pictured leaving her Sydenham home in the company of police officers, her head bowed, arms folded across her chest.

'Christopher Darling,' the presenter said, 'is the son of a former soldier. The police say they are following all avenues of investigation.'

Immediately I picked up the telephone. I dialled Justin's home number, which I assumed rang somewhere on the gallery floor of the strange, tall house. Jacqui answered, but she was in no mood for a conversation.

'I don't know what happened,' she told me, desperation clawing at the edge of her voice. 'If we knew, we could find him. Look, talk to the police.' She held the receiver away from her ear and I could hear her talking to someone. 'It's Robin Ballantyne, I don't know what to tell her. She doesn't under-stand we don't know anything.'

'Robin.' I heard a familiar voice on the other end of the line. 'Sergeant Veronica Mann here.' Her voice was coolly pro-fessional.

'What's going on? I just saw the news.'

'Good for you.' She lowered her voice, 'Look, we cannot say anything at the moment. The baby was gone from his cot this morning. That is all we know. We are looking at every possibility.'

'Well, of course you are, but what are the possibilities?' I asked, not because I was about to broadcast anything, but because I couldn't for the life of me imagine what they could be.

'Robin, a baby has disappeared, and I have to waste my time fighting you off? I am appalled. You do not get any special treatment, no special access. Do you understand? There is a press conference at ten o'clock tomorrow morning.'

In the background I could hear a high-pitched keening sound that was as constant as the whine of a mosquito.

'Is that Anita?' I asked uncertainly, not even sure that it was human. If Christopher's mother was on the edge before, surely this would push her into a fully fledged breakdown.

'I will see you at the press conference,' Mann snapped and hung up.

I paced around, then checked on the children again. Hannah was sleeping soundly on the floor. I picked her up and put her back in bed and pulled the sheet up over her, but she kicked it off immediately. In this hot, sticky weather, they wanted nothing covering them. I left the bedroom and returned to the kitchen. I heard the front door close. There were footsteps above and then Carol's feet appeared on the open staircase, coming down to the kitchen. She was back from a date with Antonio, and her face was shining.

'Look.' she brandished a plastic bag. 'I've got all sorts of goodies.'

I peered at the waxed paper packages jostling inside.

'Parma ham, pepper salami, look at these olives, they're so fat, lovely soft bread made with sun-dried tomatoes . . . oh, and the meringues, have they survived? There's cream.'

'I think he loves you,' I told her, but I was distracted.

'He does, doesn't he?' She chortled gleefully, her eyes sparkling. 'Maybe I should have my own shelf. What do you think?'

'Carol, I'm sorry. I mean yes, do clear a shelf, of course. But

I don't know how you'd feel ... I'd really like to go out for a couple of hours,' I spoke tentatively. I was so afraid of scaring her away with excessive demands. Every time I walked out of the door to work I felt guilty. I knew it happened to every working mother, I knew it was something I had to live with. But I also knew that the moment Carol began to feel I was not keeping to my side of the bargain, that I was being less than a mother to Hannah and William, then she would leave. Without her, my life would fall apart – I have no spouse to cover for me, no margin of error – it would be me or nothing.

'They're asleep,' I concluded, apologetically, 'but if you could just keep an ear out.'

'All right.' She looked up at me, the surprise on her face illuminated by the light from the fridge. 'I'll leave my door open. I'll hear them if they call out.' Her face was round, and getting rounder by the day as Antonio fed her up. I would soon lose her, I thought as I pulled on my coat.

Even without daytime traffic it took me an hour to drive down to Sydenham Hill Wood. With all the lights on and the cars parked outside, the Tree House looked a darned sight more welcoming than it had when I had first visited. You could have been forgiven for thinking they were having a party. I parked opposite the house. There was no point in even trying to gain access. Nobody would want me there – not Mike, not Kes, and certainly not Veronica Mann. And even I – shameless as I am – would have felt a little shifty about barging into a house from which a child had been taken.

Why had I come? I drummed my fingers on the dashboard. Journalists want to be where the action is. It sounds like a cheesy recruitment ad, but it's true: it becomes second nature, instinct. Perhaps it is because once you're in the business you know how easy it is to distort news. So if you want to know what really happened, you know you have to be there yourself. Especially when it's your story. And somehow, deep in my gut, I knew this was my story. What the disappearance of Christopher had to do with the disappearance of Melanie I could not have told you, but I knew the two were not unconnected. Some people go through life expecting disaster at every turn, but of course life is not, for the most part, like that. Real disaster is rare and the chances of serious crime touching any one life are small. I thought the disappearance of Melanie and of Christopher were related, but I was basing that on nothing more than a rough calculation of probabilities.

I don't know how long I intended to sit there, but as I watched a woman emerged from the house. A cool breeze had picked up and she pulled on a jacket over her top. Sheryl, I realized. Even at a distance she gave off angry vibrations, marching down the road, then into the driveway of a neighbour's house. I wondered who lived there, then got my answer as the front door was answered by Ronald Evans, his white hair flying untidily, pyjamas covered by a dressing gown tied at the waist. He listened to whatever it was that she had to say, then stood back and waved her inside.

A few moments later a second woman came out from the Darling house, and for a moment I saw her illuminated in the light from the hallway. She was tall, her hourglass figure defined in a tailored trouser suit, its pastel blue colour light against her mahogany skin, her jacket flapping in the wind. She carried authority with her now as she had not when I first knew her, her hair cut tight against her handsome head, her neck long and straight. She did not stoop. As she came nearer I rolled down the window and leaned out.

'Veronica,' I called softly.

The woman halted, looked around and spotted me. I waved.

She crossed the road and came straight to the passenger door, first bending down to look in and reassure herself that it was indeed me, then opening the door and getting in.

'What are you doing here?'

'I don't know. It was stupid. I just have this feeling . . . is this an inside job?'

Mann sighed and stared out through the windscreen.

'The mother and daughter are both beside themselves. I am already practising in my head having to tell her he's been found dead.' She shook her head. 'The daughter, Jacqui, she's so protective of her mother that she won't let me near her. And she blew up at her mother's friend, who was really just trying to be helpful. Jacqui called her a manipulative cow. All living there like that, they are bound to get on each other's nerves. What on earth possessed them to come up with this arrangement?'

'How's Mike taking it?'

'He's in shock. He's barely able to speak.'

'Come on. One day Mike Darling's being questioned about Melanie's disappearance. The next day his baby's vanished. If nothing else, it distracts attention from him.'

'What?' Veronica turned to me, her face less shocked than she might have intended. 'You think he took his own child? Or that the mother did?'

'I can't believe she's involved. She seems to be completely out of it.'

'I'm not even sure she'd have noticed he'd gone by now if it wasn't for the daughter.'

'I've been told she has post-natal depression.'

'Her doctor said the same. He said her friend Sheryl made her come and see him, and he gave her some medication. But even he thinks she's acting strangely. He thinks maybe she's been taking more than the recommended dose, or that she's been taking something else on top of it.'

'Couldn't it just be a reaction to what's happened?'

'It's possible, I suppose.' She didn't sound convinced. 'People react to emergencies in different ways. Perhaps Anita's way is to switch off.'

I asked how they had found Christopher was gone.

'Jacqui put Christopher to bed at eight. He doesn't fall asleep easily and she had to stay with him, stroking his head, until he was asleep. Then she went to get something to eat.'

'With everyone else?'

'No, there was no mealtime as such. Everyone fed themselves when they were hungry, except for Mike and Kes, who of course expected some kind of food to be provided for them. Jacqui prepared an omelette for Justin, Mike and Anita, and Sheryl cooked a ready meal for Kes. Actually she cooked one for Justin, too, but he refused to eat it. It was Jacqui who checked on Christopher before she went to bed – I gather there's something going on between Jacqui and Justin, so I think she went to her own bed way after everyone else – she thinks at about one in the morning, which means Christopher must have been taken early in the morning, rather than late at night.

'You know she and Christopher share a room – well, I should say they share an alcove. Talk about open-plan living, I'd want a door or two in there myself. Anyway, that aside, in the morning Jacqui woke up and was surprised she hadn't been woken by Christopher. She went over to his crib, and there was a pile of blankets. I suppose they must have been roughly baby-sized and baby-shaped and she assumed Christopher had burrowed down inside his bedding. She picked up the bundle, thinking she was picking up the baby, and the blankets unravelled and slipped away, and she realized there was no baby there, which really spooked her.'

'What did she do about it?'

'She went to find her mum, obviously, and when Anita hadn't got him, she began to race around in a panic. They even thought maybe he'd got out of his crib on his own. Eventually they called us.'

I gazed out into the dark street. There were lights blazing from the ground floor of Ronald Evans's house, but the rest of the street was dark. Veronica Mann pulled a card from her pocket and handed it to me. 'I have got to go or they will think I have been abducted too. This is my mobile number and my home number has changed. Keep in contact. Don't ring me at the office. Maybe we can have a chat over the next few days as things develop. I mean a quiet chat. Nothing on the record. Don't remind anyone that we know each other.'

'They may remember.'

'Try not to jog their memories. That includes Finney.'

'OK. I didn't know you'd transferred,' I said.

'It was a promotion. Otherwise there would be no reason to leave one police station for another. There are idiots everywhere. I don't mean Finney. There was another guy.'

This wasn't the time for it, but I couldn't help myself.

'Did you ever meet Emma?' I asked.

Veronica looked at me.

'Shit,' she said. 'You didn't know she'd come back.'

'I did once you told me.'

She sighed, then shook her head in irritation.

'He should have told you ... I met Emma once at a Christmas party.'

'What's she like?'

Mann considered, then shrugged.

'She thought she was too good for him. She was all sweetness and light, but she had itchy feet, she was always unsatisfied, always on the lookout for something better. She flirted with anything in trousers just to make him jealous and got annoyed when it just made him work harder. But then I fancied him myself, so I'm hardly an objective observer.'

I stared at her.

'Oh, come on. I got over it. I'm not stupid. He was my boss. I was fine with you and him.'

Immediately her use of the past tense hit me.

'He's not your boss any more,' I pointed out.

She shrugged, opened the passenger door and twisted around.

'We've all moved on,' she said.

Seventeen

At ten o'clock the next morning Anita entered the press briefing room in front of a couple of hundred reporters. Those who had arrived earliest were on chairs, the rest of us were pressed around the edges of the room. As she climbed the three steps to a podium and took a seat, the room was silent except for the soft clatter of camera shutters.

She was flanked by women. Veronica Mann to one side of her, Sheryl to the other, her hand holding Anita's tightly, her head bent so low that I could not see her face.

Mike was nowhere to be seen and neither was Jacqui. All of which seemed to me to be ludicrous. To have the father of the missing baby absent was to raise questions with a screaming red light. And where was the missing baby's older sister?

I watched Veronica Mann's face, hoping for an indication of what was going on. When I had first met Veronica, she was a lowly PC and she wore volcanic orange and reds. With promotion had come gravitas. She wore a pinstriped trouser suit and a white shirt. I could see the toll that Christopher's disappearance was taking on her. The skin under her eyes was puffy and creased with lack of sleep, and the whites of her eyes were pink. She didn't smile. She murmured a word in Anita's ear and gave her a comforting pat on the arm. Anita sat for a moment behind the forest of microphones, as a man further along the podium identified himself as Inspector Mitford, introduced her and asked her to say a few words.

Then Anita lifted her face, and again the rustle of camera shutters sounded impatiently as her huge, startled eyes gazed out at us. The tremble of her lips, the rigidity of her jaw, would be immortalized in that second, whatever happened later.

'I haven't seen my little baby for a long time,' Anita's voice was disappointingly dead, and she was making no attempt to disguise the fact that she was reading from a script. 'Every minute apart from him is torture for both of us. I kissed him goodnight and in the morning he was gone.'

I looked at Veronica. If not a lie, this was perhaps a reinterpretation of history. From Veronica herself, I knew it was Jacqui who had put the baby to bed, Jacqui who had picked up the bundle of blankets that had fallen away empty. But Veronica's face was inscrutable.

'He's tiny and he needs me. Please, if you know anything about his whereabouts, telephone Inspector Mitford or his team.' Anita stopped and looked towards Veronica, and her agitated voice was carried by the microphone, 'You said there's a number. Where's the number?'

Veronica stepped in smoothly, repeating the request that anyone with information should speak to the police and reading the number slowly and clearly. When she had finished, Inspector Mitford ran through the bare facts in a slow, heavy voice that suggested this would be a long, thoughtful and painstaking investigation. He gave the approximate time Christopher had been put to bed, the hour at which he had been found to be missing. Then he named the person who had called in the police – Mike Darling.

I was surprised when Inspector Mitford said that Anita would take questions. I had expected the police to shield her, but of course the questions were not unfriendly. The first questioner asked whether there had been credible ransom demands.

'Well – ' Anita looked from the reporter to Veronica – 'what do you mean?'

'Has there been a letter, a demand of any sort, either verbal or written?' the journalist clarified.

'A demand?' She shook her head. 'No, there are no demands.'

There was a moment's silence in the room, journalists expecting more, waiting for a fuller answer that never came. Veronica gazed into the middle distance, while Mitford twisted his head to exchange a word with an assistant.

'Mrs Darling.' Another journalist stood up, the microphone in his hand. 'Was there any clue as to how your son was removed from the house?'

Anita did not seem unsettled by the question, nor did she seem to have any sense that time was passing, that people were waiting.

'I don't know,' she said eventually, turning to Inspector Mitford. 'Was there?'

'Christopher,' Mitford said carefully and ponderously, 'slept on the ground floor. So far we have no evidence showing how an intruder came into the house or left with the child. But some of you have seen photographs of the house – as you can see, it is being extensively renovated. There are doors and windows that do not have locks. Indeed, there are windows and doors that do not have windows or doors.' For an instant, light laughter ran around the room, then was extinguished as the journalists remembered why they were there. 'Ordinarily, because of the porous nature of the building during renovation, and because of the kind of security concerns that we all share, there is an alarm system in place. However, because the ground floor was occupied, and people were moving about on this level inside the house, it had not been switched on. Elsewhere, there were spotlights at front and rear programmed to come on if an intruder approached. They may have done so, but these particular lights do not emit an alarm, so if an intruder was sufficiently brazen he or she could simply continue to approach the building in the glare of the light.'

For more than a day now, he said, a hunt had been under way through the woods at the rear of the property, as well as through the neighbouring gardens and streets within walking distance.

'We believe,' Mitford said, 'that there is more than one person who knows what has become of Christopher. No matter what good care is being taken of him, he will be upset. He is a baby and there's nothing he wants more than to be home with his mum. There's nothing any of us wants more than for him to be home. We understand there are many reasons why people feel moved to take a child, and we can talk through those needs and provide help when someone comes forward with Christopher. But for now the most urgent thing is for him to be returned safe and well. That will show us that whoever took him has only the best of intentions towards the baby.'

The inevitable question then came. 'Mrs Darling, can we ask you where your husband and daughter are today?'

But it was Inspector Mitford who stepped in to answer smoothly.

'Mr Darling has been advised by his doctor to rest, and I believe Jacqui Darling is out looking for her brother even as we speak,' he said.

While I was listening to Inspector Mitford, I was watching Anita's face. I had expected, somehow, that her pain would be so raw that it would be almost too much for me to bear. Several times in the night I had woken with my heart pounding and my chest tight, the sense of a child missing from its bed, vanished, unreachable, so real that I could hardly breathe. But I could not fathom this on Anita's face. I saw confusion and unhappiness. But I had seen the parents of dead or missing children before and always it seemed to me that they had become a personification of fear. If Anita did not look like them, did that mean she knew something that we did not? I could sense that the journalists around me were frowning at Anita as if they too were wondering what was going on here.

*

I asked around and found Justin at St George's hospital in physiotherapy, sweating to move a prosthetic leg, lurching his upper body along metal bars that supported him. I found Jacqui there too, standing silently in the corner, her eyes swollen almost shut from crying. She was clutching Justin's sweatshirt in shaking, nervous hands, her eyes following every movement of his muscles as they bunched and stretched, dwelling on the stump, her jaw tightening as his body fought for balance and lost it. I went over and stood next to her, touching her shoulder.

'I couldn't bear to be at home,' she muttered. 'There's nothing I can do there. We're going to drive around as soon as he's finished and take another look.'

Justin's face, grey and damp with effort, had aged ten years. In the twenty minutes that I watched him working, it seemed that the naivety had gone for good, to be replaced by the knowledge that sheer willpower was the only thing that would save him. At first he didn't see me, he was concentrating so hard. When he did, he twitched his hand briefly in greeting, then carried on doing as he was told until the physiotherapist dismissed him.

Leaning on crutches, his prosthesis removed, he came over to stand next to Jacqui, and I saw her hand go to his good thigh and pull him close to her, so that the side of her face was resting against his shoulder. Clearly Justin's fear of rejection and his suspicion that his love was unrequited, were unfounded.

'How are you doing?' I asked him.

'It doesn't matter how I'm doing,' he said. 'What matters is Christopher.'

He rested his hand on Jacqui's head and started to stroke her hair.

'We've got to get going. We're going to look for him. We thought we'd try house to house and we're going to make some posters.'

Jacqui buried her face in Justin's shoulder and her hand snaked up inside his T-shirt. I heard her sob.

'I can't bear it.' Her face emerged, tears swelling. 'The police aren't going to find him and Mum's worse than useless. They can't see what's in front of their eyes.'

'What's that?' I asked her.

But Justin's hand had moved from Jacqui's head and it was resting lightly across her mouth.

'Don't listen to her,' he said with a forced smile. 'She's upset, she's imagining things.'

Jacqui swiped his hand away.

'I don't need to imagine anything,' she said, 'and neither do you.'

'Come on, she wouldn't magic Christopher away.'

'Who are you talking about?' I persisted. Jacqui would have said, I think, but she had one eye on Justin, who glared at her.

'Well, does Mike have any ideas?' I asked in exasperation.

'What do you mean does he have any ideas? We've all got the same idea, but no one will say it.'

'Jacqui, let's get out of here,' Justin said. 'You want to look for him, we should go.'

He gave her a look that told her to move, and then he turned towards me. 'Leave her alone,' he said, but it was more of a plea than an order. I stood aside as they left, Jacqui head down, he clumsily following on.

When I returned to the office, Sal was emerging from the editing suite and arguing with Penny. They had, it appeared, been watching a feed of the press conference at the same time as editing tape.

'The mother knows something – don't you agree?' Sal turned to me for support. Penny was shaking her head.

'You're mad,' she told him. 'Why would any mother kidnap her own child?'

'Or kill,' Sal corrected her. 'Let's not look on the bright side. Anyway, all I'm saying is that she knows something. Her son's gone and yet she showed so little emotion. Goldilocks, you understand women, unlike Penny.'

Penny let out a breath of exasperation.

'Penny, don't huff like that. You know yourself you're an honorary man,' Sal told her. 'You've dedicated yourself to the cause of hard news. There's no subtlety to you any more, no more nuance. You might as well be a man dealing in the pseudo-certainties of black and white. Your jaw is too set. I, meanwhile, a man of some sensitivity—'

'And idiocy,' Penny managed to interject.

'. . . of some sensitivity, despite the coarseness of the profession I find myself required to pursue – am appealing to Robin, the mummy-meister.'

Penny rolled her eyes at me and made murderous gesticulations behind Sal's back.

'You're stirring, Sal,' I said sternly.

'Well, of course I'm stirring. Do you think I'm serious?' He turned to Penny, who glared at him. 'We disagree, so naturally I have to be offensive to you. Goldilocks, you agree with me, I can tell, so I adore you.'

'I have problems with the concept of Anita knowing what day of the week it is, let alone who kidnapped Christopher,' I said.

'The police think she knows something,' Sal taunted. 'Sources, my dear girl, sources. They are our life blood. You should be sleeping with a police officer. Oops, I forgot. You are.'

Eighteen

The next morning the rain was hammering down with an intensity that lent a background hiss to everything. I'd had to turn on every light in the kitchen just so that we could see our breakfast. I was out of the habit of trying to listen to the news over breakfast because it was, in general, such a frustrating experience. But that day, shut in by the weather and desperate for news of Christopher Darling – hope triumphing over experience – I switched the radio on. I shushed the children when I heard Christopher's name. Hannah, naturally, responded with an ear-splitting shriek that left William giggling hysterically. By the time I reached the volume control, the news bulletin was already over.

Afterwards, as I spoonfed cereal to Hannah and put William back on his chair a dozen times, I heard the baby's name again. This time William reached across the table and wiggled the volume control as he had seen me do. Now the report boomed out over the kitchen and Hannah clapped her hands over her ears in alarm, then clambered down from her chair to hide under the table. I adjusted the volume to a more reasonable level and concentrated, holding my finger to my mouth, silently begging the children to be quiet.

'Police are staying tight-lipped about the exact nature of developments in the case because they don't want to compromise Christopher Darling's safety. What they are prepared to say is that they have received a communication that relates to the baby's disappearance and that they continue to hope for his early return. We don't yet know any details about the communication – we don't, for instance, know whether it is a ransom note or a message from an informant – and the police stress that it will be kept under wraps until such time as they feel it is safe to release it. The police, of course, have set up camp inside the house Christopher disappeared from. There's pretty much a permanent police presence in there, monitoring calls and so on. And I can tell you that this morning there have been lots of comings and goings, and there is no doubt that the police feel that there is movement on this case today in a way that we did not see yesterday.'

'Do you get any sense of optimism on the part of the police?' the interviewer asked.

'Well, we can take it, I think, that the communication, whatever it is, hasn't dashed hopes that Christopher is still alive. But I would have to say that I sense a great deal of anxiety as well. There is a sense of urgency here this morning, but the police officers I've tried to speak to today are looking fairly grim. Christopher, after all, has now been missing for forty-eight hours, and I would say that this awful wait is entering a critical stage.'

They moved on to other news, and I sat and watched Hannah and William, now both underneath the table, competing to see which of them could put their fingers further up their nostrils. And I thought how fragile it all was.

I couldn't – or wouldn't – ring Finney. Even if he had been able to drag himself away from Emma (my imagination was working overtime), he had never been keen to share information with me. So I rang Veronica's mobile repeatedly, leaving messages each time her voicemail invited me to. In the end, I annoyed her into phoning me back.

'Come on, Veronica, you know I know the family. You know

you can trust me, Christopher's abduction isn't even my story. You have to have a coffee break. Or lunch. You have to eat.'

'I don't, actually. But I am intrigued that you're begging me to talk to you when, as you say, you're not working on the story.'

'You know what I think,' I told her. 'You know I think that Mike Darling is connected with the disappearance of Melanie Jacobs, so everything about him interests me. And you think that Christopher's kidnap is an inside job—'

'Do not repeat that. Do not even say it, don't think it. There is not a scrap of evidence—'

'At least let's pool our thinking.'

'I will be fired if I'm found conspiring with journalists.'

'But you'll be promoted if I'm right.'

She agreed, eventually, to meet me by the sphinx in Crystal Palace park.

'Not a word to Finney.'

'OK,' I agreed at once. Not difficult, given the state of play.

It was still raining an hour later when we met, Veronica hurrying towards me, picking her way around the puddles, the sky so dark it felt like early evening. Her umbrella, like mine, was being tugged by the wind.

'This thing is more trouble than it's worth,' she grumbled, by way of greeting.

We seemed to be the only ones in the park. We walked below the shrubbery, along the terraces, our route punctuated by crumbling Victorian statuary. Much of south London was stretched out beneath us, its plain face veiled by the sheet of rain. Veronica didn't give the view so much as a glance. She scarcely even gave me a glance.

'You've had a ransom note,' I said.

'Off the record.'

'Sure.'

'No, not just sure.' Irritated, she turned to look at me. 'I mean it. Off the record.'

'Off the record,' I agreed.

'It arrived this morning. Of course, there have been others, obviously hoaxes, but we're taking this one seriously because it came with one of Christopher Darling's teeth.'

'A tooth?' A finger, an ear – these were the things of horror movies. A tooth was as prosaic as a stubbed toe.

'His tooth . . . his dentist has had a look at it. Jacqui says he tried to climb onto a chair and fell off and knocked his tooth, and it was wobbling. So we don't think much force was involved, if any, but it was there in the envelope and we're pretty sure it's his. It's certainly tiny enough.'

'Tell me about the letter.'

'Handwritten, in capitals, black biro on WH Smith notepaper. Addressed to Mike Darling. Mailed from Victoria. Less than half an hour away on the train.'

'What about DNA on the envelope?'

'We'll try, but unless we have DNA to compare it with it does us no good.'

'And the wording?'

She had memorized it. '"We have Christopher. Safety assured with full compliance. Discretion above all. Instructions re cash to follow."'

'We?'

Veronica shrugged.

'The "we" may be there to mislead. Or maybe there's more than one of them. We have no way of knowing.'

'What do you think?'

'About the note? I think it's remarkably straightforward. It isn't misspelled, it doesn't adopt a fake accent. It reads efficiently – Mitford doesn't like it. He says it's too confident, too comfortable. The kidnapper seems to feel he has the upper hand. He doesn't seem panicky, he's not in a rush.'

'It doesn't specify a sum of money.'

'Exactly.' Dryly. 'So, yeah, what was the point?'

'Who opened the letter?'

'Sheryl ... Mitford's pissed off. We had a whole system in place, anything was supposed to go straight to us. But somehow it broke down and Sheryl got hold of the letter. Then, instead of handing it to us she gave it to Anita, who gave it to Mike, who was forced to give it to us.'

'Forced?'

'Sheryl seemed to be insisting, and for once in his life Mike Darling didn't know what to do. The letter demanded confidentiality, but he knows we're the ones with experience of this kind of thing. He must have been terrified.' She drew a breath. 'OK. It's your turn. Tell me your theory. How does the kidnap of Christopher fit in with Melanie's disappearance?'

I felt sheepish.

'It's not so much a theory as ...'

She turned and took a look at my face, and rolled her eyes without amusement.

'Lord preserve us, it's a hunch,' she said, her voice heavy with sarcasm. 'That's great, very valuable information Robin, this is time well spent. Thanks a bunch. I'm heading back. What a waste of my lunch hour.'

We turned and headed back the way we'd come, not speaking, and Veronica pulled a cereal bar from her pocket, ripped open the packaging and took a bite. I must have looked hungry because she relented.

'You want one?' she asked. 'I carry these things around by the dozen.'

I shook my head.

'Are you sick?' she asked glancing at me.

'I have no appetite.'

'You're lovesick,' she said in between bites.

'Maybe I am.'

She gave me a sharp look.

'And you're not doing anything about it?' She shook her head. 'He's worth fighting for, my girl. Go chase that blonde ex-wife of his out of town.'

I shook my head. 'It's up to Finney.'

Veronica gave me a cool look. 'All right,' she said, 'I'm not going to waste my time.' She was already moving away from me when her mobile rang. I turned and walked along with her out of sheer nosiness. She apologized – she wasn't where she should be – then listened for a long time without saying a word, then gave an assurance that she would be 'there' in a matter of minutes.

'Bugger,' she muttered as she flipped her phone shut and dropped it back into her pocket. 'What am I doing in the middle of a park? This is your fault, Robin.'

'Can I give you a lift?'

'Get lost.' She swivelled on her heel and was gone. But there was only one place she would be going, only one place that she could be 'there in a couple of minutes'. At least, I hoped there was only one place, or I was on a wild goose chase.

I parked around the corner from the Darlings' house, and only then saw that, whatever was happening, it was happening not at the Darlings' house but at the house I had seen Sheryl vanish into two nights before, the home of Ronald Evans. The police had cordoned it off, and the press who had been gathered previously outside the Darling household had simply moved twenty yards further down the road and were now setting up camp outside. I went to join them.

'What's going on?' I asked a photographer.

He shrugged.

'They're not saying. Looks like they think the baby's in there.'

'Dead or alive,' a woman next to him added. 'Anyone know who lives there?'

I stayed silent.

'I've seen an old guy go in and out,' someone else offered. 'Crazy-looking, he had holes in his trousers.'

Just then Ronald Evans appeared at the front door, flanked by Veronica Mann and a uniformed officer. He seemed diminished already. I had thought him a tall and distinguished – if somewhat threadbare – gentleman. Now, flanked by police, he looked old and frail and humiliated. A police car had pulled up on the gravel outside the house and Ronald Evans got in. Once he was gone, ducking in shame as he was driven past the cameras, Veronica turned and vanished once more inside the building, ignoring shouted questions from the press. As a young, black, female police officer, she was achieving a level of public recognition that might or might not be helpful to her. Finney had explained to me how vulnerable she was and that there were vultures circling, waiting for her to become carrion.

When Veronica re-emerged, I was astounded to see Sheryl following behind her. Sheryl, in turn, was helped into a police car and driven off, her shocked face shining palely in the window, a gift to the photographers.

I saw Jacqui at the edge of the crowd, agitatedly straining to look over the heads of the press. I caught up with her as she turned away, her face a picture of angry frustration, her lips trembling.

'Where's Christopher? Why haven't they brought him out?' she demanded. She was in tears, angry and frightened.

'Why should he be in there?'

'Oh, for Christ's sake, where else would he be?'

She turned angrily and walked away.

I waited. This wasn't my story. It wasn't my child. But there was still a feeling that we might, at any minute, witness the end. I looked at my watch, then rang Carol on my mobile and told her I would be late.

'Take your time,' she said, sarcastically. 'Hannah just called me Mummy, so we're just dandy here.'

I told her I got the message – Carol's sarcasm alarmed me far more than Hannah's slip of the tongue – and that I would be back as soon as I could.

I waited another fifteen minutes, and what had been an air of anticipation was turning to impatience as the dark day headed for dusk, and the sky began to drizzle. 'Jesus, how long can it take to find one bloody baby?' I heard a voice behind me.

'Depends how many walls they have to unbrick,' someone else said.

It was time to go. If they had not found Christopher by now, then he was not here, not alive anyway, and I had no desire to be around if he was dead. Turning, I saw Kes standing at the entrance to his home. I walked over to him. I was surprised that there were no police in evidence, but I supposed they had all been moved down the street to take part in the search of Ronald's house. With his eyes on the crowd in the street, Kes didn't even notice me until I was under his nose.

'They've detained Sheryl,' I said. I did not know how much he had seen.

'They'll have to let her go,' he said, turning away from me. 'She's got nothing to do with it.'

'Shouldn't you be trying to find out what's going on?' I found myself tagging along behind him as he walked back towards the house. If I was stating the obvious, it didn't seem to be obvious to him. 'Your wife has just been driven off in a police car.'

He came to a halt in the doorway, and turned and said, 'If you think I'm going to give you a soundbite for the evening news you're wrong.'

I was starting to protest when Mike appeared from inside the house, looking haggard. He caught sight of me and anger overwhelmed the anxiety on his face.

'Get away from here! Get away from my house!'

He advanced towards me, but Kes blocked his friend's way, standing face to face with him, their bodies just inches apart.

'They've detained Sheryl,' he told Mike in a low voice.

'Sheryl?' Mike muttered. He hesitated, looking uncertainly from me to Kes and back.

'Come on, let's go inside,' Kes jerked his head, and after a moment Mike turned and walked back into the house.

Kes turned to me. 'You too,' he said. 'You made allegations about a good man. You can defend them to his face, can't you?'

He didn't touch me. I could have walked away. This was two to one and Mike was out of his head with anxiety about his son. But Kes was right. I had pursued Mike. This was the first chance I'd had to speak to him in person since I'd hunted him down in Cambodia.

I nodded. Then, without speaking, I followed Kes into the home he shared with Mike.

Mike Darling didn't even notice me come into the room. I had never seen Mike here. He was pacing around next to the bed, which was, of course, his bed too, although I thought of it as Anita's.

He had set up what seemed to be an operations centre. He'd made a table out of a pile of bricks, and there were papers piled on top of it. He picked up a sheet of paper and waved it at Kes.

'Kes, what do I do when they send the next demand? I've got no spare cash.'

I hung back.

'Don't be an idiot, man. You're not going to pay a ransom. You don't play their game, you play yours. Take control.'

Behind me, Anita came into the room. She too looked right through me. But when I looked at her face I wasn't sure how much of anything she was able to take in. There were dark rings around her eyes and her lips and hands were shaking. She was dressed in the same clothes that she had worn at the press conference, a white T-shirt and dark jeans, but now there was an air of devastation about her that was, to my eyes, more natural. Mike glanced up at her. She collapsed onto the bed and lay behind him, paying no one any heed, her back to us all. Mike shook his head in disbelief, then strode over to the bed.

'For fuck's sake,' he roared at her, leaning over her, his hands curled into fists, 'can you even hear us? Do you know what's going on?'

I thought for a moment that he would strike her. And Kes must have had the same thought because he moved quickly to Mike's side and seized his friend's wrists in his own hands. They stood still, Mike's face red with fury, Kes gripping him tightly.

'This is what you do,' Kes told him quietly. 'You do what you've been trained to do. You play the game. They've said there will be more. So you wait. You get over-excited, you act stupid, something bad will happen. Do yourself a favour, Mike, take control. Remember the note. Christopher's safe. Just comply. Be discreet.'

Slowly, as he listened, Mike's head lifted so that he was looking Kes in the eye. His face was filled with longing and with fear. For several moments he gazed at his friend, and it was as though Kes's words were soaking in, seeping slowly into a brain already so saturated with terror for his son that it could not absorb anything more. He ran his tongue over his lips. He repeated what Kes had said.

'I've just got to take control,' he muttered.

'I'm with you, Mike, we take control together.' Kes turned to me. 'OK, let's get this crap you're spreading cleared up.'

Mike wasn't even listening. He was still staring at his friend's face.

'I don't think this is the time,' I said. 'I'll be happy to talk to Mike about Melanie when he's got Christopher back. Aren't you going to make a phone call about Sheryl?'

Kes spoke in a low voice, full of contempt. 'You accuse a man of murder and you're not going to say it to his face?'

'I haven't accused anyone of murder.'

Mike was looking at me now, his brow furrowed as though he was trying to focus on what was being said. Kes spoke to him again.

'You have to hear it, right? You can't let her go around spreading lies. You've got to defend yourself or she'll just keep badmouthing you.'

I shook my head, but I didn't say anything.

'Yeah, I want to hear what she's got to say,' Mike said. His voice was dead. 'What gives you the right?'

'I haven't accused you of anything,' I repeated.

'Why did you go sniffing around Alice Jackson?' Kes demanded, growing passionate in his defence of his friend. 'Why did you go running to the police? Just tell us and we can clear it up. We're not unreasonable. Mike's done nothing wrong. But you've got to give him the chance to defend himself. What did Alice say to get you going?'

'Alice didn't tell me anything,' I insisted. I saw that Mike was watching me now like a hawk, his eyes heavy-lidded, dark slits in his pale face. 'She just told me how her husband died in the ambush. Look.' I went on the offensive. 'Like I said, this isn't the time. All I've done is tell the police what I found out, which is that you'd met Melanie before. That's all. No accusation, nothing. And as for Alice, she didn't tell me anything that warranted the police. They can ask her themselves if they want to.'

Kes was shaking his head. 'No one even knows if the woman's alive or dead,' he said, 'but you've got Mike lined up as a murderer because he didn't get verbal diarrhoea when he talked to the police. You make me sick.'

He spoke to Mike softly. 'You see, all this crap, it's over. She doesn't know what she's talking about.'

Mike gazed at Kes.

'It's over,' he said uncertainly, then with more confidence, 'it's over, isn't it? Now I have to get Christopher back.'

His face contorted. He pushed past Kes and made for the back door, slamming it behind him.

Kes sat down on the bed, as if all the energy had drained from him, and I slipped away. I felt sickened that I had let myself be lured back into the household and I felt drained by Mike's despair. I found myself outside the back door, leaning against the pile of bricks, gasping in the damp air, my eyes closed tight, relief that I was out of the house washing over me.

Mike had left the house through the same door, but there was no sign of him. There was a garden shed and a light shone at the small window, but I couldn't think why anyone would be there in the night.

I turned and took one last look behind me, back into the house. That house, Anita's room, had an awful, magnetic quality. The glass door to the garden was propped slightly open and the lights inside shone brightly. I could see the area I had fled from. On Anita's elegant bed I could see not only Anita, still prone, but Kes, sitting with his head bowed. He turned to look at Anita. I could not see his face. He reached out and let his fingers brush the nape of her neck, but only for an instant. Then, rapidly, he withdrew his hand and touched his fingers to his mouth, then drew his palm over his face as though he was washing it clean. I heard a movement behind me and turned to find Jacqui there in the darkness. In her face I saw misery but something else as well. I saw calculation. We stared at each other. What had she seen? What had either of us seen?

Nineteen

That night Finney turned up out of the blue. He rang the bell, then turned his key in the lock and stepped tentatively inside as I reached the hallway, William in my arms.

'Hello.' I must have grinned, or shown my pleasure in some way, because relief swept over his face. He raised a supermarket bag high.

'I'm assuming you haven't eaten since I last saw you.'

'I'm quite capable of feeding myself.'

'You're a hopeless liar.' He walked past me and into the kitchen and flung open the door to the fridge. William, I saw, was watching Finney carefully. I put him down, assuming he'd run off to find Hannah, but instead he squeezed in beside Finney for a better view as Finney retrieved the one item sitting on the shelf. 'Fish for a Kid's Dish,' Finney read aloud from the packaging and William started to giggle. Finney glanced down at him, noticing him for the first time. 'Hang on, what's this?' He reached up to the top shelf, and poked around. 'Salami? Cheese? Cream? What's going on? Has your mum been shopping?' he asked William.

'It's all Carol's.'

'I rest my case.'

'Finney.' He turned, surprised by my tone, 'I tried to call you the other night and a woman answered.'

He stood there, a pack of gorgonzola in one hand, salami in the other.

'That would've been Emma,' he said. 'She'd come round to use the computer.'

'She said you couldn't talk to me, she said it was a bad time.'

'Then it probably was a bad time.' He was sounding defensive.

'You didn't phone me back.'

'I didn't know you'd phoned in the first place.'

'You mean she didn't tell you.'

I should have handled it better. I should have just trusted him. He was there, after all, in my home, with food for the fridge. No greater love, surely, hath any man than that he buy groceries for dinner. But my questions had thrown a pall over the evening.

We tried to talk, but as soon as I began to speak to him about what had happened at the Darling household, Finney became increasingly argumentative. What was I doing meddling? Didn't I realize I was walking straight into the middle of a police investigation? I nearly asked him then whether he was really worried about me meddling in the Darling case or whether he was just angry with me for challenging him about Emma. Unusually, for me, I managed to bite the question back.

'OK, OK.' I held up my hands. 'Look, I have to fly to Majorca tomorrow morning for filming. I'll have to leave early. Do you want to stay or go?'

Finney leaned back in his chair and looked at me from under heavy lids.

'I have someone staying at my place,' he said, 'I'd rather stay here.'

I gazed at him. The expression on Finney's face told me that my questions had to wait.

'OK,' I said less than graciously, 'so stay.'

The next morning Hannah was in high spirits, refusing to eat, refusing to get dressed, scuttling in and around the furniture so that I couldn't catch her and remove the ton weight of nappy around her knees. William had tipped juice down his T-shirt and was outraged and wet, yelling loudly. These things always happen when I least have the time to deal with them. My flight was at eleven-thirty, but getting to Heathrow would be a nightmare. Finney came into the kitchen, bleary-eyed, running his hand through hair that was standing on end. He didn't want to catch my eye, didn't want to get involved.

'What's your problem?' Finney's question to William was rhetorical, but William didn't see it like that.

'I'm wet!' William howled, omitting the consonants that would have given Finney the clue he needed.

'He's wet,' I interpreted, making another grab for Hannah, who was standing behind Finney aiming sharp kicks at his ankles.

Finney squinted sleepily down at my son, and eventually his investigator's eyes identified the problem. He picked up a tea towel and dabbed ineffectually at William's T-shirt. With unusually clear enunciation, William yelled, 'Don't want you!'

Finney turned to me, his jaw tight.

'Can't you give them some ice cream or something to shut them up?'

I ignored him, but Hannah had heard.

'Ice cream!' she squealed, then turned it into a chant.

I rolled my eyes at Finney, but he just turned away to pour himself some coffee. Carol walked in.

'All present and chaotic, I see,' she said approvingly. She whipped William's wet T-shirt off, produced a dry one she just happened to have with her and pulled it down over his surprised head, then swung Hannah onto her chair, telling her that if she kicked people she would have to go to her room. Hannah hung her head and Carol turned to me, looking what I can only describe as smug. She loves it when there is a crisis to be resolved, a mess to be cleared up, a scratched knee to be healed. She has a transformative ability that I simply cannot match.

'Thank you, Carol,' I said, looking hopelessly at my well-behaved children. I must be doing something wrong.

There was a hammering on the front door. I found Tanya standing there, her face pinched with misery. She barged in furiously and immediately started to berate me.

'How can you go along with this?' she demanded. 'Of all the wrong places to put that man, it's the worst.'

'I haven't gone along with anything,' I protested.

'Well, he's still there. He should never have been there in the first place. What sort of stupid games does Lorna think she's playing?'

Finney had been drawn out of the kitchen by our voices, and now stood in the hallway, sipping from a mug of coffee. He said nothing, but Tanya addressed him angrily.

'You do know that Lorna and Robin have set our criminal father up in a safe house?'

She waited for an answer, but he gave her none, his eyes flickering to me, then away again.

'I've done nothing of the—' I started to protest. But she cut me off.

'She's told you, hasn't she? That they've put him in Ma's house? Don't tell me you think it's a good idea.'

She listened to the silence that followed her declaration. I looked at the floor, but it wasn't about to open up and swallow me, so I had no alternative but to look at Finney. He stood very still, his mug of coffee still in his hand. I don't know what he saw in my eyes, but in his I saw weary frustration. He turned and disappeared in the direction of the bedroom and I saw Tanya's face fall, but then she gathered force once more and called after him.

'You're a policeman, you should send someone around to lock him away.'

The she turned and left, slamming the door behind her.

*

Finney eventually re-emerged. He'd had a go at combing his hair, but had not been able to subdue it and his chin was still unshaven.

'Check your email,' he said. 'There should be a message there from my personal account – I have a friend in the police force in Paris. I asked him to help me with a little research. He came over – he's staying at my flat for a day or two with his girlfriend, turning it into a bit of a holiday – and he put it all together in a file attachment. He didn't want to do it in Paris. It could have got him in to trouble. Anyway, he said he'd send it last night.'

'What are you talking about?'

'Take a look. I've got to run. You may want to think about what Tanya was saying.'

He pulled open the front door, then turned to kiss me, but his heart wasn't in it. I watched him walk off down the road. If he was losing faith in me, I had only myself to blame.

I raced around, throwing a change of clothes in a bag to go to Majorca. At the same time, I printed out the message which was, as Finney had promised, sitting in my inbox. There was no indication of the author's name. I had no time to read it, so I stuffed the pages into my bag.

It wasn't until I was sitting on the plane next to Dave, who was snoring even before take-off, that I had a chance to take a look. I thumbed through the sheets. My father's name, Gilbert Ballantyne, appeared every few lines. Most of the documents were in French. Some were transcripts of newspaper articles, some appeared to be police statements. As I read, I pieced the story together.

Here then, was the school, a small, private girls' school specializing in foreign languages. And here the scandal, as described in a news magazine. It began with the arrival of a man at the school gate one day and his request to see the principal. Somehow, although it was not entirely clear what the man had said to give this impression, the principal's secretary was under the impression that the gentleman had a daughter he wished to enrol in the school. When admitted, the man had said, in perfect French, that he wished to apply for the post of teacher of conversational English. Questioned by a confused principal about the daughter, the gentleman said that he did indeed have a daughter, that her mother had recently died and that his intention in seeking a job – although he was beyond retirement age – was to be able to pay for an education for this girl, who was called Sabine. The principal was a principled man, who also had a daughter called Sabine. Indeed, one of his principles was to provide a high-quality private education for what he considered a reasonable price, so that girls such as the motherless Sabine could attend.

He asked Gilbert Ballantyne for a curriculum vitae, which Ballantyne provided the very next day. It was thick with teaching experience in several countries with obscure dialling codes and uncertain email access, and rich in praise for his mastery of English and English grammar, his precision of explanation, his prowess as a motivator. Gilbert Ballantyne was invited to bring Sabine along for an interview and to conduct a trial class so that the principal could watch.

Sabine, charming and modest, her eyes still full of hurt at the death of her mother, was immediately welcomed into the bosom of the school. Meanwhile, her father gave his trial lesson and it was a class of sheer brilliance, as Gilbert teased English even from those who could scarcely say, 'How are you?' Their knowledge of English varied widely, but Gilbert had them working together so that the more advanced taught the less advanced, and the trouble-makers were given a pep talk which filled them with new purpose and direction.

For six months Gilbert injected new life into the school. Only later did some of the staff look back and wonder at some of the things Sabine had said. Once she was overheard to talk fondly of her mother as though she was still alive. On another occasion she recounted the death of her mother, who had died in a car accident. And yet, the very next week, she told the story again, and this time her mother died as a blessed relief after a painful and lingering illness. Sabine was a good student with a quick mind and an ear for languages, although some of the teachers noticed the young girl's disturbing tendency to draw a tight clique of friends around her and then to play this clique off against those she did not like. Sabine even picked off those inside her clique whom she had marked out as traitors, and inducted new members who swore terrified but exhilarated allegiance to her. Despite all this, the teachers understood that this mysterious girl had experienced tragedy too young and must be given time to heal and mature. Certainly, she never caused trouble in class, unless one counted the subtle loss of morale in some of those she had been close to and was close to no longer.

Meanwhile Gilbert was a consistently popular teacher. When the principal suffered a heart attack, the school was plunged into chaos because he had taken on so much responsibility. When Gilbert modestly offered his services in whatever capacity was useful, his offer was welcomed with a Gallic sigh of relief. Of course there were various contributions that Gilbert Ballantyne could make, several of which were discussed.

No one, at this point, is quite clear how it came to pass that Gilbert Ballantyne, a man with no financial qualifications, even on the curriculum vitae held by the school, came to be given such responsibility, but that he was seemed a reflection of the high esteem in which he was held by the school community. In particular, the school secretary, a lonely married woman of some glamour, felt a deep bond with Gilbert, a man of a similar age, who looked a little lonely and who treated her with the utmost respect, unlike her husband. Everyone was also admiring of

Sabine, who worked hard and had by now entered into all the
school activities, especially the community welfare projects, at
which she would help her father distribute soup to the poor in
the winter. If there was, at that point, any criticism of Gilbert,
it was only that he was in danger of exhausting himself with
work. They diagnosed his excess of involvement thus.

'C'est parce que sa femme, elle est morte depuis deux ans.'

For six months, while the principal was first in intensive care
and then convalescing at home, Gilbert Ballantyne was, in effect,
in control of the entire school budget. The teachers were surprised, but pleased, in his second month of tenure, to read an
announcement (signed by the principal) that in fact the budget
allowed for modest bonuses to be paid to all staff. The bonuses
appeared in their pay packets at the end of the next month. There
was also a staff party at a reasonably priced restaurant, at which
a certain amount of red wine was supplied and consumed.

For some months these bonuses continued. Later one or two
of the staff would question where the money came from. But at
the time it was deemed better not to enquire. There was even,
among some members of staff, a certain amount of resentment
that the excess in the budget had not been recognized and
distributed earlier. One of the junior teachers was able now to
put down a deposit on a house, another allowed herself to
become pregnant, although she was later to regret it.

The week that the principal returned to work, Gilbert organ-
ized another party, a success like the first. He, however, was
absent, sending a message that he had caught a bug and was
unwell. Sabine, it transpired, had the same bug, a nasty virus
that lingered. When, the next day, the school secretary rang
Gilbert at home with a billing question about the party the
phone rang and rang and she had the strange sensation that it
was ringing into an empty space.

The next week, dealing with the same billing issue, the
principal pointed to the signature on the catering order form,
and asked the school secretary, 'C'est à qui, ça?'

'Mais c'est à vous, non?'

When the principal shook his head gravely, the blood drained from the school secretary's face. She hurried to the filing cabinets, from where she retrieved a large stack of documents, all bearing the same signature. She collapsed onto her chair and stared at the documents. At the top of the pile was the letter authorizing the staff bonuses. She knew, also, that somewhere in that pile of paper was a letter signed by the principal informing parents of the annual school trip, to London, and detailing costs and requesting that payment be made direct to the organizer, Gilbert Ballantyne. It was a letter Gilbert had professed himself most unhappy with.

'I don't like to use my personal account for the girls' money,' he'd protested. 'Isn't there some other way that we can do it?'

But for some reason – the school secretary had forgotten now what the reason was – it transpired that the only sensible way to do it was through Gilbert's account. Were there tickets to show for this? An itinerary? She rang the airline advertised and then the hotel. There were reservations, certainly, in the girls' names. A non-refundable deposit, indeed, had been paid. The balance of the tickets should have been paid for a week earlier, but they had heard nothing from Mr Ballantyne. Did he still require the seats?

Her heart so heavy that it had taken refuge somewhere in her gut, the school secretary carried the documents through to the principal, and placed them one by one in front of him, forgetting his heart condition, and failing to note the pallor of the man, and the drops of sweat that developed on his brow as they proceeded. She showed him the signature on the bonus notification.

'Est-ce que cela est la votre?'

'Non. Ce n'est pas la mienne.' His voice was clipped, tense, quite unlike his usual tone.

She showed him the letter about payment for the school trip. He read it without comment.

'Non. Je ne l'ai jamais vu.'

He reached his hand for the next document, read through it. It was a notification to teachers of the upcoming visit of the school inspectors. He had signed it during one of Gilbert's regular visits to his house. Gilbert always carried a briefcase with him and would usually produce some piece of paper or other for his signature. For the most part these were, like the notification of the school inspection, things of no great financial import.

'Oui,' he nodded at the signature, 'c'est la mienne.'

Relieved, his secretary handed him the next document. If it was only the bonuses, well, the teachers would just have to pay them back, although she did not want to have to be the one to tell them. If the parents had lost the money on the school trip, there would be a huge loss of confidence in the school, and some very angry calls that she would have to field, but the school would survive.

Silently he read. And then he read again. With an angry jerk, and a shake of the head that looked as though he was fighting off the hangman, he handed the document back to her and stood, pushing back his chair so that it fell over on the carpet behind him. The school secretary glanced down at the paper, and felt nausea overwhelm her as she saw a list of numbers that represented the school bank accounts, and a transfer order, another bank account number, a bank address in the Virgin islands, and the principal's signature.

'Appelez la police,' the principal barked at her, before his knees buckled and, gasping, he collapsed.

Twenty

We landed in Majorca, and I had to drag myself away from my father's crimes in France and concentrate on my missing teenager. What I had feared would be a grim and distressing day turned into something else entirely. She had been found, quite happy and not much wiser, after an absorbing holiday romance abruptly ended. Instead of interviewing worried police, I ended up interviewing the teenager herself, who was surprised to find herself missing. She was funny and frank about what she'd been up to, and I wouldn't have had it any other way, but the fact that she was alive and available for interview meant that filming took longer than we expected. We spent that night in an uninspiring hotel, and headed back to the airport the next morning.

On the plane home I read the English papers. Inspector Mitford had admitted that the raid on Ronald Evans's house and the detention of both Ronald and Sheryl had been 'regrettable'. Evans was said to be staying with relatives, 'devastated' by what had happened.

'We carried out the search with what we hoped would be minimum disruption to Ronald Evans and to Sheryl Laver, who was a guest in his house at the time of our visit,' Inspector Mitford said in a statement issued to the press. 'Because of the information one of my officers had received, and because of the grave anxiety we felt about the well-being of Christopher Darling, we felt that it was vital to give no prior warning that

the police would be searching the premises. In the event, we
regret the distress we caused to Mr Evans and Mrs Laver. We
would repeat that no incriminating evidence of any kind was
found during this search. We would like to thank Mr Evans
and Mrs Laver for their cooperation, and assure them both that
we will not be troubling them again.'

A second article noted that Fred Sevi, 'psychiatrist and
companion of missing camerawoman Melanie Jacobs', had been
questioned for a second time by police after 'new information'
had surfaced.

I shifted uncomfortably in the cramped airplane seat. Dave
had nodded off, and his head was threatening to land on my
shoulder. We were circling over London, waiting our turn to
land, bumping through clouds, the view from the window in
turn obscured, then clearing so that I could see the city below.

I got back to find that William was throwing up, his pale
little body shaking and shuddering with misery. Carol, who had
been clearing up vomit all morning, was exhausted.

'He's thrown up everywhere,' she wailed. 'The poor thing
can't understand what's happening to him.'

All afternoon and evening I did vomit duty, ferrying him
to and from the bathroom, lying him on a bed of towels. In
between bouts of sickness he slept, and I used the time to load
up the washing machine and the tumble dryer, then shower the
vomit out of my hair and change my clothes. When he had not
woken for an hour, I knew the worst was over. But I was so
awake, so conditioned to the idea that I would not sleep that
night, that I was not surprised when the telephone call came.
I glanced at the clock as I picked up the receiver and rubbed
my eyes. It was nearly ten and it felt like midnight.

It was Justin, desperately apologetic as only Justin could be,
but upset and angry too.

'I need your help,' he said. 'Jacqui's gone with her dad to

meet the kidnappers. They just left. They've gone to get Christopher back.'

'I don't understand. What do you mean?'

'To get Christopher back from the kidnapper.'

'How do they know where he is?'

'There was a ransom demand. They're going to pay it.'

'Where did they get the cash?'

'Sheryl gave it to them. Everyone's been screaming at each other. Dad shouted at Sheryl for giving Mike the money. He told Mike not to pay the ransom – he said there's no guarantee he'll get Christopher back. Look, you have to hurry. I can't move, I can't drive, I'm stuck here and I'm afraid Jacqui's going to get hurt. Her dad's taken a gun.'

'Has Mike told the police what he's doing?'

'Of course not, and you mustn't, he'll kill me. Please. Hurry. There's a warehouse in Morden, Revender's warehouse on Blodale Road.'

I grabbed an *A–Z* from the bookshelf, and looked up the address as we spoke. I'd have liked to tell Justin I couldn't possibly get there before dawn, but I could probably make it in about the same time that Mike could make it from Sydenham.

'You need to call the police,' I told Justin. 'Tell them what you've told me.'

'I can't,' Justin moaned. 'Jacqui made me promise.'

'Well, if Jacqui gets killed it's your fault,' I told him harshly. 'There's nothing I can do to protect her.'

'OK, OK,' he said. 'I'll call the police. But you will go too, won't you?'

I took a deep breath.

'I'll go and take a look,' I told him.

I had moved William into my bedroom so that he didn't disturb Hannah. Now I switched on the bedside light and lay down on the bed beside him. I felt his forehead. He was cool. His breathing was slow and peaceful, his arms thrown out in deep, comfortable, sleep. Whatever it was, he had got rid of it. I kissed him lightly and he didn't stir.

I ran up the stairs and tapped on Carol's door. I heard a light being switched on, then slow, reluctant footsteps. She appeared in a dressing gown, pushing her hair out of eyes barely open.

'I'm sorry. You were asleep.'

'I was trying to get an early night. Is William OK?'

'He's sleeping. He's stopped throwing up. But I have to . . .' I couldn't bring myself to finish. She stared at me.

'You're going out?'

'Could you possibly . . . possibly go and sleep in my bed, so you'll be there if he wakes?'

She looked at me, and I knew I had to tell her about the phone call so that she would know that this wasn't nothing. She listened and she nodded. She tightened her dressing-gown end and pulled her bedroom door closed behind her, then padded down the stairs without another word.

I parked in Morden. I leaned across to the passenger seat and picked up my bag. Inside I had a MiniDV camera, tape already inside. I'd had no time to check whether the battery was charged. I pulled the strap of my bag over my shoulder and got out of the car. The street was deserted, the shops padlocked, windows barred. Revender's warehouse was a large, dark profile set just off the road. There was a bright security light shining over its yard. It looked like a football stadium all lit up for the game.

My route took me past a pub. It was chucking-out time, and one guy was chucking up in the gutter. He recovered enough to yell an obscenity after me. In my pocket I wrapped my keys around my knuckles and carried on walking. I pulled my mobile out of my pocket and called Veronica's number, but an anonymous voice informed me the phone had been switched off. I swore softly. What was Veronica doing turning her phone off? I called the Sydenham police switchboard, gave my name and asked for Mitford, but they put me on hold for so long that I lost patience.

I circled the warehouse, looking for a vantage point. I settled, in the end, on an alley that ran along the side of the warehouse and opened onto wasteland at the far end. It wasn't an obvious access point because the alley ended in a pile of builder's rubble. But I didn't want access. I wanted to be able to see.

I clambered up the pile of rubble and discovered that once on top I could see the warehouse yard, illuminated under the security light, which bathed the concreted area in a sickly white glare. The gates, I saw, had been left open to the road. After a few minutes a white SUV drove into the yard. It stopped at the north-east corner of the yard and switched its engine off. From where I was placed I could see one figure inside. Where, I wondered, was Jacqui? I waited, settling the MiniDV camera into a position where, I hoped, its lens would not catch the light. I started to film. Wait until something happens and it's always too late.

I filmed the man in the car waiting. I waited. There was silence. For the first time it occurred to me that this enterprise might end not in success or tragedy, but in sheer bloody boredom. Then, quite suddenly, I saw that there was someone else in the car park. He or she – it was impossible to tell in the dark – had emerged from a low door in the warehouse. The person stood there, nothing but a dark shape against the dark metal of the building. The figure in the car also moved, emerging into the light, and then I could see that it was Darling.

'Where is he?' In the still night air Darling's voice carried easily. He didn't shout, just spoke, and if I could hear then so could the person at the door to the warehouse.

'Where's the cash?' I'd have said the voice was male, but the night air and my nerves served as distortion.

Darling raised a bag high over his head.

The wraith slipped back inside the warehouse. Darling's gaze never wavered from the door. After a moment it reopened and the figure re-emerged. Now I could see that he or she was dressed in black from head to toe, and that even the face was covered. The figure carried a baby against its chest.

I swore softly. The tiny scrap of flesh had been missing for days, but he had never seemed as vulnerable as he did now in the harsh glare of the searchlight, his fate in the hands of these two people.

I forced my eyes to move away from the baby back to his father, and tried to listen over the pounding of my heart. With sight of the baby, Darling's voice had assumed the authority of a soldier. 'I put the money down. You take the money, you leave him.'

Darling moved so that for the first time his back was towards me. I saw – although the figure at the warehouse could not have seen – the handgun strapped to the back of his thigh.

Where were the police? If Justin had called them as he promised, they should be here by now. They would have alerted a local patrol, no need to drive across London as we had. I cursed Justin under my breath. Why had he not kept his side of the bargain?

Darling walked to the point he had indicated and placed the holdall on the ground. When he had moved back some ten yards, the figure carried the child forward, coming to a halt by the bag and squatting to put him down on the ground carefully. I could see the child more clearly now, eyes closed in sleep or something worse, small fists relaxed.

Still squatting, the figure investigated the bag. Then, picking it up, he moved away rapidly, leaving Christopher where he lay. As he retreated, never turning his back on Darling, so Darling approached the tiny sleeping form until, at the last moment, the figure in black finally turned and ran for the doorway.

But Darling was already firing, shots bouncing off the metal door. Twice, three times, shots rang out, the last two hitting the warehouse door with a metallic report as the figure disappeared back inside. It seemed to me for a moment that Darling would give chase, and I abandoned my camera and started to scramble down the pile of rubble towards the child.

But Darling had wheeled around, and then he saw me, and he held the gun on me while I got to my feet and raised my hands. There was such contempt and fear in his eyes that for a long moment I thought he would kill me. I waited, paralysed, forgetting to breathe, as he silently made his point, the gun trained at my chest. He could get rid of me if he chose. He would like nothing better.

Then abruptly he turned away from me. For a moment I just stood there, eyes closed, gathering myself, listening to my heart pound. I opened my eyes. Darling was kneeling by the baby.

I dialled Veronica's number again while Darling gathered up his son in his arms. Then Jacqui appeared from the gateway, running across the tarmac towards her father and brother. I listened to the ringing tone and watched the family huddle together, hugging each other tightly.

Veronica answered sleepily.

'Your phone was turned off,' I burst out. 'You're supposed to be here. The police are supposed to be here. Justin's been trying to get hold of you too.'

'Hey, don't you speak to me like that,' Veronica snapped back. 'My grandmother had a stroke. Mitford knew exactly where I was. And I've got my phone right in front of me. The only calls I missed were from you. No one else tried to ring.'

'Well, why . . .?' I started to ask why she hadn't rung me back, but I knew why. She would think I was just calling to hassle her for more information. And then slowly my brain picked up on what Veronica had said. 'Is she all right?'

'No. But she's alive. What do you want?'

I told her what had happened and she muttered an expletive. Then she asked about Christopher.

I turned to look. Christopher was in Jacqui's arms, as she climbed into the passenger seat.

'It looks as though he's sleeping,' I told Veronica.

'Good,' Veronica heaved a sigh, but when she spoke she still sounded agitated. 'Good. Look, I'm glad he's alive. But because of what Mike's done, a kidnapper is out there on a high, thinking he's won.'

As if he could hear what she was saying, Mike turned to me, his face suffused with victory. He raised his hand and made a fist, punching it into the air.

'We got him back,' he crowed, 'tell her that. Left to them, he'd be dead.'

He got into the driving seat and raised his hand to me as he switched the engine on. I stood in the middle of the yard under the spotlight, and I watched his tail lights as he drove through the gates. I turned round and looked back at the dark warehouse, its metal doors swinging in the wind, no sign of life inside.

'You have to send someone over here,' I told Veronica, 'and a doctor to the house to get him checked over.'

'Don't tell me how to do my job.' Her voice was uneven. I could tell she was getting dressed as we spoke.

'Darling was shooting at him,' I told her. 'You might have someone dead or injured here.'

I closed my ears to Veronica's curses and ended the call.

Twenty-One

I didn't get home until dawn. A police patrol had arrived within seconds of my phone call to Veronica, not dispatched by her but answering calls from nearby residents who'd heard gunfire. I ended up going to the police station to give a statement, and while I was there I was given a long lecture on how I should have called the police before I set out with my camera. They were right, of course. I shouldn't have left it to Justin. I didn't argue. They also wanted to see the film and I let them copy it. I couldn't see why not. There was no secret.

Carol woke up when she heard me come in and she told me that William had slept soundly. Still I didn't go to bed. My head was spinning but my synapses were still buzzing, random thoughts splintering and racing off at tangents.

I rang Maeve. I got her at home, in bed, about to get up. I told her what had happened. I told her I had film of Mike Darling paying a ransom to a kidnapper and of Christopher being returned. I told her that, as far as I knew, the child was at least alive, but more than that I could not say. I told her that Darling had shot at the kidnapper and that as far as I knew the kidnapper had escaped unharmed.

'What do I do with the film?' I asked.

'I don't understand why you're even asking. Hand it over to News. Why didn't you ring them there and then?'

'The whole thing stinks, in my opinion.'

'It's a straightforward news story. Darling paid up, Darling got the baby back.'

'I know, I know.'

'Robin we could have been first with the story and you've been sitting on it as though it's an egg. The story is out there now. The film might as well be too. Hand it over.'

She was right, but I knew that showing the film would make a difference to the way people perceived what had happened, it would give the words substance. I couldn't explain why I was uncomfortable about releasing it. I did not know what I had witnessed, I did not know what it meant, and I wasn't sure what the value was of releasing a piece of film if we could not adequately describe it. But Maeve was determined. If I wasn't going into the office, she said, she would send a courier round for the tape.

I said goodbye and hung up, still unhappy. I saw that Carol had appeared in her dressing gown and was making tea.

'I heard,' she said.

I shook my head and sat, exhausted, at the table, laying my head on my arms. She put a cup of tea in front of me.

'The baby's alive, that's the main thing, isn't it?' she reminded me.

And, of course, it was.

William carried on sleeping, worn out by his sickness the night before. Hannah woke up and behaved like an angel, delighted to have me to herself. I played for a while, but I felt almost sick with tiredness and couldn't keep it up. I lay on the sofa and Hannah came and stroked my forehead, her lovely face just above mine. Her eyes, so like her dead father's, looking down at me with exaggerated concern. Carol urged me to go to bed, but I was too wound up to sleep. In the end I sat at the dining table, getting in Carol's way, listening to radio accounts of what had happened the night before and waiting for the courier to pick up the tape. The minutes ticked by.

I thumbed through the newspaper, and saw again the article reporting that Fred Sevi had been questioned for a second time by police. I wished I had some direct line to DCI Coburn, but all my information from the investigation into Melanie's disappearance had come through Veronica or Finney, and I knew that it wasn't the right time to call either of them.

I took the phone to the sofa and rang Beatrice. I had assumed that DCI Coburn would have kept her informed about developments in the investigation into her daughter's disappearance. In fact, Beatrice had seen the same article that I had and had contacted the police herself, demanding details.

'It's something to do with mobile phone records,' she told me, 'that's all he would tell me, and he told me not to tell any journalists, so please, if you would—'

'We know Fred called Melanie on the night of January the ninth from the gate of HazPrep,' I said. 'He admits it, so there can't be any question about that.'

'I'm at a loss,' Beatrice said. Something was tugging at my memory. Sevi shifting uncomfortably in his chair, saying that he had tried calling Melanie the next day from central London after attending the public lecture at the Wolfson Theatre. I asked Beatrice whether Fred had said anything to her about trying to call Melanie on 10 January, the day she disappeared.

'I don't think so.' Beatrice sounded mystified and I told her what Fred had told me, that he had called Melanie but that the connection had been so bad that the call had lasted only a matter of seconds.

'I wonder if he told the police that,' she said, 'although, of course, it doesn't really get us anywhere.' Beatrice had started out calm enough, but now I could hear the frustration in her voice. She had few illusions about Melanie's fate, but she wanted to know what had happened and why, and at every turn there was a dead end. We said goodbye.

I got slowly to my feet.

'I'm going out,' I told Carol.

'You'll make yourself ill,' she told me disapprovingly. She nodded at the MiniDV tape lying on the table. 'Do you want me to give that to the courier man?'

I looked at it lying there. I picked it up, put it in my bag.

'No. Tell him the order's been cancelled.'

She shrugged and watched as I picked up my keys and checked the battery of my mobile phone.

'It's all very well,' she said quietly, 'but if you get ill you know who picks up the pieces?'

I gazed at her.

'I'm sorry,' I said. 'I promise I won't get ill.'

'Right.'

It took a lot of asking, but eventually I found Justin and Jacqui in the hospital canteen, his crutches propped next to the table, toppled paper cups rolling around on the table in front of them. At the next table sat a weary-looking man and a pale woman with tubes protruding from bandages at her neck.

The two young lovers were separated by the tabletop, but scarcely. Their hands were clasped together in front of them, and as I approached I saw that Jacqui had kicked off her pumps, and that her two bare feet rested on Justin's one good remaining foot. Her head was bowed and Justin was leaning forward so that his lips pressed against her forehead.

'Hello.' I sat down, unasked, at their table. 'How's Christopher?'

'Sergeant Mann took Mum over to Lewisham hospital to get him checked over,' Jacqui said. 'He looks thinner and he keeps crying, but I think he's just confused, poor thing.'

I had no idea what kind of psychological scar an abduction would leave. It was hard to believe that the child would ever completely recover from being removed from his family and from his home. But Jacqui seemed upbeat about Christopher's return and I didn't want to pour cold water on that.

'I'm really glad you've got him back,' I said. 'Your mother must be over the moon.'

Jacqui didn't respond directly.

'Mum seems better,' she said.

'But Justin,' I said, 'I have a bone to pick with you. We had a deal and you reneged.'

They looked at each other.

'You told me you'd call the police and you didn't.' I spelled it out for him.

He shot a glance at Jacqui.

'Well, it was OK in the end,' he said.

'You weren't to know that.'

'I told him not to call the police,' Jacqui intervened. 'Dad knows how to handle himself. There was never going to be a problem. If the police arrived, they'd have got involved, they'd never just have let it happen.'

Justin sat there with such a pained expression on his face that I couldn't berate him further.

'I want to know how the kidnappers made contact,' I said.

'There was another note,' Jacqui said, 'but this time Dad didn't show it to anyone except Kes and me and Sheryl. I mean not the police, or Anita. It asked for a hundred thousand pounds.'

'How was it delivered?'

'I don't know. I was out. When I got back, Dad told me there'd been this huge row with Kes and that Sheryl was giving him the money against Kes's wishes.'

'I'm sure Sheryl had something to do with it,' Jacqui muttered.

'Sheryl paid the ransom. Why would she pay money to herself?' I was exasperated. 'Why on earth this fixation on Sheryl? What harm has she ever done anyone?'

Jacqui looked at Justin, and he shrugged.

'Everyone knows. We all know and the police know,' he said and gestured to Jacqui that she might as well go ahead and tell me.

'She snatched a baby.'

'Years ago,' Justin added, with a warning look at Jacqui. 'It was years ago. I was just a kid. She was one of Mum's friends. She was always around before Mum died, helping out, cooking, cleaning, ironing. I must have been ten or eleven because that's when Mum died. Sheryl was pregnant, only she lost the baby; she had a breakdown and she took a baby. She was at her friend's house, having coffee, and her friend asked her to look after her baby while she ran to the shops. When she got back, Sheryl was gone and so was the baby. She went crazy looking all over for them and she called in the police. They found them in the park later that day, Sheryl pushing the pram around like it was her baby. Sheryl acted all offended, like she didn't know what all the fuss was about. She said she was going to take the baby back and her friend should have known she wouldn't hurt it. The police wanted to charge her, but once the friend had got her baby back she was so relieved. She felt bad about getting Sheryl into trouble, so she told the police maybe she'd misled Sheryl, maybe she'd talked about going to the park and Sheryl had misunderstood her.'

'But nobody believed that,' I said.

'Nah. Nobody believed it. Everyone knew about the miscarriage. Nobody wanted to talk to her after that.'

'Except your dad,' I said. 'He must have ignored what everyone was saying.'

For a moment Justin said nothing, but his face contorted with the effort of putting complex things into words.

'Dad says she needed him,' Justin said eventually, 'although I don't know why that means he had to marry her.'

'He obviously doesn't love her,' Jacqui said, then looked away, unwilling to venture down the path that would lead to what she and I had both witnessed. 'So you see? She's a baby snatcher,' she insisted, changing the subject.

'And someone told the police and that's why they raided Ronald Evans's house.'

'They had to know,' she said.

'Yes.' I pushed my chair back and got up to go. 'I suppose they did.'

'I've got to go too,' Jacqui said, checking her watch.

'You have?' Justin looked surprised. 'Where are you going?'

'It's nothing, I've just got go and do something,' Jacqui told him, looking embarrassed. 'I thought I told you. Anyway, I've got a few minutes.'

I left them there.

Once I was in my car I had an urge to sit and wait for Jacqui to emerge. What was it she had to do that didn't involve Justin? When she appeared, she walked towards me, pulling a mobile phone from her pocket, dialling, speaking. Then she put the phone away and pulled keys from her pocket, and I saw that she was driving Anita's green Mini.

She pulled out of her parking space and headed into town. She was driving impatiently but not particularly fast, and I easily followed on behind.

My heart sank as she pulled into a multi-storey car park. Surely, I thought, she was not going to celebrate the reappearance of her little brother with a clothes-shopping trip. I could see myself trailing behind her to Gap and H&M, and kicking myself for the wasted time.

I followed her on a pedestrian walkway out of the car park and into the mall, then down an escalator to the basement. She seemed to know exactly where she was going. If this was shopping, it was at least focused shopping. Again my heart plummeted as she headed for Burger King. There was a coffee concession opposite, and I sat down with a lukewarm espresso. I could see her quite clearly inside Burger King through the glass frontage. She approached the counter, handed over some money and picked up a tray bearing what looked like a paper cup and a bag of chips. She stood and turned her head this way and that, as though she was looking for someone. Then she made for a table in the corner, where a woman was already sitting, her head bowed over a magazine, a paper cup in front of her.

Jacqui put her tray down on her table, and when the woman looked up I recognized her. Jacqui squeezed into the chair next to Sheryl, and the older woman shifted away from her. These two were sworn enemies. What's more, they lived in the same house. What was it they were discussing that they could not say in front of the others? Sheryl spoke and Jacqui replied at length, moving her head as though she was issuing an ultimatum. Sheryl shrugged. She seemed to be arguing and now it was Jacqui's turn to look annoyed. Sheryl stood up. She swept the paper cup onto the floor, tea spilling across the tabletop, and walked out.

I went into the office. I told Sal that if anyone came by looking for me, he should say he hadn't seen me. I took refuge in the editing suite. I got the tape of the ransom payment out of my bag, put it in the machine and watched it through a few times. I gazed at the figure in black. My gut instinct was that the figure was male and tall. But the loose clothing blurred the outlines of the body. And without reference points it was difficult to judge size. I rewound it time and time again. I still had the sense that the whole event had been staged, but any handover of that sort must, by its nature, be staged. I was being ridiculous. Maeve could have her pictures. I looked at my watch. She'd missed the midday news, but she could pass it to the newsroom for the six. She was the head of Documentaries, not News, but she would get brownie points for being the one to pass the film on and it might keep her off my back for a while. I ejected the tape from the machine and took it back out into the office to put in an envelope for the internal mail. Sal was talking to a young man. He was short, casually dressed in a Garfield T-shirt, jeans and running shoes.

'Robin.' Sal introduced us. 'This is Edwin Rochester. I just convinced him that you weren't here. Robin – ' he turned to Edwin – 'is an illusion. But you may shake her hand.'

'I'm sorry, I was trying to avoid my boss,' I explained. 'I'm so glad you dropped in.'

'Yeah, well, I know you've been digging around and I'd really like to help if I can,' he said. He had an attractive, easy, smile. He pulled up a chair.

'You spent a lot of time with Melanie,' I said.

He shrugged.

'We got on pretty well, so we travelled together when we could. We kept bashing into each other around the place. We pushed things a bit further than some people would. Melanie could talk her way into anything. Her bosses would have been horrified at some of the things she did. Not that they complained about her pictures. They supplied her with all this stuff, helmets, body armour, as though she's going to wear twenty-pound ceramic plates all the time. If she'd been doing things by the book she'd have been travelling with a bodyguard – they call them security consultants – but she preferred not to.'

Again I was hearing that past tense. But I didn't pull him up on it. Who of us by now really believed that Melanie was alive?

'I keep hearing that Melanie was suffering from post-traumatic stress,' I said.

Edwin gave me a look that suggested he didn't like what he was hearing. He leaned forward to rest his elbows on my desk and picked at the edge of a newspaper while he thought about his answer.

'I suppose it's a possibility,' he said carefully, 'but she was always as solid as a rock when we worked together. Not that I saw much of her in the last year or so before she disappeared. I saw her maybe twice after Afghanistan.'

'Tell me more about Afghanistan.'

'It's like stepping back in time.' He leaned back in his chair, swinging it gently to and fro as he spoke. 'Scarcely any roads and those there are are mined, bridges gone, mud houses, cloth on the windows, no glass. Anything modern is Russian – tanks, trucks, jeeps, weaponry. And the Afghans. There they are working as drivers and fixers for foreign journalists, and they're qualified doctors and lawyers. Intelligent, handsome, with these aquiline noses, melancholy as hell. Crazy drivers. The women are all in burkas, of course. But hey, you know, the sky is this deep azure blue, and you sit on top of one of those flat-rooved houses in the evening, and you look up and the sky is full of stars, and it's the closest you can get to heaven.'

Edwin had raised his face towards the ceiling and he was smiling. It was all very romantic, but it wasn't what I had meant.

'I mean did Melanie ever talk to you about what happened in Afghanistan after you left? Like when you showed her the photos. What did she say?'

Edwin looked at me.

'She made some comment, like that something went wrong, or she didn't want to talk about it. But that was it.'

'You took some beautiful pictures of her.'

'Yeah, well, she was a beautiful person. Not everyone saw it, but I like that look, you know. She played up to it, too. She knew what I was looking for. She used to mess around like everyone else, but as soon as I pointed a camera at her she'd do this aloof, watchful thing. It was so cool.'

He stopped talking and watched my face for a moment.

'You don't have the first clue what happened to her, do you?'

I sighed. My head was pounding and I was exhausted after my sleepless night. Christopher and Melanie. Why had I tied them together in my head? It seemed an empty hypothesis when I examined it more closely, and I feared that I was concocting links and conspiracy theories simply because since Adam's death I was prone to see them everywhere.

'No,' I said. 'I haven't got a clue.'

I asked him whether Melanie had talked about Fred Sevi or

her friend Stella Smith. But Melanie had lived two separate lives. One she had lived back in Britain, where she had at least attempted to have a normal life. The other life she had lived abroad, frequently in hostile environments, away from safety.

After Edwin had gone, I addressed the envelope for the internal mail and wrote a brief account of what had happened the night before. Once the envelope had started on its way I spoke to the news desk about the film I had shot. The editor was bemused that I had not handed the film over earlier, but he would still have it for the prime-time news slot.

I returned home, still feeling uncomfortable about the film of the ransom payment. My meeting with Edwin had also made me feel deeply sorry that I had achieved nothing for Melanie. I wanted nothing more than to speak to Finney and to take comfort in his huge good sense. I wasn't playing hard to get. I had tried calling him. Several times. But he'd been in turn, busy, in a meeting, unavailable, out to lunch, and engaged.

I put the children to bed, enjoying William's good spirits. Hannah, jealous of the attention that William received, was trying to convince me that she was sick too. She kept making disgusting but unproductive retching sounds that had William in stitches.

Eventually, I got them into bed, switched off their light and sat down at the computer. I could hear Hannah in the bedroom still making retching sounds and William giggling. I ignored them.

My mother had emailed me to wish me a happy birthday. Which came as a surprise, because I had forgotten what day it was. Actually, so had she. She was a day early.

Many Happy Returns, but I'm busy trying to persuade myself I'm 21 again, so I'd be grateful if you wouldn't remind me how Old you are. I have been Working Out. My Butt is getting Tighter

(I am assured. I can't actually see it without putting my neck out). I have an ADMIRER. He is American, but he's a Democrat so that's all right. Wish me luck.
PS would you like some Birkenstocks for your birthday? I believe they're quite the Thing.

I saw there were two attachments, and I opened them to find my mother had emailed me two pictures. One was of a pair of very sensible sandals that would soon belong to me. The other was of her paramour, a man with a big smile who must have been in his fifties. This attachment was titled 'Randy'. There was another email from her. I opened it up.

PPS I have just read on the Internet about the missing Baby being Found. What Wonderful News.

It was, of course, quite simply Wonderful News. I held on to that thought, and went to sleep.

Twenty-Two

I spent the morning in Crawley, home to another of my family of missing people. Lindy Mason, a forty-three-year-old woman, had disappeared six weeks earlier while out food shopping two months exactly after her husband of twenty-five years had died of leukaemia. Her car had been found abandoned in the supermarket car park. Her son, Tony, was devastated. I spent an hour with him in his small terraced house. His wife was out at work and his three young children were hurtling around the lights Dave had set up to film our conversation.

'She was coping, you know? She was doing all right without Dad, she was holding things together,' he told me, bouncing a two-year-old on his knee. 'The only thing I can think is that something happened or that she lost her memory. I think that's the most likely thing, don't you? I'd say it can happen when people have had a shock.'

Lindy had not vanished entirely without trace. There had been debit-card withdrawals from her account. But the police had told Tony it was possible that the card had been stolen and it was being used by someone other than his mother. Then the bank informed Tony that, because of the doubts about his mother's whereabouts, the account was to be frozen.

'To be honest,' he told me, 'I liked to think she had some cash, if it was her taking it out. What will she do if she can't buy things?'

Tony seemed to me to be trying to ignore the bleaker aspects of his mother's disappearance. She was a woman of mercurial mood, abrasive and warm by turns, who had made great friends of some neighbours and enemies of others. She had also been in and out of psychiatric institutions for the past twenty years. Twice she had tried to kill herself. After speaking to Tony, we interviewed Lindy's neighbours. Everyone who knew her agreed that it was her husband who had been holding her together. He had looked after her not with indulgence but with infinite patience. Those who knew Lindy could not imagine her without him. On the day he died, one woman told us, Lindy had argued with a door-to-door salesman so violently, kicking and hitting him, that the salesman had called the police. But everyone agreed she was more of a danger to herself than to anyone else.

After filming, Dave and I grabbed a quick pub lunch, then we got back in the car and headed north on the M23 back towards London, Dave driving so that I could make some calls. I rang Veronica's mobile, and was surprised she took the call.

'I've given you more than twenty-four hours to forgive me,' I said.

She grunted.

'How's Christopher?'

'He's alive. He was drugged to keep him quiet. Which could mean that there was only one person involved. It's possible he was left alone somewhere, but even so whoever held him could have come and gone knowing he wasn't going to scream. Anyway, he's alive. He's going to be OK.'

'Are there any long-term effects?'

'There are no guarantees. It's not the kind of experiment drug companies get permission to do and we don't know what doses he was given.'

'Whoever had him risked doing him real damage.'

'Even more so if he really was left for long periods of time on his own. But you don't have to have a medical degree these days to get hold of information about dosage, you can just type the name of some drug into your search engine and away you go. You can probably buy it the same way and have it delivered to your door.'

'Did you find anything in the warehouse?'

'No. Whoever was there was careful not to leave finger-prints, shoeprints, any kind of print. There were no bloodstains and there's no indication that Darling's bullets touched him, which we find strange.'

'I'm not sure he ever got a clear shot at him.'

'Still,' she said dryly, 'we expect more of our soldiers. Hit the target at least.'

'Are you suggesting that he wasn't trying? Or that it was for show?'

There was a moment's pause before Veronica answered, 'A show for who? He didn't know you were there.'

'He knew Jacqui was.'

'Does she care about displays of machismo by her father?'

'She just cares about her little brother,' I said. A picture of Jacqui came unbidden to my mind, walking up to Sheryl, sitting down next to her, saying something that Sheryl did not want to hear.

'I understand the cash came from Sheryl,' I said.

'Against her husband's wishes, yes.'

I thought back to Mike's rescue of his son. His face, victori-ous, his fist punching the air, gloating as he rubbed Veronica's nose in it. 'Left to them, he'd be dead.'

'Now Christopher's back are you going to question Mike again?'

There was silence on the line for a moment and I thought I'd lost the connection.

'Mike came to us while the baby was gone,' Veronica told me. 'He's given us a full statement concerning that earlier meeting with Melanie Jacobs.'

'Oh, really?'

'He said he wanted to get things straight with us because we were working with him on the kidnap. He said it was preying on his mind.'

'He told you about the ambush?'

'You already know about it, I gather.'

'What do you think?'

'What is there to think? He was with Melanie when his friend was killed. He didn't feel like talking about it. He didn't think he needed to. He's very apologetic about not coming clean in the first place. I don't think there's any great secret: he just got stupid when she disappeared and, once he hadn't told us, he couldn't go back on it. It happens more than you'd think.'

When we had hung up, I told Dave what she had said. He shrugged and said, 'So I guess that's that,' and I'd have been stupid to argue the point. I sat back and watched the countryside glide by. Why had I become so obsessed with Mike's supposed guilt? Perhaps it was just that I hated not to know. If there was no good answer, I would invent one and try to make it fit. It didn't make me feel good about myself. I had cursed the people who'd done just the same to me. I closed my eyes.

My mobile trilled into the quiet of the car. It was Tanya. She apologized for shouting at me and invited me round for a birthday dinner.

'I'm inviting Lorna as well,' she said. 'I'm still angry with her, but I can't bear that we're not all friends.'

Lorna, I could have said, would have held out much longer. Tanya, the youngest of us, is the most forgiving, except where our father is concerned. Instead I just thanked her for the invitation and promised to be there as early as I could.

Then, as Dave and I got closer to London and the traffic slowed, I called Sal. There had been a new sighting of Melanie in the Lake District. A woman of her description, but looking unkempt, had been seen in a supermarket buying groceries and an armful of newspapers. As she paid at the checkout, the cashier pointed out a picture of Melanie that had been posted on the noticeboard, and commented on the likeness. The woman had left the store in some distress, taking her shopping but failing to pay.

I caught sight of a sign for Sydenham and I thought of Jacqui badmouthing Sheryl then going straight to a meeting with her. I thought of Justin, and how he'd begged me to go to Morden, and the way he'd broken his promise to me to call the police. And I decided I was owed some answers.

'Dave,' I said, 'would you mind dropping me off in Sydenham?'

There had been a light rain, and the wet grass clung to my sandalled feet, wrapping itself around my toes. I went round to the back of the house and hammered on the glass door. I saw Jacqui emerge from the alcove she shared with Christopher, the baby on her hip, so at home it seemed he had never left. He was holding the palm of his hand against Jacqui's face, as if for security.

She opened the door.

'What are you doing here?'

I fancied that Christopher had become thinner. He had never been a fat baby but now his cheeks looked sunken, his fingers as thin as chopsticks.

'I'm pleased to see Christopher,' I said. I put my hand out to touch Christopher's head, but he flinched away and started to whine anxiously.

'He's still jumpy,' she told me, lowering her voice. 'They drugged him with Valium. Talk about sickos. Just like the stuff Sheryl gives to Mum.'

Anita's mental state was not at the top of my list of priorities. As I didn't want to be distracted from my purpose, I didn't follow up on this, but I made a mental note of what Jacqui had said. Jacqui turned back inside the house, and I wasn't sure what I was expected to do, so I stepped inside without being invited.

'Sheryl's exactly what I want to talk about,' I said quietly. 'I want to know what you were doing meeting her in Burger King.'

She stood there, still holding the door open, too shocked to remember to shut it behind me.

'It's none of your business,' she said, recovering. 'I can talk to who I want.'

She pushed the door shut – she was too considerate to Christopher to slam it – and turned away from me, back towards the alcove she had come from. I paused at the entrance while she laid Christopher in his crib. I turned my head, my eyes caught by something in Anita's alcove. I stared. On the wall that faced me there was a violent stain. For an instant I thought I must be looking at art. But the smears of paint were ugly, and they were surrounded by a larger wet mark. The whole area stank of turpentine. On the floor lay the remains of a bottle that must, I thought, have been smashed against the wall.

Pots and brushes, a canvas, even an easel, lay untidily on the floor where they had been hurled. Then I saw that Anita lay on the bed, on top of the tangled sheets, propped against pillows, her eyes wide, staring at the ceiling, her hand plucking at the silky nightdress that was twisted up around her thighs.

'What happened?' I murmured.

Jacqui looked up, then realized what I could see and her face flushed.

'Mum lost it,' she said. She bit her lip. 'It all got too much for her.'

Without thinking, I took a step closer. I must have made some sound, or disturbed a shadow, because suddenly Anita half sat up and saw me.

'I'm sorry,' I said and took a step back.

She collapsed onto the pillows and I ventured to her bedside.

She stared up at me. Tears were flowing down her face and soaking the pillow.

'What is it?'

'It's my own fault,' she muttered, her words slurring. 'The whole thing's my fault. What was I thinking?' Then her voice turned into a wail. 'What on earth was I thinking?'

She buried her face in the pillow and beat her fist against it.

Behind me Jacqui spoke, and Anita pulled another pillow over her head to block out her daughter's voice.

'Leave her be,' Jacqui said, 'you should go. Stop sticking your nose into our business. Christopher is back, so there's no need for us to be public property any more. I'm not going to tell you what I said to Sheryl and that's final.'

She held the door open for me and I had no option but to leave.

I didn't arrive as early as I'd intended at Tanya's, but apparently I was the first. We were greeted by her three girls, who had prepared little packages for Hannah and William.

'I know it's your birthday, but we don't know what to make for old people,' Chloë said, as the twins ripped the paper from packets of chocolate drops. 'We only know what little kids like.'

'I told them,' said Patrick, appearing behind them, 'that their present to you was to look after Hannah and William this evening.'

I kissed Patrick on the cheek. 'I like that present.'

I watched the twins follow Chloë and her sisters eagerly up the stairs. I knew I would not see them for some time. Then I followed Patrick into the kitchen and Tanya greeted me as though she had not, just days before, charged yelling into my house. She kissed me, then pointed me towards a pile of onions. The onions, I decided, as I picked up the chopper, were probably my punishment for not telling Tanya that Gilbert had been staying in Ma's house. I decided to take it on the chin. Not because I thought I had been treacherous, but because someone had to chop the onions and it might as well be me.

When the doorbell rang I blinked the tears from my eyes, wiped my hands on my jeans and went to let Lorna in, but she was not alone. For a moment I didn't recognize her dinner guest.

'I thought of bringing Dad, but I decided Joe was less controversial,' Lorna said defensively. I found my tongue and welcomed them both in, noting – silently and to myself – that Lorna had dispensed with the priest's title. I led them into Tanya's tiny kitchen. They made a gorgeous couple. Lorna looked pre-Raphaelite with her ringlets, her pale skin and fine bone structure. Father Joe had shaved off his beard – an act surely calculated to make himself look less ascetic – to reveal what could only be described as a gorgeous mouth and chin. Lorna was assessing the situation in the kitchen.

'Joe, chop the mushrooms,' she ordered. 'I'll wash the salad. Tanya, what are you doing with that chicken?'

Tanya turned and put her hands on her hips.

'Is that it? What am I doing with the chicken? How about hello, thank you for the invitation, and sorry for offending you. Because that's what it was. Offensive. She's my mother too – you can't just go doing what you did.'

I realized, then, that I had got off lightly with the onions. Lorna stood stock-still, staring at her little sister. I heard Joe cough softly. It was a subtle clearing of the throat, no more. But it was communication, and the kind of communication that happens between lovers, when other things take the place of words. I wondered whether they had stopped at coughing.

'Of course,' Lorna said mechanically and not entirely graciously. 'Hello, thank you for the invitation. I regret anything I've ever said or done that might conceivably have offended anyone in this room.'

Lorna and Tanya watched each other for a moment, while the rest of us held our breath.

'You know Dad's gone, don't you?' Lorna said.

'Good.' And then, despite herself, my little sister asked, 'Where to?'

'I don't know. I went to Ma's, but he's not there and all his things are gone. I thought you might know. Robin?'

I thought of the information Finney had given me about Gilbert's devastation of the school in Paris.

'I don't know. He's a grown man. I'm sure he can look after himself.'

The doorbell rang and I went to get it, mostly because I wanted to get out of the kitchen.

Finney was standing there, his hands in his pockets.

'I'm here on a mission of destruction to pay you back for what you did on my birthday,' he said. We smiled at each other and I stood back to let him in. He took off his jacket and kissed me.

'OK,' I said, 'but my family doesn't really need any help. It's quite capable of self-destructing.'

I led him through to the dining room, where Patrick, who had grown up a Roman Catholic was berating Father Joe about the impossibility of the celibacy of the priesthood, much to the delight of Lorna.

'I agree with you,' Father Joe said, in a voice calculated politely to put the subject to rest, 'the present situation is untenable. But these things don't work themselves out overnight.'

Lorna's eyes were shining. Had Father Joe given her cause to hope? I could not see it, but then I was not looking for it as hard as she was. We talked about other things, in particular about Ma and her romance with Randy, and the tone of conversation lightened.

As Tanya brought on coffee at the end of the meal, I noticed that Lorna was slumped in her chair as though she could not hold herself upright. She had not taken part in the conversation for some time. Father Joe's eyes were on her too. He pushed back his chair, got up and went over to her, squatting down beside her chair and speaking to her quietly, not making a scene. Nevertheless, conversation dried up as the rest of us realized what was happening. Lorna nodded, a tiny inclination of her head.

'If you'll excuse us,' he said, 'Lorna's wiped out. Can I call for a cab?'

'I'll run you home,' Finney said, 'I've got to be at work by seven tomorrow, so I have to go too.'

Father Joe nodded his thanks and held out his hand to Lorna. She took it, but she couldn't pull herself up, so without any hesitation he leaned over, reaching one arm around her shoulders and the other under her knees. He scooped her off her chair and stood there holding her like a babe in arms. She didn't protest. Instead, with a small smile on her face, she rested her head on his shoulder, her red-gold curls draping his arm. We all stood to say goodnight and Finney followed them out of the room, thanking Tanya for dinner.

When they had gone, Tanya and I looked at each other. She bit her lip, she shook her head.

'Whatever,' she asked, 'is he thinking?'

I helped Tanya with the washing up, enjoying the opportunity to gossip more, mostly about Lorna and Father Joe. What was he thinking? What was she thinking? Less luridly, we worried that Lorna's sudden and dramatic exhaustion was an indication of just how much she had been pushing herself recently. We talked about Ma and Randy, like parents discussing their children. Could there be any real future in such a long-distance romance? Were they compatible or was this just the lure of the exotic?

'And while we're on the subject, what about you and Finney?' Tanya asked. 'Do you have any plans, or are you just going to tease each other on like this until you're sixty?'

My mobile rang. I grabbed it from the table, eager for any

excuse not to answer the question. It was Mike, although he didn't stop to introduce himself but launched into a tirade. I pulled a face of disbelief at Tanya.

'What do you want from me?' he shouted. 'Why are you coming here to harass my wife? Leave me alone, leave my family alone and leave my friends alone. If this goes on, I swear you will be sorry.'

He hung up.

'What was that?' Tanya asked. She was standing stock still. 'I could hear him from here.'

'He's upset,' I said. 'He doesn't mean anything by it.'

But we didn't gossip any more after that, and when I gathered up the sleeping twins to put them in the car, Tanya helped me with them and watched me get into the driver's seat, hugging her arms around her against the evening chill.

'I wish you had Finney with you,' she said. 'Take care.'

She waved me off. When I looked in the mirror she was already back inside, closing her front door.

Twenty-Three

I got home and locked up, hardly able to stay awake. When the phone rang I snatched the receiver up, ready to snap at whoever was ringing. I was afraid it would be Mike with more warnings to stay away. But when I heard Justin, as apologetic and anxious as ever, I staggered as far as the sofa and lay down, with my eyes closed, to listen.

'I've got Jacqui with me,' he said. 'She's really scared and she wants to talk to you so someone knows what's happened. The police won't listen to her any more. I think maybe she's imagining it—'

At this point, the telephone was grabbed out of his hand and Jacqui started to tell me her story.

Justin and Jacqui have established what can only be called a love nest in the grounds of the house at the edge of the wood. In fact it's a garden shed, but like a bird building a home Jacqui has stolen cushions and blankets, one by one, from the house, and piled them high in the tiny wooden shack. Jacqui's need to create this warm and soft environment for their lovemaking springs from something deep inside her, something that is made more urgent by Justin's severed limb. She wants to surround him with the comfort he has longed for ever since his mother died.

They have created this haven in secret – which fact on its own lends it an erotic frisson. The atmosphere inside the house is now so oppressive that neither of them feel they can breathe. They know, without discussing it, that their respective parents will freak out if their precious child sleeps with the other parents' respective precious child inside the house. But they also know that their respective parents are so distracted that they don't give a damn what goes on in the garden shed.

Justin, his time filled with doctors and physiotherapy, challenged by his own impaired and painful body and, his loins on fire for Jacqui, pays only glancing attention to the eddies and flows of misery inside the house. When they lie down together there is nothing on Justin's mind except his body, made whole, her body, and the fact that he loves her.

Jacqui's body is equally consumed. Their frequent bouts of sex distract her intermittently from the fact that she is terribly frightened. She has developed a quick, soft way of walking around the house that gets her from room to room discreetly. She watches her mother and father, and sees that the return of Christopher, which she thought would save them, has not done so.

Jacqui is also frightened of Ronald Evans, who passed her in the street two days after the police raid on his house and laid into her.

'Are you aware of what I have been through because of you?'

Jacqui tries to walk past him, but he grabs her upper arm in a surprisingly tight and painful grip.

'What?' Jacqui demands. 'I haven't done anything to you.'

'It was you who told the police you thought I had the boy,' Ronald continues furiously. 'Trying to make yourself important. I've never hurt a fly. The idea of abducting a child is abhorrent.'

'So what if it was me?' Jacqui says, and pulls her arm out of his grasp and runs off.

'You won't be allowed to get away with it,' his voice calls after her.

Jacqui has come in for worse abuse from Sheryl.

'He's an old man,' Sheryl tells her, quietly and white with

anger, 'a frail old man, and you set the police on him, and you humiliated me.'

'I don't know why you think it was me.' Jacqui is defiant, even as she retreats. But later she sits sobbing on the step just outside the back door and rings Veronica Mann on her mobile.

'You told them it was me,' she cries. 'You said it would be a secret.'

'I have not told them a thing,' Veronica Mann sounds impatient, as though she has better things to be doing. 'They must have worked it out for themselves. It won't have been difficult.'

'Ronald said they wouldn't let me get away with it.' Jacqui's voice rises. 'But I was just trying to do the right thing for Christopher. I know you don't believe me, but—'

'Listen Jacqui, they're upset. But Christopher is back now – that's all that matters. Isn't that right?'

Jacqui hangs her head. She takes a deep breath.

'I really think you shouldn't give up trying to find out who took Christopher,' she says to Veronica.

'We have not given up,' Veronica tells her. But the police have many things on their plate, she does not say.

Jacqui bites her lip.

'I mean there are things you should know about what's going on here. I know you think I wasn't right before, but I want to talk to you again.'

'I will be there tomorrow,' Veronica tells her, and thinks, resigned: And I will hear another grand conspiracy theory.

'Tomorrow,' Jacqui repeats, thinking about Justin's physiotherapy sessions, 'OK. I'll be here.'

Jacqui puts her phone back in her pocket dejectedly, staring at the ground and rubbing her eyes clear of tears. She sees the flicker of a shadow on the ground, as though something or someone has moved at the window to her right.

That night Jacqui and Justin are entangled in the blankets in the garden shed, their only illumination a powerful torch that they have propped in the corner, and across which Jacqui has draped a pair of red knickers. The torch, thus clad, casts a semicircle of red light across the timber roof. Jacqui has brought two or three torches to the shed by now, but they get lost, one by one, in the bedding.

Justin is propped against a wall of cushions. Jacqui lies across his naked chest, the blankets are pulled tight around them, and they are silent, kissing, when a loud groan of hunger from Justin's stomach makes them collapse in giggles.

'What've we got to eat?' he asks.

Jacqui scrabbles around in a box by the door.

'Eggs,' she offers helpfully, holding up a carton.

'What are we going to do with those?'

They laugh again. When Jacqui's with Justin, the fear recedes.

Jacqui delves into the box again, but shakes her head.

'That's all there is. I'll go and get you something.'

'Nah. I'll be all right.'

'You can't go to sleep hungry,' she tells him. 'I'll go and get some biscuits or something. I'll be back in a minute. Can I take the torch?'

There is a minute hesitation before he says, 'Yeah, take it. I'm not going anywhere.'

Jacqui removes the knickers from the torch, pulls on a T-shirt, and heads out into the night. Justin waits in the sudden pitch dark, counting the seconds to her return, feeling a terrible pain in his missing leg. He has been trying to limit the number of painkillers he takes, because he can't think clearly when he's full of them. In the dark, strange, unpleasant thoughts occur to him about the people he loves. He becomes panicky. He won't even let himself think about the future. His prosthesis is lying somewhere, abandoned, buried in the blankets. He begins to search for it in the dark.

*

Jacqui makes her way across the lawn, enjoying the breeze and the damp grass on her bare feet. There are few lights on in the house, it must be nearly midnight. Just one in her parents' bedroom and two at Kes and Sheryl's end of the house. She finds this interesting. She has been wondering how Kes and Sheryl can sleep together. She finds it more credible that her own parents can at least continue to sleep in the same bed since they seem to be in denial. Probably, she thinks, they can lie in the same bed and each pretend they're on their own. The light in Christopher's room is out, presumably he was asleep hours ago. She lets herself in through the back door.

Jacqui goes to what passes for the kitchen, and is pleased to see that amid the meagre supplies – no one seems to be thinking about grocery shopping, or even about eating, these days – there is a packet of chocolate digestives. She seizes this and two cans of beer, then runs lightly on the same noiseless feet back the way she has come, proud of her spoils.

She tracks back across the lawn, taking a different path this time, perhaps a little shorter. Now, walking away from the illuminated house and into the darkness, she feels suddenly afraid. She is aware of a tiny knot of panic sitting under her ribs. Suddenly she comes to a halt. She has heard something. She listens. Perhaps the noise came from the garden shed, perhaps it is Justin moving around.

She starts to walk again, but the sound is closer at hand. She can hear breathing, and now she begins to run and, behind her, feet pound. She feels a hand grab for her, but manages to evade it, slithering like a snake from its grasp. She is a dancer and she pushes her bare feet into the earth and springs to one side, wrong-footing her assailant. She calls for help and suddenly Justin's voice is shouting her name, and she can just make out his shape in the doorframe of the shed, a torch in his hand, shining it across the orchard so that it reaches her. And suddenly she is alone again, her assailant vanished into the night.

She races to Justin and almost bowls him over.

'What was that all about?' he wants to know. 'And where's the food?'

'I dropped it. Out there,' she gasps. 'Didn't you see her?'

'See who?' Justin sometimes thinks Jacqui's paranoid. All that stuff about Sheryl and Ronald Evans had been an embarrassment.

'Sheryl,' Jacqui says, her voice high and panicked, 'Sheryl was trying to kill me.'

Twenty-Four

The next morning I rang Veronica and told her about Jacqui's telephone call.

'That explains it then.' Her voice didn't express surprise.

'That explains what?'

'They've gone. They've been camping out in the garden, but the shed is abandoned. They've taken Anita's Mini. No one saw them go, which probably means they didn't want to be seen. They've taken clothes and food. It looks as though they've moved out.'

'Who was it who noticed they'd gone?'

'Sheryl, of all people. The only adult who isn't a parent of one of them.'

'And there was no note? Nothing? Jacqui usually rents with friends. Could they have gone there?'

'They've checked, she hasn't.'

'Where, then?'

'Your guess is as good as mine.'

As we said goodbye, I realized she had given up telling me this was none of my business. Anyway, my guess was pretty straightforward. I dialled Justin's mobile number. When he answered I asked where I could find him. He hesitated for an instant and then he gave me an address.

*

Outside the Europa supermarket men were unloading loaves of
bread in wire trolleys from a van. It meant that the tradesman's
entrance was open and I managed to slip in and up the stairs.
On the first floor there were small, dusty offices, none of which
seemed to be manned. I walked up another flight of stairs. This,
Justin had told me, was Sheryl and Kes's old flat, abandoned
when they moved to Sydenham. I tried to imagine Sheryl here:
Sheryl supervising men carrying a leopard-skin sofa up the
narrow stairs; Sheryl tottering up in high heels and leather
trousers; Sheryl lugging up a carrier bag with a chandelier
clanking around inside. The stairs were steep and claustropho-
bic, with small high windows and years of grunge washed into
the seams. Voices, the noises of a supermarket and of the busy
street outside, wafted up inside the building.

On the second floor I found three flats. Number 1C, Justin
had said. I rang the bell. The door looked pretty solid, a heavy,
grey, forbidding metal. But it vibrated gently to a soul beat.
Nobody came, so I tried knocking, once politely and then a
second time hard enough to hurt my fist. I waited again and
eventually the door opened on a chain, the music got louder
and Jacqui peered out. When she saw me her face twisted. I
waited while she went through her by now familiar internal
argument: was I friend or foe? More help or hindrance?

'May I come in?' I asked. She had told me, after all, about
the attempt on her life. She had chosen me – or had allowed
Justin to choose me – as her confidante. She didn't know who to
trust, but she needed to trust someone. She took a step back and
opened the door.

Inside, the flat showed signs of earlier occupation by Sheryl.
There was a swagged curtain at a tiny metal-framed window
and something that might have called itself an armoire stood
hunched under the low ceiling. The paint was peeling and the
distinctive smell of mould came from a doorway that opened

onto a bathroom. Justin emerged, leaning on his crutches. When he saw me, he stopped still. How, I wondered, had he got up the stairs?

'How did she know?' Jacqui asked him.

He shrugged. 'I told her.'

Jacqui looked awful, unwashed, unbrushed, still dressed, clearly, in yesterday's clothes.

'They've probably all guessed where we are,' she said.

'Well, none of them can be bothered to come looking for us.'

Jacqui gave him a dark, dismissive look.

'She came,' she said.

She turned her back on me and walked past Justin. I followed her into what turned out to be both bedroom and sitting room, barely furnished with what Sheryl had decided to leave behind: a sofabed extended to its full width. The walls, a nasty shade of pink, were naked. There was a small table here, too, which probably counted as the dining area, but there were no chairs. Jacqui sat on the edge of the bed. There was a sleeping bag laid out on top of it and dirty cushions that had served as pillows, but otherwise no bedding. It struck me that there was a strange odour about the place, as though it had been closed up too long with too many bodies inside. Had it really built up in the few hours that Jacqui and Justin had been there?

'Why did you leave?'

'You know. I told you.'

'Why on earth would Sheryl want to kill you?' To me, the idea of Sheryl barrelling across the lawn in camouflage and on tiptoes was ridiculous.

Jacqui slumped, if possible, even further. I remembered how I had first seen her, sitting in the garden with Christopher, poised and confident. Now she just looked scared. Justin came to sit by her on the grimy bed.

'Tell her,' he urged, no longer taunting. He took her hand and held it on his lap.

'It was Sheryl who took Christopher,' she said.

Gently, I reminded her that the police had checked Ronald Evans's house and questioned Sheryl, and had decided that neither of them had anything to do with the kidnapping.

'But we were wrong – she didn't keep him there, she kept him here,' Jacqui said. 'I suddenly realized Sheryl still has this flat. She put it on the market when they moved out, but so far they haven't found a buyer. So we came here last night.'

'We found this.' Justin came forward, holding a scrap of plastic. He handed it to me. It was a turquoise blue, with white lettering, part of a letter M.

'It's come from a packet of nappies,' he said.

'It might have,' I agreed. There wasn't enough lettering to be sure. 'Where did you find it?'

'It was stuck to the edge of the bin under the sink,' Justin said.

I went into the kitchen, opened the cupboard under the sink and put my head inside, but there was nothing else to be seen.

'What do you think?' Jacqui asked. She might not have wanted me there, but she wanted vindication. To me the smell of bodies in the flat was more persuasive than the scrap of plastic, but that was evidence of nothing. I looked around me, trying to imagine Sheryl here with a small baby, drugging its milk, leaving it alone, not caring, ultimately, whether it lived or died. And this not any old baby, but Anita's. I couldn't imagine it and yet I knew that this was quite possibly a failure of imagination on my part. I could not imagine half the horrors Melanie had witnessed and yet they had occurred.

'I can't believe Sheryl would do that to Anita or to a baby,' I said. 'I've never seen Sheryl be cruel. Have you?'

Jacqui gazed at me, and once again I could see her keen intelligence at work. She glanced at Justin. 'She could have stolen Christopher for herself, then lost her nerve,' she said. 'You say she's not cruel, but nobody likes her. Justin doesn't, Kes doesn't.'

Justin shook his head and turned away. He moved like a caged animal.

'The stairs . . .' I said to him, 'how can you cope with the stairs here?'

'I can't,' he said. 'It took me forever to get up here. I can't go out. It's like a bloody prison. C'm on Jacqui, no one's after you. I'm going to go back to the house. I can't stay in here. I'll go mad.'

Jacqui looked impatient.

'Don't you think Christopher was here?' she asked me.

I shook my head. 'It's possible, I suppose,' I said.

'You should be going.' Jacqui jumped up. 'I'll walk you down.'

In the corridor she closed the door to the apartment and led the way down the stairs to the next landing, where she stopped and spoke in hushed, urgent tones.

'You think I'm paranoid about Sheryl,' she said. My heart sank. I could not endure another conversation about Sheryl. I shrugged in agreement.

'OK, you do. You saw us the other day, right?'

I nodded.

'All right, I'm going to tell you what that was about and then you'll understand. I asked her to meet me away from the house like that because I decided to tell her about Kes and Mum.'

'What?'

'Kes and Mum – don't pretend you don't know what I mean. You saw what I saw.'

'What did I see?'

'Kes, on the bed, with my mother,' she hissed.

'He scarcely even touched her,' I protested. 'She was in a terrible state. He felt sorry for her.'

'Oh, come on, they're – ' her face contorted – 'they're having sex.'

I looked at her in disbelief. Jacqui, I thought, had become as unhinged as her mother. First this obsessive suspicion of Sheryl and now this fantasy about her mother.

'I thought if I told Sheryl what Kes was up to, she'd put a stop to it.' Jacqui hurried on, her voice still low, casting anxious looks at the door. No wonder, I thought, she did not want Justin to hear this. The news that Jacqui thought his father was sleeping with her mother would be instant death to their relationship. 'She was angry—'

'I saw her walk out,' I said.

'But I think she already knew what was going on between Kes and Mum,' Jacqui insisted, 'and if that's true, she's got a good reason to want to hurt Mum.'

She looked at me expectantly. My brain slowly caught up with hers.

'You mean you think she could have taken Christopher to get back at Anita for sleeping . . . as you think . . . with her husband.'

'Exactly,' Jacqui agreed. 'Then the next day I think she overheard me saying to Sergeant Mann that I had information for her. That night she tried to kill me in the garden.'

She looked at me with huge, worried eyes.

'Jacqui,' I said, 'you've been under a lot of pressure. I'm not saying there's nothing to what you're suggesting. But . . . this thing in the garden. Frankly, it seems unlikely.'

Jacqui turned away from me impatiently.

'Jacqui,' I told her, 'you've got to get Justin out of here. He can't stay. He can't get in and out. He'll go crazy.'

Jacqui turned to the wall, shaking her head, and eventually I realized she was crying.

'I can't go back there,' she said, sobbing. 'I can't go back.'

I spent the afternoon in the editing suite, going through the rushes I had gathered for the documentary. I would continue to gather interviews over the next two weeks, but I was beginning to get a feel for how the film would look.

I took a break from the rushes to call Lorna. Usually the bouts of exhaustion that she suffers from pass in a few hours, and I wanted to check that she had recovered after she left my birthday dinner in Father Joe's arms.

'I'm fine, thank you,' she said in her determinedly upbeat way, 'completely back to normal.' But I could tell there was something wrong and I asked what it was.

'Joe's gone back, that's all,' she said.

'I see. Well—'

'I don't want to talk about it now. I just can't.'

We said goodbye.

Sal called to me from the office. He sat at his desk, reading from the screen.

'Look at this. Fred Sevi's in the shit,' he said. 'The minicab driver who reported taking him home from the Elephant and Castle now says that he was paid to say it. The driver's called Paul Dreyer. He says he never saw Sevi before Sevi walked into the minicab offices on January the eleventh and asked for a cab to Barnet. On the way he struck up a conversation and offered a payment of five hundred pounds if Dreyer said he'd had him in his cab the night before.'

'Why would the driver change his story now?'

Sal turned away from the screen and swung around on his chair.

'Perhaps he got scared.'

I sat down opposite Sal, thinking it through.

'The only reason for Sevi to fabricate an alibi would be because he had something to hide,' I said slowly. I knew I was stating the obvious. And of course both Sal and I knew the next logical leap – that he was guilty of something. If you have nothing to hide, why hide? But these were the same arguments that I had found myself making about Mike.

'Well?' Sal was excited by the news.

I found myself speechless, shook my head, shrugged.

'Well?' he demanded again.

'Well, I don't know,' I said, throwing up my hands. 'We're going round in circles here. I feel like you do, but it's exactly what we were saying about Mike. Why would Mike lie about knowing Melanie if he's not guilty of something? And we don't even know she hasn't just flipped and run off.'

Sal's face soured. He didn't like me throwing cold water on him.

There was a long, tense silence.

'I'm going home,' I said.

'PC Plod waiting for you, is he?'

'Yes,' I said. 'As a matter of fact he is.'

In Ulverston, on a street of forbidding Victorian architecture, a woman with long dark hair that is matted by the rain is trying to find a police officer to ask for help. It is pouring, as it has poured for the last two days, and she is at her wit's end, her vast capacity for living rough now having reached its limit. She has knocked on the police-station door, but no one answers, and there is no light inside; indeed when she peers at the notice posted next to the door, she understands that it is closed for the night. Her face twists as she realizes the irony of her situation. For days now she has wanted to do this, and hour after hour she has resisted. Now, at last, when she has made up her mind, it is too late.

The rain is easing up, and she lowers her backpack from her shoulders, sits down heavily on the wet step, unzips the pack and looks for her cigarettes. The packet is buried deep, below a sweater, below a folded newspaper. She pulls out a lighter, too, and with a shaking hand she produces a shuddering flame and puts it to her cigarette. She draws a smoke-filled breath through lips that tremble too. There are people who love her who are waiting for her. Well, they won't see her tonight. Not now. She will spend another night in her damp tent.

Footsteps sound on the rain-soaked pavement. They come to a halt in front of her. She looks up. A man is standing there, dressed in a raincoat.

'Are you all right, love?'

She nods, incapable of speech, gestures with the hand that holds the cigarette that he is free to go.

Twenty-Five

I had just got the children to bed when Finney turned up. His timing is usually immaculate. On occasion he will ring at six-thirty or seven to see what stage the children have reached so that he can calculate at what time he should appear – a bath is thirty minutes, a bedtime story fifteen. We took a candle and a bottle of wine outside into the garden. It had been a hot, clammy day, and it was still uncomfortably warm inside the house. Outside, a breeze had begun to stir.

We were still awkward with each other, extra nice, aware of how we still tottered on the edge of the abyss. Finney volunteered to cook, so he set about roasting a mound of pink sausages and dunking pale strips of potato in boiling oil.

William came to find me in the garden, wanting water. I sent him back to his bed clutching a beaker, his little feet placing themselves carefully, toes splayed. Then Hannah bounded out, giggling, reporting that she'd had a bad dream. She accepted a brief hug, beamed at me, stuck her tongue out at Finney and was sent bounding back to bed. William reappeared in tears, to tell me that Hannah had spilt water all over his bed, which she had. I went in to change the sheets and settle the children again. I waited outside their room for a few minutes to see if they would reappear. Then I checked my email. There was a message from my mother.

Trouble in Paradise, I'm afraid. Today a grim silence at the dinner table. Nancy and DeeDee have had an argument, and it has something to do with the menfolk, but quite Who, When, Where, I can't say. I feel a little awkward. They need their Privacy.

I joined Finney at the garden table, in the light of the candle. He brought out a roasting pan of browned sausages, a bowl of golden chips and a pot of yellow mustard. The silence suited us well. We ate, and then there was a moment when we both found ourselves just sitting and looking at each other.

'We're still here,' Finney said.

'We are.'

The phone rang. Or rather phones rang. My landline, my mobile, Finney's mobile, all at once. They all told the same story.

In Reigate a middle-ranking factory manager named Ryan had been made redundant. Distraught, he paced his house. His wife, Izzy, was worried but sympathetic. They would be all right, she reassured him, she would take on more hours at her temping agency, the kids would be fine, they might even earn some money themselves one day. He must retrain, learn how to use computers. She looked ahead to light at the end of the tunnel. Still he paced. He felt closed in. All he could see from the windows of their house was the brickwork of other people's houses.

'Come on, let's you and me go for a walk while the kids are at school,' Izzy said. 'We'll get a pub lunch, and we'll have a walk in the fields. It's a beautiful day and my laundry can wait. I don't feel like doing it anyway in this heat – all that bending down.'

They didn't go for walks in the countryside very often. Never mind, they found a pretty village and, after a lunch of fish and chips, Izzy asked the barmaid and the barmaid asked the barman to recommend a walk.

'Go out the back,' he said. 'You'll see a path. It goes through the woods and then up onto the hill, and you'll have a lovely view over the valley.'

They found the body in the woods. They hadn't been looking. It was the last thing either of them would have expected to happen that day, or indeed on any day of their lives. And their interest in the countryside was straightforward: fresh air and sunshine, perhaps a view. They weren't digging around for rare mushroom species or plucking at leaves for their scrapbooks. They didn't even have a dog to take for a walk. There was a dog, a cheerful Dalmatian, but he was running ahead of his owner, coming the other way. Izzy and Ryan stopped to admire the animal's handsome spots and his fine face as he came to an abrupt stop and sniffed the movement of air that was almost a breeze.

'Mind you, there are sheep around. You wouldn't have thought you'd let a dog off the lead here,' Izzy said.

The dog set off, away from the path and into the undergrowth. They heard him barking and thought little of it. But the dog emerged and stopped in front of them, hackles raised, and barked again, ran off again, returned to bark, and so on.

'It's as if he's trying to get our attention,' Izzy said. She thought Ryan would think her silly for saying that. But it was Ryan who crashed off into the undergrowth behind the dog while she waited on the path. She thought maybe there was a sheep in trouble. Either that or a dead rabbit.

She heard the dog barking again and then Ryan's voice.

'Izzy, Izzy.' He was calling for her desperately. He plunged out of the undergrowth, a sheen of nausea coating his face. He'd grabbed the dog by its collar, and seemed to be trying to restrain it, stopping it from running back in. But as he saw Izzy, he dropped to his knees and the dog escaped his grip and plunged back in again.

'There's something in there,' he cried. 'Dear God, oh, my God. Izzy, help me.'

The grave was outside the HazPrep estate, further down the valley, but the route, along a little-used track through the woods, would have been quick and easy in a four-wheel drive. Despite the razor wire at the main entrance to HazPrep, there was no such boundary to the estate land running through the woods.

'It was a shallow grave,' Veronica told Finney. 'Maybe the killer didn't have much time to dig, but more likely he was slowed down because the ground was frozen in January. Then, when the summer came, the rain washed the earth downhill.'

It wasn't Veronica's case, but she'd rung Finney as soon as she heard.

'It will take a while to make an identification,' she said. 'It's been so wet this year and hot on top of that, but there are some shreds of clothing, a belt buckle and a watch. There's a mobile phone, too. Coburn is pretty sure this is Melanie Jacobs. There's not much doubt.'

While he was talking to Veronica, I was on the landline with Maeve. Clearly upset, she described to me the discovery of Melanie's body, and gave me the same précis that Veronica had given Finney, but embroidered with miserable speculation.

Sal had left a message on my mobile, so I called him back. This man, who had seen so much death so very close up and who had reported it on national television, was so distraught by the news of Melanie's death that he was almost unable to communicate. He sobbed uncontrollably. We did not speak for long. We said goodbye and I hung up worried by this sudden dam-burst of grief.

I sat back down at the table. The candle had blown out in the breeze and Finney was trying to relight it. I watched its struggling flame. It kept going out and Finney kept relighting it, until in the end he threw the matches down in exasperation on the table and left it as it was. I didn't even realize I'd started to shake until Finney went and fetched me a jacket and I could scarcely get my arms into it. I turned and tried to smile at him, but that didn't work either.

'I failed her,' I said.

'Don't be ridiculous.'

'I was supposed to find out what had happened.'

'Well, now you know, there's nothing you could have done for her.'

'But the sightings—'

'It's classic. Power of suggestion. Perfectly decent people, no one trying it on, it's just a kind of mass hallucination.'

Before I went to bed, I checked my email. There was an FYI from the Cumbria police.

The following is a press release: Cumbria police stated today that a woman answering Melanie Jacobs's description sighted on several occasions in Cumbria has been otherwise identified as Lindy Mason, a forty-three-year-old housewife from Crawley who was reported missing by her son six weeks ago and who has been sleeping rough. Mrs Mason, who had run out of money, approached the police in Ulverston to request help in contacting her son.

I brought up onto the screen pictures of Lindy Mason and Melanie Jacobs. There was a good five years between them, but both of them kept their distance from the camera, both of them tied their long dark hair back, away from their pale, high-boned cheeks, and both of them had a row of gold studs in their left ear. I was glad Tony had his mother back.

Twenty-Six

'Come away with me for the weekend,' Finney said next morning, leaning over me as I lay staring at the wall. 'We both need a break.'

I rolled over and gazed up at him. I had not slept all night. Hannah and William had crawled into my bed in the early morning. Usually when Finney is there they cling grimly to the outer edge of my side of the bed, but this time they had set up camp in the valley between my pillows and Finney's. They were still asleep, squashed together, a mountain range of arms and legs.

'Come on,' he said. 'I'll talk to Carol. She'll understand.'

'I've been away a lot. William's not keen.' Did Finney understand, I wondered, that this kind of competition for my time and attention was one of the things that frightened me.

'Give me two nights.'

Taking my leave of Hannah and William was a long-drawn-out affair. There were so many final hugs and kisses that I nearly missed the last call. At Heathrow I ran through the departure hall and at last caught sight of Finney. I shouted his name and he looked to see that I was carrying luggage, and it was only then, when I hoisted my bag over my head so that he could see, that he allowed himself to smile.

It was a short, bumpy ride to Paris, an hour of enforced

closeness, Finney's knees jammed up against the seat in front, our shoulders pressed together.

We checked into a small hotel on the Rue de Seine on the Left Bank, where Finney surprised me by addressing the receptionist in more than passable French. Our room was tiny, on the fifth floor. The wallpaper was decorated with little pink flowers and there were plump embroidered cushions on the bed. I opened the window and looked out at the street, the warm noise of city traffic wrapping itself around me. I had spoken that morning to Beatrice on the telephone, and the conversation had been going around and around in my head ever since. Finally Beatrice had some of her answers. She had a body to bury. But the discovery had only made her other questions more urgent. Who could have done this to her daughter? Finney came and stood behind me. I closed my eyes and leaned back into him.

'I have a life-affirming idea,' I said eventually. 'Let's eat.'

We ate in a small restaurant in the maze of streets off the Boulevard St Germain. I could not face crowds, so we chose a restaurant that was quiet and expensive, decorated not in the rich colours of the tourist bistro, but in shades of grey. There were a few tables of affluent local residents at a comfortable distance from us, whose conversations provided an agreeable background noise for our meal. We ate and drank in almost total silence.

Afterwards, we walked by the Seine, below the golden gothic spires of Notre Dame and then went back to the hotel, to our womblike room. Finney opened the windows to let the city in, and we undressed in silence and went to bed.

The next morning, breakfast consisted of coffee and toast at a cafe on a cobbled street, tourists gathering around us, one group looking noisily for eggs and bacon and English tea.

'So how do you know where to stay in Paris?'

He smiled at me. He looked less like a police officer than ever here in the sun, relaxed, happy. I realized how much my view of him was defined by the way I had met him.

'You think I'm a philistine, don't you?'

'No . . . Well, a little bit.'

'I spent six months here with the Paris police force, supposedly coordinating our efforts to curtail drug-smuggling operations.'

'Supposedly?'

'Coordinating is a fine art.'

I sipped at my coffee.

'Why did you join the police, Finney?'

'Why not? You don't share your father's view of the police as the reactionary forces of oppression, do you?'

'No . . . Well . . . a little bit.'

He scowled. 'We're a necessity.'

'So are sewers.'

He raised his eyebrows. There was an irritated glint in his eye.

'Thank you. Look. I'm a steady guy. It's a steady job, a steady income, steady demand,' he told me. 'Isn't that what your media friends think?'

'You like to stick your nose into other people's business, just like me,' I said. 'You lot are no different from journalists.'

'Now that,' he said, 'is below the belt.'

Across the street a table of backpackers were photographing each other, their poses getting a little more raunchy with each click of the shutter, their laughter getting louder, reaching a crescendo of delight when one of the girls hitched her skirt up, sat astride the lap of another girl and kissed her. Finney had his back to them.

'What are we going to do?' he asked.

'I don't know,' I said vaguely, not wanting to apply my mind. 'More of the same, I suppose.'

We smiled at each other. We had agreed, in the middle of

the night, that we would not be distracted. With Melanie dead, the urgency of my quest was gone anyway. I had wanted to save her, not to find out who had killed her. The shock of the discovery of her body had receded, and in its wake I realized that we had, all her friends, been mourning her for months. It was her body, decayed and destroyed, that was the shock, that and the knowledge – now a certainty, not a suspicion – that she had died at someone else's hand, with real violence. It had been a long and lingering death for those left behind. But at least we knew it had not been a long or lingering death for Melanie.

Despite our resolution not to be distracted by her, we had used the hotel computer to check the news on the Internet. We learned that initial indications were that she had been killed by a gunshot wound to the back of the head. It had been a clean, professional killing. The remnants of a hood remained covering her head. There were no indications of rape or of mutilation. One newspaper was reporting that the last call to Melanie's mobile phone was from Fred Sevi, at two minutes to ten in the evening on the 10 January.

'It was him,' I muttered. 'Why did I get so hung up on Mike?'

I buried my head in my hands. I felt panic overwhelm me. I had made a man's life hell. I had repeated history, only this time I was the predator.

'Stop jumping to conclusions,' Finney said. 'It's a mobile phone, not a gun. Sevi could have been calling her from Dundee. They'll go over all that.'

I heaved a sigh.

'I know that,' I said, 'but why did she come out of the bar if not to speak on the phone? You heard Andrew Bentley – why did she walk outside, if it wasn't to speak on the phone?'

'You heard Bentley too. She may just have wanted a cigarette.'

I shook my head.

'Whoever wanted to kill her needed to get her outside. He couldn't just hang around and wait.'

'It's not impossible.'

We walked by the Seine for an hour and every time I tried to bring up Melanie's death, Finney blocked me. Eventually I gave up. And when I had been silent for a long time Finney spoke again.

'I thought,' Finney said carefully, 'that we might try to track down the mysterious Sabine.'

'I thought,' I said equally carefully, 'that you were fed up with my crazy family.'

'You are all barking mad. With the exception of Patrick.'

'Patrick? Why should he be let off the hook?'

'He's male and he has no Ballantyne blood,' Finney said, with forensic accuracy. He made a gesture, resting his case, and I scowled.

'Anyway,' Finney went on, 'if, as seems possible, I'm stuck with them – you – then it follows that I should know the worst.'

I gazed at him.

'If you know about Gilbert, you know the worst.'

Adding Gilbert to our holiday was like igniting a stick of dynamite. But if there is one thing that united Finney and I (and surely there must always be one thing, beyond sex, that keeps unlikely couples together) it was a restless curiosity. So if a stone presented itself, however innocent it looked, we were both incapable of leaving it unturned.

'You have your sources,' I suggested.

'I have my sources.'

We took the subway to Montmartre, to the Rue Ravignan. I expected little, and expected even less when we found ourselves faced with a locked door and an entrance buzzer. Finney pressed an apartment number and, when a woman answered, said, again in good French, that we had been sent by Gilbert Ballantyne. To my surprise, the woman buzzed us in. We climbed a winding, red-carpeted staircase to the second floor, where a girl dressed in black was already waiting for us at an open door. She looked at us with mousey eyes half hidden by lank hair, obviously disappointed that Finney was not who she had expected.

'Sabine?'

'Maman?' she called back into the apartment and an older woman appeared, her blonde hair swept up onto her head, pale, sun-spotted skin stretched tight over high cheekbones, long earrings dangling almost to her shoulders, a younger, thinner, taller version of my mother. And living in an alternative universe. She stood, an elegant and sophisticated woman, in an elegant and sophisticated hallway. My mother would not have endured this lack of clutter. It was indecently tidy.

Finney filled the gap left by my confusion, introducing us as friends of Gilbert Ballantyne. The woman's face fell. She flapped her hand, urging us inside, and looking up and down the corridor outside to check that no one had seen or heard us.

'Gilbert, il n'est pas ici,' she said defensively. I took in polished wood, gilt-framed glass, pretty pictures, flowers.

'Do you know where he is?'

The woman looked helplessly at Sabine.

'Il a disparu,' she said, and made an explosive sound that she matched with her hands, and that I guessed meant 'just like that'. 'Mais, c'est normal.'

'Normal?' I echoed.

'Lui, c'est comme le soleil. Un jour il est la et un autre il disparait.'

I stared at Sabine. She regarded me with something that I could only describe as malice.

The woman was examining Finney.

'Vous êtes de la police?' she asked nervously.

Finney shook his head. Not here, not technically. He pulled a face that suggested the very thought was laughable.

'Alors?' She raised her hands. She was not being impolite. She simply did not know what to do with us. And nor did we know what to do with her. Finney kept her chatting – no, she had no idea when Gilbert would be back. No, she had no forwarding address for him. Did Gilbert owe us money? It sometimes happened that people would come to this door claiming that Gilbert had borrowed from them. Were we journalists? I knew Finney was giving me time to think, time to decide how much to tell her of my identity. The daughter – this girl I now realized must be my half-sister – watched me through narrowed eyes. She knows, I thought. And she wants nothing to do with me. Nor I with her.

'We're late,' I said quietly to Finney. 'It's time for us to go.'

He nodded. We made our excuses.

'You don't want to get to know them better?' he asked me, as we walked away. We could feel the eyes of Sabine and her mother on us from the doorway. I remembered the accounts Finney had gathered for me, the suggestion of Sabine's facility with lying.

'I know enough already,' I told him. 'The woman is nothing to me. And the girl . . . her mother's a charming romantic and her father's a petty crook. But she's something else altogether. Something nasty.'

We walked in silence for a moment, and I thought Finney might be thinking me mad. But eventually he said, 'You may be right.'

I wondered what more he knew about Sabine, but this time I resisted the urge to find out. Did I envy Sabine and her mother their shrug of the shoulder, the lack of accusation? I couldn't imagine any one of my family comparing Gilbert to the sun. Not with a straight face.

Finney had little patience with sightseeing. By early evening we had abandoned the queue at the Louvre and walked instead by the river. I lit a candle for Melanie in Notre Dame. Then I surprised myself by lighting one for my father.

We returned to the hotel to shower and found ourselves once more in bed, and later we lay there and watched the sun set slowly over the city. Eventually, as hunger reminded us that it was dinnertime, we pulled our clothes back on. When my mobile rang, I seized it up from the floor where it had fallen, my imagination suddenly, guiltily, with the children. It was Jane. I breathed again. Then immediately I wondered why she was calling me here. I assumed she was wallowing in cosy domesticity with Q and baby Rosemary. I could hear the baby crying.

'Hi.' I could hardly hear her voice. 'Rosemary sounds unhappy.'

'She's got colic. I don't know what to do about it – she doesn't sleep, I don't sleep . . .' I could hear the shudder of real exhaustion in her voice. I realized guiltily that my hugely competent friend Jane had joined the ranks of mothers on the edge of collapse, and that I had been leaving her to get on with it. 'Anyway – ' Jane's voice dragged on wearily – 'I know you're not interested in colic. Did you hear the news?'

'What news?'

'Q just called me. Ridiculous, he's halfway around the world and he knows more than me about what's going on here. Mike Darling has run off.'

'What do you mean, run off?' The phrase makes me think of a child.

'I don't know any more than that.'

I sat down hard on the bed. Finney paused in the act of buttoning his shirt and turned to me.

'Where did he go?'

'They don't know. He seems to have vanished.'

Behind Jane the sound of Rosemary's crying rose again, high-pitched and insistent.

'I have to go.' Jane sounded at the end of her tether.

'Where's Q?'

'In Washington, with the prime minister,' Jane's voice was distant, as though she was pulling away from the telephone. 'He'll be back next week.' And then the phone went dead.

I leant against the balcony, looking back into the room as Finney dialled Mann's number, and smiled, spoke, then listened. He glanced across at me. When he hung up, he came out onto the balcony and we stood side by side, looking out over the city.

'No phone calls to your buddies in the newsroom. That's the deal.'

I rolled my eyes.

'Take it or leave it.'

'OK, OK. Tell me.'

'She's right. Darling's on the run. He's taken the boy. DCI Coburn rang to ask Darling to come in and answer more questions.'

'Was there something about Melanie's body that made them want to talk to him?'

'It was buried on land bordering HazPrep, of course they want to talk to him. Perhaps they wanted to rattle him.'

'They must have succeeded.'

'Anita was out at the doctor's, but Sheryl was there when he got the phone call. Apparently he put the receiver down and just grabbed up Christopher and went outside. She followed him out to the car. She says he was clearly in a state of panic, and she demanded to know where he was going, but she says he wouldn't tell her. He pushed her away, fastened Christopher in the car seat and drove off.'

Just then Sal rang me on my mobile and he said aloud what I was thinking.

'He bloody did it.' Sal was exultant. I wondered what had happened to his grief. 'The bloody bastard killed her. He's on the run.'

Finney was glaring at me, warning me not to say too much.

But it was impossible to cool the level of Sal's speculation. And the connection was inevitable. There were no television pictures, the police had lost him, but Mike Darling's car was a white SUV. Even in the imagination, history was reborn. The man in this car was fleeing because he had been found out.

'Mike Darling bloody killed her,' Sal insisted. When I refused to be persuaded, he hung up on me, upset, as though I was betraying Melanie.

'It's time to go back,' I said to Finney. 'It's not just Mike Darling, it's everything. It's Jane, she's sounding exhausted, Rosemary's screaming. I feel as though there are things I should be doing. We can come back some other time.'

He nodded.

'We can come back,' he agreed. He turned away. We packed in silence.

Twenty-Seven

I'd rung Jane when we arrived back in London and found her on the way to the hospital with Rosemary, who was burning with fever. She had called her mother in Perth and Q in Washington. Both had said they would come home, but it would take hours. Now I sat in the hospital corridor, my eyes glued wearily to the television bracketed to the wall. The volume was turned down low. The pictures were of Mike Darling's house, the driveway empty of the large white vehicle that was usually parked there.

Jane and Rosemary had vanished into a room for tests. We had been there for hours. Jane, usually so utterly in charge, was like a lamb here, being sweet as pie to everyone, desperate for them to help her child. In my role as stand-in for Q, I had been her muscle, constantly reminding staff that we were waiting, making sure we weren't forgotten.

I wanted to talk to Finney, but I'd had to turn my mobile off. I wanted to see the twins, but for now Jane was my priority. Baby Rosemary's temperature was dangerously high by the time she got her to the hospital. She was no longer crying. She was floppy and quiet, and her skin was covered in purple blotches. A Dr Yenz was checking her now to eliminate meningitis as a possibility.

Jane reappeared with Rosemary in her arms. She gave me a wobbly smile.

'They think she's fine,' she told me, 'it's just a virus. But we have to wait until her temperature comes down.'

And so I sat with her while she tried to pull herself together, digging paper hankies from my bag so she could wipe her eyes. Jane had peeled off Rosemary's hot outer clothes, and now the baby was lying on a blanket on her lap.

'This is so silly,' Jane said. 'Q's on a plane for nothing. Can you hold Rosemary while I go and ring him?'

I held Rosemary on my lap while Jane disappeared. She came back a few minutes later, looking sober. 'He hadn't even set out for the airport. He's been on air solidly since I called . . . I thought he'd just have walked out. But I suppose he couldn't. Still,' she breathed in, 'at least he didn't race off for nothing.'

All the time I was aware, in the margins, of the news pictures on the television. Q, doing a stand-upper in front of some huge public gathering in Washington, a great frown of worry on his face, as though he was worried about the state of the world, whereas I knew that he was worried about the state of his child. Then pictures of HazPrep estate, a file photo of Melanie, then a picture of Mike Darling in uniform.

There were well-thumbed magazines in the room and a coffee machine in the corner. Once in a while a nurse came in to check Rosemary's temperature.

'Her colour's nice and even now,' the nurse told us cheerfully. 'She's going to be fine.'

I worked my way through a stack of magazines. They seemed to be published on some other planet. I tried to bend my head around the diary of a catwalk model, but I couldn't work out why the poor skinny thing had bothered to write it, let alone why anyone agreed to publish it. I peered at photos of the latest fashions. There was a great deal of over-sized turquoise jewellery worn with flamenco-style skirts. I glanced down to confirm what I was wearing. Jeans, faded through wear rather than through design, raffishly threadbare at the knee. I looked briefly at the travel section, which featured Paris. I looked at my watch. If we'd stuck to our plan, we would only now be heading for the airport.

'I'm going outside for a minute to call Finney,' I told Jane, touching her shoulder. 'I'll be right back.'

Outside, there was a small garden, with a fountain that wasn't working, and a bench surrounded by flowers. I kicked off my shoes and rested my feet in the dry grass. The air was heavy, as though another thunderstorm was gathering. I was about to dial Finney's number when he rang me.

He was at home. I could hear music in the background. I told him what was going on and that I would stay with Jane until Rosemary was allowed to go home.

'Is there any news of Darling?' I asked.

'There's been a sighting or two, according to the TV,' Finney told me, 'but there must be thousands of men in Nissan people carriers with baby seats in the back. His mother is up north – maybe he's going up to see her. But look.' He lowered his voice. 'There's one thing. You were right. Fred Sevi has admitted to Coburn that he went out to HazPrep on the night of the tenth.'

'What happened?'

'He'd already told the police that he'd tried ringing Melanie at around ten, but that the connection was terrible and they had hung up. That fitted with the records for Melanie's number, and because it seemed to fit they didn't look at the call log more closely at that point. Anyway, after the taxi driver came forward, they checked the call records again, and this time they realized that although Sevi's call went through a different transmitter than the one Melanie's phone was logged onto, in fact the transmitter his phone was using covered the area surrounding HazPrep. So there was no way he could have been calling from the centre of London. Sevi now admits that he left the party at the Elephant and Castle after about half an hour and that he drove out to HazPrep again on the tenth, like he did the night before, and that he rang her from outside just before ten, and begged her to allow him in, or to come out. He said she refused again.'

'Why didn't the guard see him like he did the night before?'

'Sevi says he pulled off the road about half a mile from the gatehouse. Says it was too humiliating to have the guard see him there a second night pleading with Melanie to come out.'

'Does Coburn believe him?' I asked.

'Hard to say. He hasn't arrested him yet. Sevi says that once Melanie refused to come out, he turned around and drove home.'

'I thought reception was bad.'

'Good enough for her to refuse.' He paused, then said heavily, 'If you believe Sevi. The bare facts are that we know he called her from outside on the road, that she left the building, and that she disappeared and he manufactured an alibi. It doesn't look good.'

'Maybe that's why he manufactured the alibi,' I said.

I promised to call him later and I thought about our conversation as I headed back to the waiting room. I don't know why I felt I had to defend Sevi, except that Finney had so many times told me not to jump to conclusions, and now it seemed to me that he was doing just that. Perhaps I just had a guilty conscience. I had dismissed Stella's allegations that Sevi had said he would kill Melanie. But now I was wondering whether I should have put pressure on Stella to go to the police.

Baby Rosemary's temperature was coming down rapidly and Jane was returning to combative normal.

'If we're here, we might as well talk. I want to know why you've been avoiding me.'

'Avoiding you?' I was genuinely shocked. 'Is that what you think?'

'You've scarcely come near us.' Her voice was accusatory, all the tension bursting out of her. 'You haven't even rung me. You were supposed to be the one who knew about all this stuff. You were the one who was going to tell me what to do. I was relying on you. I don't know anyone else with babies. All my friends have five year olds.'

I stared at her and slowly the truth of what she was saying

dawned on me. I'd been so excited when Jane became pregnant. I'd as good as promised to go through childbirth for her. I tried to explain. The truth was I'd thought Jane could do anything and I'd thought she had Q with her, which she didn't, not really. I told her all this and she looked mildly mollified.

As we talked, and I watched Jane with Rosemary, I saw how they had become part of each other. Jane was exhausted by sleeplessness, but she touched Rosemary and talked to her with an instinctive understanding of what she needed. I thought of Anita and sensed that in her there was a deeper problem. Perhaps it was a combination of the years of stress worrying about her husband at war, and post-natal depression and Valium. But where Jane and Rosemary were an organic whole, Anita and Christopher seemed dislocated.

Eventually an impossibly young doctor came and spoke to us. Rosemary's temperature was back to normal, she could go home. He smiled at us sympathetically. He hadn't come across many parents in his short career. Had we been worried?

Jane's mother arrived. She shook herself like a dog, then removed her headscarf and wrung it out, creating a pool on the floor.

'It's pissing it down,' she said, her Perth accent even stronger than her daughter's. She was even more imperious than Jane and fiercely protective of her only grandchild. She dismissed me and I left ahead of them, leaving Jane to gather up her baby's things.

I stepped out of the hospital into driving rain. The warmth had gone out of the air when the sun went down and the clouds broke. It was like stepping into a cold shower in a dark bathroom. I ran to the car, my head lowered into my collar, yanked open the door and threw myself into the driver's seat. About half a gallon of rain came in with me.

I sat there for a moment, listening to the rain pounding on the roof. Then I called Carol to tell her I was on my way home. The children had been in bed for hours and I told myself that I would take the day off tomorrow so that I could spend some time with them. I tried to call Finney. We were like young lovers, calling each other all the time. We would be texting each other before we knew it. His line was busy. I dropped my phone on my lap and put the key in the ignition.

As I was about to turn the key, there was a movement from the back seat. Startled, I twisted round, and as I turned, a hand snaked in front of me and snatched my mobile phone from my lap. I cried out, but another hand came from behind and fixed itself over my mouth.

My heart was pounding so hard it threatened to explode through my ribs. I squirmed and hit out blindly behind me, trying to make contact, trying to dislodge the hand, all without success. I bit hard into leather and had the satisfaction of a grunt of pain. The hand loosened and I lunged for the door, but then he had me again, slamming my head back against the headrest.

'Don't fuck with me,' he hissed. Out of the corner of my eye, I saw a figure approach the car, a man in overalls, a hospital employee. I drew breath to scream, but then I felt the cold hard metal of a knife against the soft flesh under my chin.

'Drive,' he instructed. Shaking, my pulse racing, I clutched the steering wheel and tried to steady my feet on the pedals, pulling jerkily out of the parking bay.

He indicated with his hand which way I should go, and I complied, driving out of the main gates of the hospital to the right and then turning left. He had lowered the knife and it jabbed into my side. I could feel it slicing through the fibres of my clothing, scratching my skin, drawing blood. It filled my head with fear.

'Who are you?' I demanded. My voice was shaking, but I knew I must speak, knew I should engage him, distract him from his purpose. He didn't answer, but I couldn't bear to be silent. It made me feel better to hear my own voice.

'Who are you? What's your name? Why are you doing this?' With every question I could sense his irritation growing, but

I knew he would not kill me here. There were too many people. Too many cars. We turned right, then right again, then left, and now the roads were emptier. I fell silent. At every junction, every set of lights, I was tortured with indecision. At every turn, I chose to obey. But now I knew I'd made a mistake. Better to have fought while there were people around. Better to have risked it. I thought of Hannah and William, asleep in bed. What had I done? We were on a small road with trees on one side and on the other side, below us, the Thames. Panic rose, my heart pounded, my throat constricted with terror. I had driven myself to my own grave.

He indicated that I should pull over to the side of the road. I stared, appalled, at the oily black waters heaving gently at their banks, as though they were breathing. Raindrops pockmarked the surface. A body could fall from this car and tumble carelessly into those waters, and they would swallow it up and spit out the bones. I felt sick with fear. If I did not act, it would paralyse me.

I reached for the door handle, but he slammed the lock down. He took my head in his hands and yanked my head around to look at him, but I could see only the dull glimmer of his eyes. His face, his hair, everything that could have identified him to me, was covered in a balaclava. The car was dark, but I could feel his eyes and the grip of his fingers. The rest of his face, the rest of his body, seemed to have no shape to it, melting into the darkness.

'Who are you?' I tried again, forcing my voice out, 'Why are you doing this?'

But he wasn't listening. I allowed myself to follow his eyes and hope sprang up inside me. In this deserted place a young couple were walking towards us, along the path next to the river. They were sheltering under an umbrella, holding hands, swinging their arms, deep in conversation. So deep in conversation that they might not see us. The man glanced up towards us. Time slowed. I felt my attacker's hand slip from my head, saw the same hand move to the lock of the door, covering it. I sensed him shift slightly away from me, I perceived that the focus of his attention had also shifted to these outsiders. The man looked down again, said something to the woman. I heard a small sigh of satisfaction from behind me. The tip of the knife still scratched my side.

My mind did not race so much as scream towards escape. In desperation I rallied what was left of my courage and I leaned forward, grinding my teeth against the stab of pain from the knife in my side as I moved, and I flicked on the lights inside the car. In the same movement, even as I felt his hand on my shoulder, pulling me back, I shook him off, reached out again and turned on the car radio and twisted the dial, and music rang out, distorted by the volume. I saw the heads of both the man and the woman jerk upwards, frowning, mystified as my car turned into a mobile nightclub. He grabbed at me.

'Get out,' I screamed at him, tearing his hand from my shoulder. 'Get out now.'

The couple were hurrying towards us. My attacker made a noise that was part hiss of fury, part sob of frustration. Then, suddenly, he opened the door and levered himself out and away, breaking into a run.

The couple approached the car at a jog. I wound down the window and they bent down to talk to me. Had I been hurt? Was everything all right? Did I want to call the police? I calmed my breathing, but still my heart was pounding and my hands were shaking. I told them I would call the police myself, thanked them for their concern. I should have told them they had saved my life. Uncertain, they moved on, occasionally looking back at me over their shoulders.

I wound up the window and gazed into my rear-view mirror. Might he come back? I was still shaking, but I could not stay here.

I drove slowly past the couple, raising a hand in thanks, my eyes raking the darkness at the side of the road for my attacker.

But if he was there, I did not see him. I drove in circles, I think, for some time. My brain wasn't working and I didn't know this part of west London. All I wanted was to find a place where there were people and lights. And on a night like this it wasn't going to be easy.

At last I saw a supermarket car park. It was busy, well lit, people coming and going. I parked in one of the families-only spaces nearest the entrance, nearest the lights and the people. Oh, how I loved those people. I watched them for a moment, in the glow of neon, no children at this time of night, mostly young men in T-shirts, running in through the rain with their car keys and wallets in their hands. Then emerging with plastic bags of pizzas and beer, hurrying back to their car, heads still dipped against the rain.

I lifted my shirt. My side was bloodied, and I dug around for a packet of tissues, and dabbed, shakily, at the wound. There was no one deep cut, but a series of small punctures and one nasty gash that must have happened when I reached forward.

I rummaged around on the floor in the back to find my mobile phone. My attacker had turned it off. As soon as I turned it on, it started to ring, the sudden noise making me jump.

I tried to calm my breathing. I nearly wept when I heard Sal's voice.

'At last,' he said. 'Everybody's trying to get hold of you.'

I closed my eyes, trying to calm the panic. Who could I trust?

'Robin? Are you still there?'

I grunted into the phone.

'Jacqui called.'

'Did you tell her where I was?'

'She said you'd turned off your mobile, and asked how could she get hold of you, so I told her if it was urgent she could try calling the switchboard at the hospital. I've been fielding calls all day. Next time you turn off your mobile, you get yourself a secretary. Fred Sevi was trying to reach you too. To tell you not to use the interview he gave you.'

'And you told him the same thing?'

'Right. I told him the same thing I told Jacqui. And, let me see, I wrote it down, an Alice Jackson. She has something to tell you about Anita.'

'About Anita?'

'That's what I said.'

Behind me, I saw a tall man in dark clothing emerge from the car parked behind me, his head lowered as he walked towards my car.

'Gotta go, Sal.' I ended the call, switched on the ignition and backed out of the parking bay. As I pulled out and drove away, I saw a woman approach the man who had alarmed me with his dark clothing. She ran to catch up with him, then slipped her hand into his and they headed into the supermarket.

My mobile rang again. I pulled in to the side of the road and answered, expecting Finney.

'Robin Ballantyne?' A voice asked. I shook my head. The voice was familiar, but it took me a moment to place it. I'd heard this voice angry, threatening and distressed, but now it was unnaturally calm.

'Is this Mike Darling?'

'I have something to give you,' he said. 'It's about Melanie.'

'Where are you?'

'That doesn't matter. We'll meet at the warehouse—'

'No way.' My voice matched his for icy calm. 'If you're innocent, show me. Go home.'

'Go home?' he repeated, his voice full of confusion.

'If you've got nothing to hide, go home,' I said again. And I severed the connection.

Twenty-Eight

When I reached Sydenham, the rain had turned into a thunder-storm, and the house was illuminated in all its decrepitude by lightning. I slowed as I drove past it. There was no sign of Mike's car. I parked further on between two large vans, where I would be inconspicuous but still have a clear view of anyone arriving at the Darling house.

I rang Finney.

'Where are you?' He was annoyed, but I could hear the anxiety behind it. 'I rang Jane and she's already back home. She said you'd left the hospital ages ago. I thought you'd vanished off the face of the earth.'

'I nearly did,' I said, and then I told him about the man who had waited for me in the car, and how he had me drive to the river, and how I believed my life had been saved by passers by. Finney swore softly as I spoke.

'Do you know who it was?'

This question, above all others, distressed me. That I had sat in this enclosed space and had my life threatened by a man I could not identify was something my brain would not accept. My lips were shaking as I told Finney I didn't know.

'Where are you now?'

I told him about the call from Mike.

'You wait for me, all right? Don't set foot outside your car until I get there.'

I was in no condition to fight and anyway, as far as I could see, Mike had not yet returned.

I sat and I waited, my side throbbing, and I watched the house. There was no movement.

My mobile rang, startling me again. My nerves were not in a good state. It was Jacqui in tears.

'I've moved back in with my friends. I've split up with Justin,' she told me, between sobs, 'I told him everything.'

'What everything?'

'About what his dad's doing to Mum.'

I winced.

'What happened?'

'He went ballistic.'

'I bet he did.'

'No, but you don't understand.' Jacqui's voice rose. 'I've never seen him like that. He went mad. He was shouting and screaming and throwing things around. And I thought maybe the doctor was right, when he said Justin's psychotic.'

I shook my head. I was keeping my eye on the road, waiting for Mike and for Finney. I didn't want to get embroiled in young love, or indeed in Jacqui's fevered imagination, where Sheryl was a kidnapper, Kes was forcing sex on Anita and now Justin was mad.

'He's not psychotic,' I spelled it out, as if to a child. 'Jacqui, he's lost his leg. It's going to take him years to get over it. I know you were trying to make everything all right for him, but he's going to get angry sometimes, even when there's no reason.'

'I hate Mum.' She was sobbing. 'And I hate Kes. If it wasn't for them, we'd be together.'

I heaved a breath. I couldn't deal with this right now.

'Jacqui,' I told her, 'go and have a drink with your friends and then sleep on it. I'll talk to you tomorrow.'

I ended the call. It had started to rain again. The drops

splashed onto my windscreen. In my wing mirror I could see Mike's car driving slowly up to the house. He parked in the driveway. After a moment he stepped down from the driver's seat into the rain and walked around the side of the house, presumably to the glass door at the back. I expected the intruder light to come on as he approached the house, but it didn't. Even that half-hearted attempt at security, it seemed, had been abandoned.

'So where the hell is Christopher?' I muttered.

For all my good intentions, I could not wait for Finney. I opened the car door and stepped out into the rain, following where Mike had gone, around the side of the house towards the back door.

Mike has not closed the door behind him, but I hang back. I watch as Mike flicks a switch and Anita's bedroom is bathed in light. I see Mike's face, hear his roar of anguish even before I take in what he has seen, Anita and Kes naked on the bed. Kes leaping up, leaving Anita cowering against the headboard, pulling the sheets to cover herself. Kes twists away from Mike, and launches himself towards the glass door where I am standing. The two men hurtle out and I step backwards, but not fast enough. Kes blunders into me and we fall against the pile of bricks. I try to pull myself up and away from him, but he grabs my hair and then he wrenches my arm behind me so that I cry out in pain. He holds me in a lock against him, then stretches behind him and picks up a brick, which he holds poised above my head.

Mike is only steps away from us. Fury is written all over his face, but he cannot launch himself at Kes because his friend holds me hostage.

'I lied for you,' Mike snarls.

I see his eyes flicker beyond me, to something or someone behind me, and all at once I am knocked to the floor, and Kes's legs are knocked from under him, and Mike is lunging forward to get at Kes, and as I raise my head from the ground, all I see are bodies tangled and a naked arm lifting a brick to smash it down on Finney's chest. Finney, I think, who I have dragged into this.

I leap to my feet and shout and start to run to Finney as the brick rises and crashes down again. The garden fills with people, many of them uniformed. Kes is being grappled away from Mike and Finney. Finney rolls away. He pulls himself onto his elbow, spits blood into the grass and then he collapses. I kneel down beside him.

Behind me, Mike and Kes are locked in a fight that is more violent than anything I have ever seen. As police officers tear them apart, Mike has seized his friend's head and is bashing it against the brick that Kes held against my head and that he used on Finney. By the time Mike is pulled away from him, Kes is lying still, his face covered in blood, the back of his head a mass of battered, torn flesh and hair and blood. His eyes are open, fixed on Mike. His lips seem to move, and Mike yells something unintelligible and strains back toward the naked body on the ground, but the police officers who have hold of him drag him away.

Moments later, as Finney and Kes are loaded into the ambulance, I glance back, and I see Mike standing, handcuffed, flanked by police officers, and Anita kneeling at his feet, sobbing and begging for forgiveness. He stares down at her as though he does not know her.

Twenty-Nine

I waited outside the operating theatre. At one point a nurse came out, peeling off blood-covered gloves, and I begged for news.

'He picked the wrong men to scrap with,' he said and hurried off.

After I had been waiting forever, Veronica Mann arrived and came to sit beside me, patting my knee.

'Do you want news, or do you want to be left to worry?'

I looked at her.

'I always want news,' I said tightly. 'I want to know where Christopher is.'

'He's safe with Mike's friends in Carlisle,' Veronica said. 'We've sent people to check. He's fine.'

'And I want to know what happened to Melanie.'

'I could lose my job for this,' Veronica said. She took a buff envelope from her bag and put it on my lap. 'But I want you to read it. It's a statement Mike prepared before he came back tonight. That's why he wanted to see you. He was going to give you this and then give himself up. You have to remember he wrote it before he found Kes in bed with Anita.'

Veronica ran her tongue over her lip. She glanced up as Sheryl walked uncertainly into the waiting room. 'Perhaps you could read it somewhere a little more private.'

I nodded and Veronica rubbed me on the shoulder and told me she must go, she was absent without leave.

Sheryl sat down opposite, pulling her jacket around her defensively. Her face was bare of make-up and she looked more vulnerable, younger.

'How is Kes doing?' I forced myself to ask.

She frowned at me as though she couldn't place me.

'I don't know.' Then she added, with great precision and even more bitterness, 'I decided some years ago that it was better not to know how Kes is doing, or what he's doing. Or who.'

'You were out this evening,' I said.

She nodded, face set.

'I was at the pub with Ronald.'

For a moment neither of us spoke. I wanted her to go away so that I could concentrate on Finney. I did not want to hear about Kes, I did not want to hear about her.

'I have known Ronald for less than a year,' Sheryl continued, her voice gathering in anger, 'but he is more of a friend than Kes has ever been. And that little bitch Jacqui, and her silly accusations—'

I interrupted her impatiently. 'You must have known about Anita and Kes.'

'I was out at Ronald's, often, in the evening.'

'You knew. Jacqui told me. I didn't believe her, but I do now.'

'All right, say, just say, that I knew.' Sheryl was annoyed at me, and her voice quickened. 'Or that I suspected. What could I have done about it? Men don't change. I knew what I was getting when I married Kes. He needed someone to look after Justin while he was away and I thought that at least I'd have companionship sometimes, when he was in the country. But he doesn't notice me any more, just my friends. Why do you think I want Ronald as my friend? Because he's a man, so Kes can't have him. What Kes did to Anita, it wasn't the first time. I've watched him do it again and again and again . . .'

She crumpled and, as her shoulders heaved, I realized she was sobbing.

I went over to sit next to her. She had tried to do things for the best. But I felt so sick with worry for Finney that I had no sympathy to give her.

'Why don't you ring Ronald, and ask him to come and sit with you?' I suggested. She nodded and after a moment went to find a telephone.

I unsealed the envelope, glanced at the document inside, then let it fall into my lap. What will I do if Finney dies? How will I bear it? I have been so very lucky to find him. Why did I drag him into this? I forced myself to start reading. The first section of Mike's statement repeated things that I already knew: that he has known Kes for twenty years, that they have fought together and saved each other's skins more times than they can count. That three years before Melanie and Edwin had come upon Mike's patrol, the vehicle bogged down in potholed terrain off the road. It was then that the SAS patrol, as well as Melanie and Edwin, had come under RPG fire from Taliban forces on a ridge above them, and that the SAS had responded with the vehicle-mounted GPMG and a 40mm grenade launcher.

It was then, of course, that Edwin had taken his photograph of Mike firing above the low wall and Melanie lying in the ditch by his side. The Taliban withdrew and Mike's patrol moved rapidly on, reluctantly but chivalrously allowing Melanie to hitch a ride, with the proviso that she be dumped at the earliest relatively safe opportunity.

We pressed ahead with a reconnaissance patrol in a small settlement to our east. Our instructions were to make contact with a man who would introduce us to the local warlord, who was reportedly willing to work with our forces. We proceeded to this settlement successfully and we waited until dark, then proceeded according to Kes's navigational instructions.

Kes objected to Melanie accompanying us, but at this point she had nowhere to go and no transport, and we were in hostile territory. Like us, she disguised herself in local clothing.

She carried a small hand-held camera, and she was instructed to hide this under her clothing as we made our way into the town. I know she filmed us as we prepared for the mission – she undertook to disguise our faces if she ever used the film – but after that the rules were that she would be allowed to film only on our specific instruction.

As we approached on foot, I began to think we were in the wrong place. The streets were in the wrong formation and the feel of the place was wrong. Kes knocked on the door of the house which he believed to be our target. An elderly woman opened the door to us with children at her knees. As soon as we saw the expression of fear on their faces, we realized that Kes had brought us to the wrong place. The woman slammed the door, and from inside we heard them shouting to their neighbours.

We moved away fast, back in the direction of our vehicle, but soon we heard shooting behind us. We spread out and ran along the edges of the street to make ourselves harder targets. Alan was out in front, then Kes. Behind Kes was Melanie and, behind her, Ray and I were on opposite sides of the street, Ray to the rear of Melanie.

The gunfire was sporadic and we would have made it without incident if Kes had not panicked.

I saw Kes turn to check on the rest of us behind him. When he saw movement behind Melanie, he fired. Ray fell to the ground with half his head missing. I was no distance from him. I saw his brain spill onto the road. Melanie saw it too. I shouted out Ray's name and Kes stopped in the middle of the road. I don't think he could believe it. He started to run back towards us, but I pushed him on. If we had gone back for Ray's body we would have died too.

We made it back to our vehicle and we were able to drive out of the area without being pursued. We were all very upset by the loss of Ray. Alan could not understand what had happened, he hadn't seen him fall. Kes told him Ray had fallen to enemy fire. Melanie started to protest, but I told her to shut up.

Later, when we were alone, Melanie said she had seen Kes shoot Ray. I told her that he had been trying to save her life and that she should never have been there in the first place, and that Ray's wife must never know that her husband had been killed by one of his best friends.

As for Kes, he wouldn't talk about Ray's death. But I know Kes, and I know how hard this hit him because it was all his fault.

When we reported Ray's death Kes blamed Melanie, saying that snipers had sight of her camera and opened fire.

That is not true.

Within the next year, Kes and I both left the army. Alan left a few months after us. When I saw Melanie Jacobs at HazPrep, it was the first time in three years. We arranged to go out for a drink on 9 January. I drove her to Sydenham, near my house, to my local pub. I wanted to get away from HazPrep because drinking with clients is frowned on, and I didn't want to explain to anyone about the situation in which we had first met. While we were in the pub, Melanie took a call from her boyfriend, who had driven out to HazPrep to see her. She told him she was unable to see him. She didn't tell him she was with me.

I should have realized that Kes Laver might come into the pub. As soon as I saw his face, I knew we were in for trouble. The moment she saw him, Melanie walked out of the pub. Kes criticized me for socializing with Melanie because he said she was responsible for Ray's death.

Even if she was originally prepared to stay silent about Kes's part in Ray's death, I think Melanie changed her mind when she saw him in the pub. Kes knew that, if she started to talk, his reputation as a soldier would be on the line. Kes makes a lot of money from security work. If word gets around about taking patrols the wrong way, or shooting one of your own men dead, you're finished. But I don't think it was about that. I think he just wanted Melanie dead because he blamed her for Ray's death.

The next day, on 10 January, I went over to sit with Melanie at the bar when she again received a phone call, but she got up and turned away from me, so I couldn't hear what she said. It was short. Probably reception was bad. Almost immediately, she excused herself and got up to go outside. I do not know whether this was to make a phone call or whether it was to get away from me because of what had happened with Kes the night before.

After Melanie disappeared, I questioned Kes and he denied any involvement. I did not believe him. Furthermore he told me that, if the police asked, I was not to disclose that we had all known each other in Afghanistan.

If it was Kes who killed Melanie, he must have waited outside the building, observing her movements inside and seizing the opportunity when she went outside. He's trained to do that. He can't always read a map, and he never does things to the letter, but he can wait for hours. We call him Kes, for Kestrel. He parachutes like a bird, but even when he's on the ground he waits like a kestrel hovering with his eye on some weak animal. Like he's anticipating the pleasure of the kill.

After that night I did not want to be in close proximity to Kes. I took a job abroad, although my family were begging me to stay with them.

On my return, I realized quickly that Kes blamed his son's accident on me too.

When the police found out that I had known Melanie and called me in for more questioning, Kes was furious, and I was furious with him for putting me in this position.

Shortly afterwards, my son Christopher was kidnapped. Kes never told me that he had Christopher – he must have known I would kill him with my bare hands – but he found ways of letting me know that Christopher's safety relied on what I told the police. He made me volunteer a statement to the police. I told them about Ray Jackson's death, but nothing about Kes's involvement. I said exactly what Kes told me to say.

Then Kes told me he had made contact with the kidnappers, and he gave me a letter that said my son would be returned on payment of a ransom, which his wife Sheryl agreed to loan me. He argued with me and with Sheryl about paying the ransom, but I now believe that was for show, in order to distance himself from the kidnapping, and so that I would not ask him to go with me when I went to pay the ransom. In this way, he was able to hand Christopher back to me. I have only gradually worked this out. At the time I was mad with worry about my son.

When I heard on the radio that Melanie Jacobs's body had been found near HazPrep, I knew that I would be questioned again and I was terrified that Kes would use my son as a hold over me again. I panicked. I didn't even wait for my wife to come home. I just took my son and left immediately, and went to a friend's house near Carlisle. While I was there I did a lot of thinking. I cannot go through my life in fear of Kes. I am certain that he killed Melanie and that he must answer for it.

At the bottom, in his own hand, Mike had scrawled a note. 'I returned last night intending to make this statement available through the press and to the police. When I returned home and found Kes in my bed with my wife, I lost it. I do not blame my wife. I blame Kes. He is a predator.'

When I look up, a doctor is standing there, asking whether I am with Thomas Finney. For a moment I stare at her. Shame washes over me that I have let myself be distracted.

'Yes, yes, I am.' She looks so formal that for an instant I think my legs are going to give way.

'Are you the next of kin?'

'He has no kin. There's only me.'

'Well, he's out of surgery. He has broken four ribs in two places, he's suffered pneumothorax, which is a collapsed lung, in this case from a chest wound.'

I am speechless. She smiles and takes my hands.

'He'll be in pain for some time. We'll see how things go, but eventually you'll be able to take him home in one piece. If you hang on for an hour or so, you'll be able to see him.'

And then I surprise myself by hugging her.

As I head outside to get some fresh air, I pass a small room set off the corridor, and through an open door I see Sheryl seated with Ronald beside her, his head bent close to hers. Justin is there, too. A doctor is speaking to them. He has pulled his chair up close to theirs. He is shaking his head.

Thirty

Ivor Collins stood up when I approached, shook my hand and stood behind me to adjust the positioning of my chair as I took my seat, rather as I did for the twins so that their food had a better chance of reaching their mouths. His welcome verged on the unctuous. He had invited me to lunch at his club. It was a sweltering day, but he did not remove his jacket or tie. It was a classy way to bury the hatchet and a sweaty one, since the club did not indulge in anything so modern as air conditioning.

'I'm not a monster,' he said as he sat down opposite me and clasped his hands together on the linen cloth. 'I don't pull out the fingernails of my journalists. I feed them fine food and wine in an atmosphere of calm sophistication.'

These last few words had an ironic ring to them. Collins, for all his chair adjusting, came from a background where the men's clubs were nothing like this leather and dark wood confection. I would have said that neither of us belonged there.

He handed me a menu. He looked very fine in a slate-grey suit with a faint pale line running through it. His blue eyes shone like sapphires in his narrow face, and his white cropped hair was a sprinkling of snow on the sandy beach of his tanned skin.

I put the menu, unopened, on the table in front of me. 'I wish you'd been straight with me from the start. I saw the file on Sean Howie's death, but I think you had another complaint from the military about Melanie, accusing her of being to blame for Ray Jackson's death.'

He took a deep breath through his nose and lifted a hand discreetly to a waiter.

'We did,' he told me. I noticed that Collins kept his voice low, as did everyone else in the dining room. It was not clear whether this was from habit, or a rule of the house, or a self-perpetuating fiction that they all had important secrets to keep. 'But I had to take decisions about how to proceed on the assumption that she was alive. It was the only honourable course. She had a right to privacy as any of us do.'

He broke off to order water for both of us, tap water. It was, I thought, a nice way to put me in my place: in one fell swoop he reinforced his superiority by ordering on my behalf, and by ordering tap water he reminded me that this was a business lunch, that the Corporation was paying, and that he was a man of the people. Collins took up his story again, still speaking so quietly that I had to lean in close to hear what he was saying.

'When the complaint came to us from the Ministry of Defence – and that's more than two and a half years ago now – I had a meeting with Melanie. She took it very hard. She swore to me that she was not to blame for Ray Jackson's death. She told me that the leader had taken the patrol to the wrong place and had drawn fire. She talked about Ray Jackson dying from friendly fire. I advised her that we would con- tinue fully to support her, but that we should not antagonize the military by making counter-claims. I warned her that if the matter escalated it would inevitably become public, and that whatever the truth of the matter the military was a powerful organization that protected its own. And there the matter rested. What would have happened if, the moment she disap- peared, I had made public this complaint that we'd had about her and ruined her reputation, and then she'd turned up alive? As far as I knew, none of this had any bearing on her dis- appearance.'

'If only you had told me about the complaint we might have made the link with Kes Laver,' I told him.

'It would have been a leap,' he said, sipping and approving the tap water with a nod of his head. 'I'm not sure that Kes Laver's name ever came to my attention.'

'We'd have got there eventually. You could have trusted me with this information.'

'Would you have wanted it? You wouldn't have known what to do with it. Ignore it? Report it? Ignore it and, if anyone found out, you'd have been accused of being dishonest. Report the allegations and they would have stuck. I was genuinely trying to defend her reputation when I warned you off.'

'Her reputation and the Corporation's.'

'They are indivisible. Anyway, this is irrelevant. If I had been open with you, it wouldn't have changed anything. She was already dead. And she was not killed because of any demand that we made on her. She was an outstanding woman, but the demands she made on herself were just that, demands she made on herself. We begged her to do things by the book. We ordered her to take greater precautions.'

'Of course,' I said, 'you employed her because she made those demands on herself.'

'Of course.'

A waiter hovered. Collins beckoned him over with a minute movement of his fingers. We ordered.

'And so,' Collins said, 'I'm half expecting that you're going to tell me now that you want to make a documentary about Melanie and how she died.'

I looked around me, at the opulence and the elegance, at the suits and the ties, and the leather sofas. I wondered how many viewers would be able to understand Melanie and the life she had led. And Collins was right. Allegations have a way of sticking. Now that Mike had beaten Kes to death, his account of that night in Afghanistan might be disputed.

'I think I'm going to leave her in peace,' I said.

Collins nodded approvingly.

Food arrived, tiny perfect portions of colour-coordinated worthiness. We ate. It didn't take long.

'Why,' he asked me, 'do you think Kes Laver acted as he did? Soldiers do crack up, of course, and so do journalists. They get very close to very terrible things. But they don't usually end up murdering people.'

'I don't know,' I said, 'and now Kes is dead, we won't ever know. But from the way that people talk about him, Kes found in the army a sense of family that he couldn't find anywhere else. When he caused Ray's death, although it was a mistake, it really felt as though he'd killed a brother. In order to survive he had to create a fiction that it was Melanie's fault not his. She was the only one who wasn't one of them. The fact that he'd thought he was saving her life when he shot Ray just made it worse. He really began to believe that the whole thing was her fault. When they met in the pub, he must have seen her as a threat to him. He killed her out of revenge for something he did himself. But mostly I think he just hated her because he blamed her for Ray's death. Everything else after that was self-defence. Self-defence, and a strange kind of psychological battle with Mike Darling that culminated in the kidnapping of Christopher.'

'And why did he attack you? I gather there was an incident in your car.'

'He tried to kill Mike's daughter too. Jacqui suspected Sheryl of taking Mike's son and, although she was wrong, her suspicions were leading her too close to Kes. It was Jacqui who realized the baby had been kept in Sheryl's old flat, and that Kes and Anita were having an affair. As for me, that afternoon Jacqui told Justin what she'd told me, and he went to his father and challenged him. Kes denied it, but he knew that I'd put it all together sooner or later. Kes decided to track me down, and Sal told him I was at the hospital. Sal didn't even mention it to me, he'd been fielding so many calls for me.

'Kes must have felt as though he was losing control. Mike

had gone on the run with Christopher and Kes was afraid that Mike would crack. Perhaps Kes even thought that if he killed again it would scare Mike back into silence.'

Later, when Collins and I had finished our coffee and returned to the office, I received a call from Beatrice. She asked after Finney, as she did every day when she rang, and she thanked me for helping, as she put it, to track down Melanie's killer. This she also did every day when she rang. And every time she said it I felt that I should say that it was more a case of him tracking me down. I was deeply unhappy about my own role. I felt that I had missed too much and that I should have paid more attention to some of the things that had been said to me.

'I won't ring you every day,' she said to me, 'but I just wanted to tell you that I had a telephone call from another of Melanie's classmates this morning. This friend, Ann, told me that Stella had always been very . . . competitive with Melanie. She told me that Stella has known Sevi for a long time – it was at her house that Sevi and Melanie met. And according to Ann, Stella liked Sevi herself, but he turned her down for Melanie and ever since she's been trying to stir up trouble between them.'

'So you think she lied?'

'I don't know about lying, but I think she certainly embroidered the truth, or exaggerated. People do say the most terrible things – perhaps Sevi did say something he shouldn't have and she made the most of it. But of course she never did want to involve the police, she just wanted to sow distrust of Sevi among Melanie's friends.'

'As if he didn't get himself in enough of a mess by faking an alibi.'

'Poor man,' Beatrice said. 'I keep thinking of him sitting in his car waiting for Melanie to call him back, and just yards away that man . . .'

In their brief conversation with the terrible reception, Sevi had asked Melanie to ring him back. Melanie had left Mike at the bar and gone outside to try and get a clear line. For an hour Sevi had sat there, waiting. And when she didn't ring he thought it was because she didn't want to speak to him. When he realized, the next day, that Melanie had disappeared, he panicked. The police would never believe his story, he thought, so he concocted an alternative

As soon as I had said goodbye to Beatrice, the phone rang again. This time it was Alice Jackson.

'I heard about what happened,' she said. 'I think I need to talk to you.'

We met during her tea break and we sat on a bench in Green Park again. Alice didn't have much time. She was still in her Boots overall, attracting glances from tourists.

'I tried to tell you that day. I rang you, but I couldn't get hold of you, so I left a message with someone, a man with a woman's name.'

'Sal,' I said. 'He told me you had something to tell me about Anita.'

'That's it. He was very nice, but I couldn't really tell him what I wanted to tell you. It was partly about Anita and partly about me. When you came to see me, I told you how kind Kes and Sheryl were after Ray's death, but I was too embarrassed to tell you that Kes kept touching me. It was so awful, I didn't know what to do. Sheryl could see what was going on. I couldn't believe she let him behave like that. In the end I told him not to come and see me again. It was so soon after Ray's death. It was completely inappropriate.'

'As though he could see you were vulnerable, and he took advantage,' I said, thinking aloud.

'Exactly. And that's what Alan's wife Kay told me was happening with Anita too. She went over there to see Anita and saw what was happening. She rang me and told me about it, and that's what made me ring you. And then, when I heard that he'd tried to kill you, I realized it was partly because of all this. Because that day, after Kay rang me to tell me about Anita, and I told her that I would speak to you, she rang Kes and said I was going to tell you all about how he'd tried to sleep with me. I think that's why he tried to kill you. It's strange . . . that he didn't manage it. Don't you think?'

I told her I still wasn't sure whether Kes wanted to kill me or scare me. The same went for his attack on Jacqui. Could he have killed his best friend's daughter?

'I hope they'll take into account what Kes did to Mike,' Alice said, 'just for Anita's sake. If only they could have each other back. They used to be so good together . . . she hasn't been herself.'

'Sheryl gave her Valium, and she was taking that on top of whatever it was the doctor had given her for post-natal depression. I don't think Sheryl realized what was going on and I'm not even sure Anita did. She just took whatever pills were around.'

Alice chewed her lip and stared ahead of her.

'I was thinking . . .' she said eventually, 'you don't think she knew, do you, that it was Kes who took Christopher?'

'Apparently she seemed genuinely shocked and upset when the police told her,' I said and Alice looked relieved. Shortly after that she had to rush off, and when she had gone I sat for a while on the bench in the sun. I remembered Anita lying in bed and saying that it was all her fault, and I wondered whether at some level she had realized what was going on. I didn't want to think so, but the truth is that there is no way of getting at the secrets in another person's head.

Later, while I was cooking pasta and broccoli for the twins' tea, my mother called me.

'I'm at Heathrow,' she said. 'I decided it was time to come home.'

'Oh no,' I cried, thinking of my father. Had he really gone from the house? Might he have returned? 'I thought you were staying longer. What about Randy?'

'Randy is here with me, he's come to visit,' Ma said. 'Would you like to say hi?'

I rolled my eyes. Since when did my mother say 'hi'? But I couldn't say no. Perhaps this was payback time for all those people I'd forced to speak to the twins on the telephone.

'Hi,' I said, at a loss.

'Hi,' said a friendly American, voice. 'When do we get to see you?'

Without so much as an introduction.

'Perhaps tomorrow?' I said weakly.

'Sounds good. I won't force you to make conversation. I'll put your Mom back on the line,' he said.

My mother told me how much she was looking forward to being in her own house again. I got off the line as quickly as I could and rang Lorna. She still sounded down, but I had no time to be sympathetic.

'Where's Gilbert?' I demanded.

'I think he's in France,' she said. 'He has some business interests there he has to see to.'

I was speechless. Business interests? He had nothing of the sort. He had a second family. For the first time I realized that I knew more about my father's life than my sister, who has been his champion.

'You have to go round there at once and make sure he's not there,' I told her, 'and that none of his things are there. No toothbrushes, no laundry, nothing.'

'Shouldn't we just tell her?' Lorna asked. 'I never meant to do it behind her back.'

'OK,' I said bluntly. 'You tell her.'

There was silence for a moment and then she said, in a low voice, that she would go round and check on the house. When I hung up I reflected that neither of us was used to me giving the orders and we were even less used to her obeying.

When the children had eaten their tea, their paternal grand-parents came around to babysit. The children were delighted. They knew there would be sweets. They knew they would not have to go to bed. They knew there would be endless games. I made a half-hearted plea for a reasonable bedtime and shut the door behind me, and thought that when I returned I might be changing life for all of us.

The last time I had visited Finney, the doctor had said to me, 'You can take him home tomorrow,' and since then the question of where 'home' is for Finney has vexed me. Is it my child-chaotic home, or his bachelor pad? Because wherever I take him now is home and home is where you stay.

Finney was the world's worst patient. It was, to him, the greatest humiliation to be flat on his back. He had spent most of his time in hospital annoying the nurses by refusing to turn his mobile off. I hadn't visited the station, but I assumed they were pretty pissed off too, to find their boss, supposedly out of action, still sticking his nose into everything.

This evening Finney has a visitor. She is blonde. Looking shifty – inasmuch as anyone can look shifty when they're propped up pathetically in bed – he introduces her as Emma. She has a slightly ditzy look to her, dimpled cheeks, attractive and unreli-able, and I can see at once how he fell in love with her.

'Hello.' I nod at her and try to smile, looking her up and down.

'Hello.' She nods back, grinning brightly. 'I've heard all about you.'

'I wish I could say the same.'

Finney winces and she look uncertainly from him to me and back again.

'I have to go,' she says and then something occurs to her. 'Oh, I'm sorry. I think I forgot to pass on a message one day when you phoned.'

'It doesn't matter. I hope we'll get a chance to talk later,' I say, trying to make up for my rudeness.

'No I mean I really have to go. I have a plane to catch. I'm going to Italy. I'm not very good at being in one place too long.'

She leans over and kisses Finney on the cheek and says, 'Get well.' Then she flaps her hand at me in a wave and leaves the room.

I sit on the edge of Finney's bed.

'Is she going to come back?'

'She's not stupid. She didn't get what she wanted and she won't waste her time again.'

'So,' I say, 'I've come to take you home.'

I look into his eyes, and see that his mind has been working on the same problem.

'And where is that?' He speaks slowly. 'I'm at your mercy.'

'Can you cook?'

'I can shop.'

'Can you iron?'

'If I have to.'

None of this is the point, of course, but I have to work myself up to this question.

'Can you live with my children?'

There is a moment's silence.

'Will William always stick spaghetti up his nose because, seriously, I can't face that.'

'Not always, no.'

'Will Hannah always kick me?'

'Very possibly.'

'Well, I can try,' he says lightly.

I force a smile, but I'm not sure it's good enough. I cannot force him. I cannot blame him either. He is joking, but these things – the kicking, the spaghetti hanging, ketchup dripping, from the nose – are not much fun. It is so much, too much, to ask, to take us all on. He would try, but to try is to admit the possibility of failure, the possibility of giving up and leaving. And what my children need is not someone who will endure them only as long as he can. There is never any guarantee of safety and security, and God knows neither Finney nor I have much experience of either. But still, it's what I need. He can see all this on my face. For an eternity, neither of us speaks.

'I have no intention of leaving,' he says, touching my face.

My eyes search his. He smiles tentatively, and I smile back, and I know I will settle for this.

Epilogue

She walked from room to room. Randy had gone out to get the newspaper, and she was glad to be on her own for a little while. She needed to reacquaint herself with her home before she introduced Randy into it and it all changed.

She sat experimentally in her favourite armchair, then got up and shoved it into its proper place, just a few inches more from the wall. It was funny, she thought, how everything looked fresh and different after her time away. It was as though her things had dissolved on her departure and reconstituted themselves for her return.

She passed the mirror in the hall and stopped and looked more carefully at her reflection. Surely she had changed too. Perhaps her molecules had melted down in the sun of California and rearranged themselves. It was not, of course, that she was looking at a blonde twenty-year-old in the mirror. But she looked ten years younger. Her orange blouse was more colour than the house had seen in a while, and there was a glint in her eye that she did not recognize.

And then she saw it. An envelope, her name written on the front in a hand that brought memories flooding back. She reached for the envelope and opened it, pulling out and unfolding a single sheet of notepaper. As she read, her knees gave way, and she sat down hard on the stairs.

My dear,

I wanted to thank you for your hospitality at a time when I was badly in need of it. You are a gracious and forgiving woman.

I also wanted to bring Lorna to your attention. She has had her heart broken and is in need of her mother. I have tried to comfort her, but I am afraid circumstances mean I shall have to pass the mantle of parental care back to you.

Yours truly,
Gilbert

She did not know how much time passed as she sat on the stairs. Only that eventually Randy rang on the doorbell, and that she let him in, his arms full of newspapers. She rallied herself and greeted him with a smile. She folded the letter and put it in her pocket. She must get on with life, even if it had altered in her absence.